There was a body
on the side of the road.

Alice Meyers saw it on her way to apply for a job.
The first thing she thought was that the highway
shoulder was a stupid place to take a nap. Then her
heart began to pound; her knees turned to water.

"Oh, God, what do I do? Don't let him be dead.
Don't let him be dead," she said as she pulled
over. Oh, Holy Mary and all the saints, why had her
mother gone to so much trouble to teach her
daughters to always ——

She left the car ——————— to touch
the man's ——————— cold, clammy, but
not dead. Swallowing hard, she knelt in the
mud and inched toward him, dragging her leaden
fingers away from his elbow to place them at his
jugular. The surge of blood through the vein beneath
her finger startled her.

Alice gulped. It wasn't a body—it was a living man.

Something pulled at the front of her clothes.
Stifling a yell, Alice looked down to see a muddy
hand getting a better grip on her blouse and slip. For
half a second, paralysis set in. Then a slight motion
drew her attention to where a gun stared her straight
in the nose....

Dear Reader,

In a world of constant dizzying change, some things, fortunately, remain the same. One of those things is the Silhouette **Special Edition** commitment to our readers—a commitment, renewed each month, to bring you six stimulating, sensitive, substantial novels of living and loving in today's world, novels blending deep, vivid emotions with high romance.

This month, six fabulous authors step up to fulfill that commitment: Terese Ramin brings you the uproarious, unforgettable and decidedly adult *Accompanying Alice;* Jo Ann Algermissen lends her unique voice—and heart—to fond family feuding in *Would You Marry Me Anyway?;* Judi Edwards stirs our deepest hunger for love and healing in *Step from a Dream;* Christine Flynn enchants the senses with a tale of legendary love in *Out of the Mist;* Pat Warren deftly balances both the fears and the courage intimacy generates in *Till I Loved You;* and Dee Holmes delivers a mature, perceptive novel of the true nature of loving and heroism in *The Return of Slade Garner*. All six novels are sterling examples of the Silhouette **Special Edition** experience: romance you can believe in.

Next month also features a sensational array of talent, including two tantalizing volumes many of you have been clamoring for, by bestselling authors Ginna Gray and Debbie Macomber.

So don't miss a moment of the Silhouette **Special Edition** experience!

From all the authors and editors of Silhouette **Special Edition**—warmest wishes.

TERESE RAMIN

Accompanying Alice

Silhouette Special Edition

Published by Silhouette Books New York

America's Publisher of Contemporary Romance

For Bill, Nathan and Brynna,
who know what it is to live with a writer
but live with me anyway
and for
Ma, Mort, Kath, Pat, Mike, Sean, Beep and Ann,
with love
and for
Meta, who sewed the seed pearls on my veil
Thanks

SILHOUETTE BOOKS
300 East 42nd St., New York, N.Y. 10017

ACCOMPANYING ALICE

Copyright © 1991 by Terese daly Ramin

ISBN: 0-373-09656-9

First Silhouette Books printing March 1991

Printed in the U.S.A.

Books by Terese Ramin

Silhouette Intimate Moments

Water from the Moon #279

Silhouette Special Edition

Accompanying Alice #656

TERESE RAMIN

has been making up stories since the day she was born. The eldest of eight children, she has always possessed a natural talent for storytelling as well as languages. While in Finland for fourteen months as an exchange student, she became fluent in Finnish and garnered an understanding of German, Spanish, French and Swedish from her summertime travels.

Now living in Michigan with her husband and two young children, she's a full-time wife and mother in addition to serving as a chapter advisor and the Literacy Committee chairperson for the Romance Writers of America. Her background includes work as a nurse, a hospital unit secretary, a newsletter editor, singer/guitarist, salesclerk, bookseller, receptionist and wine shop manager, but this versatile woman can never remember a time when she didn't want to write.

Preamble

It was a bad week.

On Monday, Alice Meyers turned thirty-five.

On Tuesday, her eighteen-year-old twins graduated from high school.

Wednesday, the rumor that the small independent bookstore—which had fed, clothed and housed her and the twins for the past fifteen years—was going out of business became a fact.

In Thursday's wash she found six square innocent-looking cellophane-wrapped packages that let her know at least one, if not both of her girls, was no longer innocent.

Friday, Allyn, the twin older by five minutes, climbed into a camper filled with "just friends, Ma"—three of whom were boys—and set off on a 3,000-mile cross-country pilgrimage to Meccan L.A., land of the stars.

On Saturday, Rebecca, the younger twin, called from East Lansing—home of the Michigan State University Spartans and her boyfriend of two years—to say "Hi, Ma! Mike and

I eloped last night hope you're not mad and oh by the way you'll be a grandma in six and a half months isn't that wonderful? 'Bye.''

At one o'clock Sunday morning, Alice sat on the couch in the living room picking at the afghan, thinking that someone hadn't bothered with those little square innocent-looking cellophane-wrapped packages.

At one o'clock Sunday afternoon, she lay where she'd crawled shortly after her late-night reflections: in bed in her darkened bedroom in her robe and slippers with the quilt drawn up to her chin and the pillows piled up on her face, assuring herself that she wasn't a bad mother, she really wasn't. Everyparent's shock rocked her hard. It was as though Allyn and Rebecca had mutated or something suddenly, overnight, turning into people she didn't know. She'd thought everything was fine—or as fine as it could be when you were the single parent of pretty, popular, opinionated and personable teenage daughters. It wasn't as though she'd ignored them—she rarely worked evenings, worked the shortest hours she could on weekends, was always there no matter what the girls needed, set them the best example she could. She never went out, never dated, never brought men home....

Funny, she didn't *feel* like Saint Alice.

She scrunched deeper under the bedclothes. Just because she'd watched over them, fed them, clothed them, lectured them, listened to them, wiped their noses and bandaged their knees for the better part of eighteen years didn't mean she knew—or had to know—everything about them. Did it? Her own mother had known nothing about her at the same age. Or so Alice remembered being bent on proving at the time...

She pulled the pillows off her face and stared at the spot where the light bulb yellowed the ceiling. Sanity told her that like everything else, knowledge was relative and mother-hood was blind. And no matter how well she'd prepared

Allyn and Rebecca for adulthood, or protected them from every possible eventuality, she couldn't keep them in a box forever, couldn't live their lives for them. She couldn't keep them from making their own decisions, their own mistakes.

Couldn't prevent them from repeating hers.

God, she thought, having children sure did make you look at yourself, didn't it?

She tried counting the water spots on the ceiling to distract herself from remembering the life-shaking mistake she'd made at the end of her junior year in high school when Matthew Dane Meyers, Pontiac Catholic football hero, had invited her to his senior prom. That had been quite a night—quite a summer, as a matter of fact, until she'd realized she was pregnant. He'd said all the right things: *Marry me, Alice, it'll be all right. I won't go to college, I'll get a job. We'll elope, it'll be all right, I swear.* He'd made all the right moves: *I, Matthew Dane Meyers, take you, Alice Marie Brannigan to be my wife . . .* Except.

There was always an *except*.

Except that even after they'd announced their impending parenthood and subsequent marital status to her parents, he hadn't told *his* parents that he'd married a pregnant girlfriend they'd never met. *Except* that he'd lied to them so that they'd think they were giving him money to get a head start on his college credits and campus life when what he was really doing was getting an apartment with his wife. *Except* that when his parents found out what he was really doing and then had come to interfere, he hadn't stood up to them, had let them verbally pound his new bride into the ground. Had let them get his marriage to her annulled.

Alice's jaw clenched. Even after all this time, thinking about it still made her angry.

Her own parents had been wonderful, sad but supportive, telling her that they believed in her, would stand behind their adult daughter as they'd stood beside their girl-child. Now it was Alice's turn to learn to think that way.

Because the bottom line was, if she hadn't managed to teach Allyn and Rebecca to be good people by now, it was too late. She'd done her best, done everything she'd known to do with them, as her parents had done with her.

She turned over in her bed and pulled the covers around her ears. The I-did-my-best philosophy didn't help.

In the rainy gray drizzle of Monday morning, she stared at her image in the bathroom mirror, taking stock. She was a thirty-five-year-old single mother of two grown children who'd gone off to start their own lives without consulting her about whether or not she was ready for it. Six days from now she was supposed to march down the aisle behind five of her sisters as a bridesmaid for Grace, the twenty-one-year-old sixth. For this occasion, her family had rather pointedly paired her with a thirty-three-year-old successful stockbroker who'd never been married, but who was now—nudge-nudge, wink-wink—ready to settle down and have two or three kids of his own. And in approximately 200 days she was going to be a grandmother.

Despite the fact that her mother came from a family where a woman's worth was measured in how many children, grandchildren and great-grandchildren she had, Alice wondered how Julia Block Brannigan would take to being a great-grandma at fifty-nine, and whether or not the thirty-three-year-old successful nudge-nudge, wink-wink had ever considered being a stepgrandpa.

Alice made a face at her reflection. He'd probably considered being a stepgrandfather about as often as her family considered the fact that she was not looking for a man to accompany her through life.

Sighing, she pulled her lower lip in over her teeth and angled her head to get a better look at her chin. Damn. Thirty-five years old and she still needed acne medication for the once-a-month pimples.

She tilted her face to the left. There were two new gray hairs at her temple, bringing the total she'd found this week to six. Scrutiny of her right profile introduced her to the fan of wrinkles where she too often squinched her right eye.

She turned sideways, slouching. Yep, just as she'd expected, her breasts drooped, and where ten days ago her tummy had still been flat, she could now see the beginnings of that getting-older womanly paunch.

What was her family thinking of, anyway, partnering her up at a wedding with some successful untried kid? What were her daughters thinking of, growing up overnight to make her face age and grandma-dom without letting her take a breath?

She sagged against the sink. Oh, God, it had really happened. In one short week she'd gotten old.

Chapter One

There was a body by the side of the road.

She saw it on her way to apply for a job. It lay on its back in the rain at right angles to the edge of the pavement, one knee raised, the other dropped, its head nearly even with the white road-shoulder-warning line as though the owner of the body had sat down to throw pebbles into the drainage ditch and simply fallen backward and gone to sleep. The first thing Alice thought was that it was a singularly stupid place to take a nap. Then her breath caught and she slammed her car to a stop on the gravel shoulder and backed up to peer out the back window.

The body belonged to a bearded man with dirty blond hair, a torn black Grateful Dead T-shirt, grease-stained brown corduroys and black harness-style motorcycle boots. A thin chain made a zigzag across his throat and trailed over his left shoulder to a small oval medal lying in a puddle; a fine coating of mud darkened his skin. Her heart began to pound, her knees turned to water, her hands locked around the steering wheel.

"Oh, God. Oh, please. Oh, what do I do? Oh, don't let him be dead, don't let him be dead...."

She couldn't stop repeating her plea as she struggled to unlock her door and get out to wobbly-knee her way cautiously around the car, then pause to look about. Traffic along this stretch of southeastern Michigan byway was normally sparse, but not usually nonexistent. She looked down at the man, the *body*. Its face seemed so ashen, so devoid of life.

She looked for his hands, anyway, before going any closer. They were at his sides, in skeletal position: empty, palms up, fingers crooked. His arms were bare, pasty beneath the grime; she imagined the tips of his fingers had a bluish cast. Oh, Holy Mary and all the saints, why had her mother gone to so much trouble to teach her daughters always to help their fellow man?

Cursing the niggling, too charitable, overprotective guardian of her conscience that had gotten her into trouble frequently in the past, she quaked nearer and stooped to touch his forehead. His skin was cold, clammy maybe, but not dead. Swallowing her sanity with the rain pooling along her upper lip, she knelt in the mud and inched closer to his side, dragging her leaden fingers away from his brow to place them at his jugular. The back of her hand accidentally knocked the matted hair at his temple, grazing blood down his cheek.

"Oh, no. Oh, holy merry Christmas. Oh, please, please, please."

She had no idea what she was pleading for. Probably to be anywhere else at any other moment as any other person doing any other thing. "Oh, somebody, ple-e-e-ase!"

The surge of blood through the vein beneath her fingers startled her. She jerked back her hand, then gathered her courage and pulled back an eyelid with her thumb. His eye reacted readily to the dim light, pupil contracting to reveal aquamarine irises.

Alice gulped. It wasn't a body, it was a man. Her hand dropped to her knee. Sweet angel Gabriel, now what did she do? Cover him up? She couldn't remember. Not if his life depended on it. She peered wildly at the sky. *Oh, please, Lord, just this once let me be good in a crisis—*

Something pulled at the front of her blouse. Stifling a yell, Alice looked down to see a muddy hand getting a better grip on the left side of her blouse and slip. For half a tick, paralysis set in, then a slight motion drew her attention to where a single hollow metallic eye stared her straight in the nose. Her eyes crossed as she peered down her nose at it in disbelief. Where had he gotten the gun? Even her mother's Good Samaritan policy didn't extend to victims who carried—

There was a clack, and the bullet she'd seen in the uppermost cylinder revolved slowly into the chamber. In that split second, Alice knew she was going to die. She'd saved his life and now he was going to kill her without so much as a by-your-leave, or time for an act of contrition. Then *she'd* be the body at the side of the road that someone else would find. Well, damn! You just couldn't help anyone these days.

In the other half of the split second it took her to think this, reflex took over where instinct should have been, and the yell she'd saved up till now erupted. She screamed and jerked backward, scrabbling to get away, but for an apparently dead man he was very strong, holding her still. While she watched in panic, he gulped breath painfully through his teeth, as though deprived of the taste for a very long time. The gun didn't waver.

"Who...who...?" It took him two ragged breaths to get the partial question out.

Alice opened her mouth to answer, but somewhere between her scream and his question her throat had frozen all sound. She shook her head jerkily at him. In a moment she would die and all that would be left of her life was a clutter of things to be gotten rid of so new owners could occupy her house. She wanted to leave more behind her than a houseful of years, two teenage daughters and an unborn grandchild. Somehow her life was supposed to mean more than that. Not to mention that she wasn't finished with it yet. She still had potential to fulfill, a mark to make on the world. She'd been too busy raising children even to take the time to figure out her life yet. So you see, she had no time to die. Not today.

The drag on her blouse increased, and the gun bobbed slightly and bumped her nose.

"Who . . . are . . . you?" The raspy voice was insistent, almost desperate.

"A-Alice." The gun wobbled again, and she shut her eyes. Just do it, she begged silently. Just do it and get it done. Oh, please, let me be brave.

Behind the gun, the man's pale face twisted painfully. "Alice what?"

"Alice Meyers."

Breath wheezed, grew stronger in his lungs. "Prove it."

Alice felt herself going giddy. Something about this whole scene seemed to be happening in another lifetime, a parallel universe—on television, perhaps, where she was watching it. "What?"

"ID," he snapped. "Driver's license, credit cards. Photo ID. Show me."

Sound throttled by fear rushed around her ears as she tried to bring some sort of sense to the situation. The distant whoosh of traffic along Waterford's Dixie highway, the slight rattle of leaves in the rain . . . Both spoke of normalcy continuing alongside abnormal circumstances. Dear God, Alice prayed, this couldn't happen; she couldn't possibly be responsible for saving the life of a bad man, and certainly never a *killer*.

Panicking at the thought, she turned too quickly, scrabbling for the purse at her side. He jerked at her blouse, using it to haul himself upright, and jabbed his weapon hard at her.

"Slowly," he hissed. "Do it slowly."

Fear anesthetized her, left her without thought or will, staring at the medal lying askew on his chest. Faintly, and from a great distance, recognition stirred her fright. St. Jude. He had St. Jude, patron saint of impossible causes, around his neck. Hope sprang eternal. She'd grown up with St. Jude, the Lives of the Saints, with a mother who believed firmly that despair was a mortal sin and that wherever there was life you'd better not quit.

She clutched at recognition like a lifeline, let it galvanize her frozen limbs and brain. Slowly, deliberately, she searched her purse, withdrew her wallet and opened it, holding first her state of Michigan driver's license, then her before-and-after-hours mall security pass up for his inspection.

"I don't have any credit cards," she began shakily, "just two video-club cards, a library card and my social security card. A-and, um, look . . . here's my car registration, health insurance and auto club . . ." While her mouth ran on, she dug through her purse for anything else that might help reassure him, anything that might buy her more time. "H-here's an envelope with my name on it for yesterday's church collection. I didn't go because my girls— Ah, here's my gas and electric bills, my voter registration—" she paused, dug deeper, unaware he'd begun to relax "—a locket with my initials that the girls gave me and—oh! Here's a birthday card and—and—"

"Enough," he said. Relief eased his grip on her blouse and the barrel of the gun dropped away from her nose. "Enough. You're not one of them. Thought you might— can't trust any—they killed—tried to kill—"

He stopped, visibly trying to collect himself. Alice tried to think, tried to breathe. The fear between the man and herself was palpable, as much his as hers. She hated fear, hated what it did to her, what it made her do.

She stole a glance at him, a fearful little jerk of her eyes in his direction, hoping he hated fear, too. Watching her, all the time. His gaze seemed to have a weight she could feel, a touch that made her shiver somehow with apprehension and anticipation. So little expression was visible behind the beard, the eyes, as though the only emotion he had left in the world was fear—and how to use it.

With a jittery, half-expectant heart, she watched him. All her life she'd longed for adventure, daydreamed about being the plain little schoolmarm swept off her feet by some masked desperado on his way to Hole-in-the-Wall or the Alamo, about how courageous she would be in the face of the terrifying and unfamiliar, how she would beat the odds against her and emerge the torch-bearing victor.

Now here she was, six days out of mother-may-I-hood and scared to death to see what might happen next. She'd often had the strange and nonsensically guilty feeling that she'd given in to Matt that night on purpose so she'd get pregnant and have to get married. That way, she'd never have to put her money where her mouth was, never have to live up to her dreams, never have to find out what she'd often suspected about herself: that she hadn't really any courage at all and she was actually a stick-in-the-mud coward.

She could have done without proof.

Rain dribbled off her bangs, dripped off her chin and down the front of her blouse, but she barely noticed it. She couldn't take her eyes off the man and his gun. Staring down at the weapon as though seeing it for the first time and wondering what to do with it, he rubbed his sore temple with the heel of his hand, jarring open his wound. Fresh blood trickled down his cheek, and he viewed his bloody fist with surprise.

"You've been hurt," Alice said tentatively. "You need a doctor, maybe the police—"

"No." Panic roused him suddenly, tightened his hold on her blouse. "*No* police, no doctor. Gunshot wound they file a report. They file a report and they find me. They find me and I'm dead. Do you understand that? They've already killed Nicky and God knows who else. I'm next, unless I stop them, and maybe even then, but I've got to try." He shook her in despair. "Do you understand? I don't have time to die right now."

Her sentiments exactly. For the barest instant Alice stared at him wildly, wondering if she'd spoken her own thought aloud. Then sheer will let him twist his legs underneath him and push himself upright, drag her up with him. "Come on," he urged. "Can't stay here. Got to leave. Got to move before they find..."

Vertigo staggered him, rocked him back. For the first time in her life, Alice recognized opportunity when it slapped her in the face: she shoved him hard, yanking away from him at the same time, making a beeline for the car. With stunning speed he recovered and caught her, tossed her against the station wagon's mud-coated tailgate and pinned her there. He breathed hard, his breath warm and human against her rain-chilled face. Gathering the courage she didn't think she had, she lifted her chin defiantly and matched him stare for stare. "I won't go quietly," she spat. "I won't lie down and let you kill me."

He recoiled as though slapped. *"Kill?"*

Stunned, he stared at her, and all at once the balance between them shifted perceptibly. Her eyes took him by surprise; where he'd expected ordinary brown he found mocha, cinnamon, flecks of chocolate.

And directness.

His mouth went dry. In a flash he saw himself the way she must see him, *not* as Gabriel Lucas Book, who'd fifteen years ago sworn to serve and protect, but as Luke Book, the corrupt cop, the bastard he portrayed, the man at home among killers, drug runners and thieves. He licked the rain off his lips, trying to moisten his tongue.

Unsettling. He wasn't prepared. He'd pegged her as a nice, naive, everyday sort of woman with a social-worker's conscience, easily mired in extraordinary circumstances, not the type of woman to make a man uncomfortable with his stray thoughts. Not the kind who could tell a man to go straight to hell and leave him standing there like a dummy asking for directions. Not the kind of woman who'd be worth that particular emotional trip.

Distracted, he looked at her again. Dark hair short enough to require little care, but long enough to tangle his fingers in, brushed her neck as she cocked her head to view him from another angle, waiting. Her eyes told him she'd had a lot of experience with waiting, with fear.

He blinked and looked elsewhere, trying to escape her eyes.

Step back, Book, he told himself—it'll eat you alive. Concentrate. This is life 'n death you're messin' with here— her life, your death. You owe her something, but don't screw it up.

"Listen, lady," he said softly, and felt his gut cramp. Telling her who and what he was violated all the rules, but he didn't see where he had much choice. He had to trust someone. If anything happened to him, someone had to know why, someone had to speak for him; someone had to forgive him. "We have to get out of here *now*. I know this is tough for you, I know you're frightened, but I'm not the killer here and I don't have time for long explanations."

He pulled her around to the open driver's door of her car and slid in across the seat, drawing her in behind him. "My name's Book, Gabriel Lucas Book. I'm a federal agent—

FBI—working internal-affairs undercover at the request of the Oakland County prosecutor's office.'' He grabbed up a pile of paper napkins that sat in a tray on the floor hump, then angled the rearview mirror and wiped the mud and blood from his face and hands. ''You'll have to take that on faith—I don't have any ID. Last night somebody killed my partner and shot me. I think it was a cop—I'm sure it was a cop. Had to be. Only three people know who I am and why I'm here. One of 'em's dead and the other two...''

He stopped, turned a blind eye to the rain rolling down the windows, looking for courage, for relief from the pain. ''The other two are friends.''

Abruptly, he tapped the keys she'd left in the ignition. ''Drive,'' he ordered. ''I have to pick up some stuff, then I need a phone. Whether I want to or not, I've got to find out whose gun this is. After that...'' He stared bleakly at the gun in his lap. ''After that,'' he said grimly, ''I'll need a new identity and a place to hide for a while. A safe place.'' He turned to her and the depth of his ocean-bay-colored eyes was intense and endless. ''Your place should do.''

''Huh?'' Alice's mouth dropped open in disbelief. She shut it with a snap, and the soft line of her jaw firmed. ''What am I supposed to do, let you waltz in and take over my life and my home at will?''

Gabriel ran a hand regretfully through his hair, wincing slightly, and fingered the gun. ''You don't have much choice right now, Alice,'' he said. ''And neither do I.''

Alice rounded on him ferociously. ''I'm tired of people telling me there's no choice. There's always a choice.'' Her voice faded abruptly. What was she doing yelling at a man with a gun in his lap—even if she did believe him?

She believed him.

With only part of herself she watched him reach across the car to turn the key in the ignition, heard the car jump to life. She looked at his hand. Beneath the mud and grease it was a neat hand, long fingered and strong, nails and cuticles trimmed—nothing ragged about it. The hand of a gentleman. Or a well-paid crook.

"Come on," he urged, voice gentle despite the tightness in it, bass-rich beneath a veneer of gravel. "We can't sit here. They're out there looking for me. We *have* to go."

Facing him, she squeezed her hands around the steering wheel until her nails cut into her palms and her knuckles ached from the strain. Oh, God, she believed him. She hadn't intended to, but she did. And that meant she'd let him stay with her. Willingly. Just another man she'd say yes to when what she really ought to do was give him a firm no. Why was it that, when she was so strong in other ways, she'd let herself get into that yes-no habit with men? First there'd been her father and the dare-to-challenge-yourself camp she hadn't wanted to attend at fourteen that had cost her a broken ankle and torn ligaments in her knee. Then there'd been Matthew in the back seat of his car when she was sixteen and fertile.

She mentally ticked them off: the real-estate agent who'd sold her the house for more than it was worth; the man at the dealership who used to work—and work and *work*—on her car; her boss five years ago when she hadn't really wanted to become manager of the bookstore; and now...

In resignation she faced forward, shifted the car into drive and pulled away from the side of the road. "Where..." She paused, suddenly knowing that, in spite of anything else, she had to help him now because instinct told her it was the right thing to do. Period, exclamation point, and damn her mother, anyway. "Where to first?"

They drove in near silence, attention focused deliberately away from one another on things that were less unnerving. The air between them was stifled, tense, unsure. Gabriel gave directions circumspectly; Alice followed them nervously. Further talk seemed inappropriate—they weren't here to get to know one another—and the rarely tongue-tied Alice couldn't seem to find anything to say, anyway. Gabriel sank inside himself, as though wrestling with the demons of his own disbelief, offering and inviting nothing.

Rain fell in sheets, cut a blinding path across the empty pawnshop parking lot as she pulled in and, at Gabriel's direction, angled the car sideways as close as she could to the front door. Across the street near the intersection of M-59 and Voorheis Road that officially divided the city of Pontiac from the city of Waterford, yellow buses stood in line at the corner waiting for traffic to clear after dropping off students in front of the old three-story grade school with the sign out front that read Home of the Dragons. Around the corner stood the steepled church and Catholic grade school Alice had attended. When the time had came for the girls to go to school, Alice had scraped together the tuition to send them there, too. Cattycorner from the pawnshop was the independent family-owned grocery store where she'd shopped all her life; a couple blocks down was the Irish pub where, on rare occasions, she met her sisters for drinks.

Her lips worked over her teeth as she struggled to collect her bearings. Funny, she'd always thought of this industrial suburb in the northwest Detroit area as a large city. Now as she really looked at it for the first time in years, Pontiac seemed suddenly small—not unlike the shrinking world around it, she supposed—unwittingly giving her more in common with the man beside her than she would have liked. Common ground usually meant common interests, and she really didn't think she wanted . . .

She licked her lips nervously, trying to un-sidetrack her thoughts, and eyed the pawnshop with misgivings. He'd said he had something important to pick up here. Proof, he'd said, evidence that would make her more comfortable about having him in her life. At a pawnshop?

In the midst of her childhood stamping grounds, the place had stood here as long as she could remember. She'd never been inside, though her family had frequented the television-repair shop adjoining it. Pawnshops belonged in sleazy, addict-populated downtown areas and detective novels, not in suburban neighborhoods. She glanced at Gabriel for direction. He'd made no further threats, either overt or implied, but she still didn't feel safe with him. He wasn't a *safe* kind of guy. He was the kind of guy who'd attract trouble in the middle of an empty field without another living soul around for miles. The intense broody type who belonged on the back of a motorcycle with Peter Fonda and Dennis Hopper. The type who attracted women because he was dangerous and needed saving.

The kind of guy who'd attracted her when she was sixteen, then frightened her so badly she'd turned tail and rabbited straight into the arms of someone safe like Matt.

Her breath stuck in her throat behind the fine bone of shame she'd never quite managed to get rid of whenever she thought of that mistake. But now was not the time to consider past mistakes, nor the time to make new ones. Especially not to make new ones. She dragged her thoughts into the present, let her eyes focus on Gabriel. He picked the gun out of his lap and tucked it into his jeans at the small of his back underneath his shirt, then took her hand and jerked his head to indicate she should follow him. Her skirt caught on the corner of the seat when she started to slide across the car. She tugged it loose and lifted herself over the slight bump in the center of the bench seat. Gabriel towed her through the rain and into the shop.

A bell rang over the door as it swung shut behind them. Voices seemed to rise at the back of the store in response to the bell. Alice looked around; the place was nothing like she'd imagined. No army-jacketed, suspicious-looking characters lurked in the shadows; no guns lay invitingly behind unbreakable aquarium-like counters; no frightened-looking chain-smoker stood behind an iron cage backed by bullet-proof glass. The store was dim, but from dust and clutter rather than furtiveness. Bicycles crammed the floor at the front of the shop, lined a side wall, hung suspended from the ceiling alongside radio-controlled miniature cars, orange pup tents, and drab camouflage tarpaulins.

Everywhere Alice looked there seemed to be a resting place for other people's cast-off hopes and dreams: camp stoves, gas heaters and propane canisters littered deep shelves piled high with typewriters, desktop copiers and radios. Expensive new fishing equipment looked as dull as the much used rods and reels that overshadowed it; army-surplus camping supplies made the unused, scientifically designed, brand-name paraphernalia beside them looked like bright, untried uptown yuppies standing next to never-been-innocent mercenaries. A glass-fronted counter to the side and behind more bicycles showcased both fine and not-so-fine jewelry. Audio and video equipment, car stereos, compact-disc players and computers filled the back wall behind a long wooden counter.

At the same time that Alice wanted to hold herself tightly away from the things other people had clutched, used and sneezed on, she found herself strangely thrilled at the discovery of a place full of buried treasure at economy prices. Whether or not she could actually get herself to come in here alone, scrounge thoroughly, then buy some of this stuff, she didn't know. She canted a tentative glance at Gabriel, who lifted his chin and indicated the back counter, stepping aside for her to precede him down the narrow aisle that led to it. Gathering a shallow breath, Alice did so.

A doorway covered by strings of wooden beads stood to the right of the counter. A man in his mid-thirties, who appeared to have been watching them, stepped through the beads in response to a cough from Gabriel. "Picking 'em up?" he asked without preamble.

Nodding, Gabriel slid two fingers into his left boot, withdrew a pawn ticket and tossed it onto the counter. "Last time," he said.

"Good thing you came in when you did, then. Had a buyer for 'em in here yesterday. Told him to come back today. Gettin' tired of movin' the damn things around." The man behind the counter picked up the ticket, fingered it. "You're almost a month late. You weren't so regular 'bout comin' back for 'em—I wouldn't even've held 'em an extra week. Would've sold 'em if you hadn't come in today."

Gabriel's knuckles whitened over the edge of the counter. "I hear you," he said softly.

The pawnbroker eyed him uncomfortably for a second, then tapped Gabriel's ticket on the counter and disappeared with it through the beads. Expression remote, Gabriel looked after him, jaw tightening and straining over thoughts Alice couldn't imagine. All at once, as though some new problem had just occurred to him, he dug into a hip pocket and pulled out a money clip, fanning quickly through the few bills on it. The pickings were a trifle slim. His mouth thinned for an instant. Then, looking like what he was, a man who'd run out of choices, he drew Alice aside and asked quietly, "You got any cash?"

"Let me check," she replied automatically, then caught herself with her hand in her purse. She should have anticipated the question, but somehow she hadn't. For all his other flaws, he didn't look like a man who took money from women he was barely acquainted with. "Do I have any *what?*"

"Cash. Money. Moola." Gabriel sent an uneasy I'd-rather-do-anything-else look toward the beaded doorway. "I'll sign a receipt. You'll get it back."

Alice stared at him. Lord, he did have nerve. What was it the Samaritan code had to say about lending money? She clamped her lips together hard. Oh, yeah. *Give it freely,* she answered herself in her mother's voice, *so beggars don't have to steal.* She pulled out her wallet, opened it and, without counting the bills, handed him its contents. "This is not an auspicious beginning for our relationship," she whispered tartly. The Samaritan code said nothing about keeping pointed comments to herself.

"We don't have a relationship," Gabriel assured her, sorting the bills and tucking them into his money clip. "You're an accident, default, luck of the draw, that's all."

"That's *all?*" By the sudden sensation that she'd burst into flame, she knew her face and neck had turned red and she was about to explode. People shouldn't treat people like pebbles in a stream bed, like mechanical drones without personality or function other than that programmed for them. That was just plain wrong. On the other hand...

She swallowed inflexible judgment with difficulty. She'd spent the thirty years since kindergarten learning to douse the fuse on her temper once it had been lit. She struggled with it double time now. "I don't know about you, but some guy sticks a gun in my face, kidnaps me, takes my money and tells me he's commandeering my house, I have a relationship with him whether I want one or not. It's not based on trust, of course, but it is a relationship."

"I told you, as soon as it's safe, you'll get your house, your life and your money back."

Alice shrugged. "Forget it. I always give my grocery money to men with guns."

With a sense of irony, Gabriel took in the line of her jaw, the soft oval cut of her chin, the disturbing quality of her eyes and his unaccustomed vulnerability to them. He knew better than to let her get to him. He didn't expect this kind of weakness from himself. At least not under the circumstances. And if he hadn't felt exactly like the kind of cheap mugger she compared him to, he'd have been able to grin and ignore—hell, *enjoy*—her barbs. Instead, he sucked air between his teeth, too tired and shaken not to snap back. But before he could say anything, the pawnbroker reappeared with two stereo speakers on a dolly and settled them in front of him. Distracted by his original purpose, Gabriel turned to inspect the speakers, momentarily giving Alice both the last word and his back.

Speechless, Alice stared at the three-dimensional brown rectangles, all fake maple and textured cloth. This was what it had been about, the gun in her face, the six miles she'd just driven with her heart quivering against her lungs, and her knees feeling like mush? This was his evidence, his proof, the embodiment of all that desperation, the intense agony of life and death? She didn't know what she'd imagined he had to pick up here, but stereo speakers? And she'd bought into his story, his emotion.

Deep inside her the little flame she thought she'd put out ignited again. Reaction hit her before she could control it. Inside her chest, her lungs compressed, refusing to let her breathe in anything more regular than shallow gasps. The reckless sensation in her stomach that always preceded her doing something brave but stupid grabbed her, tried to warn her not to do what she was already doing. Her hand slipped under the tail of his T-shirt, found the waistband of his jeans, touched the gun. Fast but casual, his hand whipped around, caught her wrist in his fist.

Holding her tight, he eased her around in front of him, tipped up her chin and smiled down at her, eyes hard. *Don't,* they warned her silently, *because I know what I'm doing here, and you haven't got a clue.* "So, what do you think, honey?" he said aloud. "Great speakers, aren't they? Come on, let's take 'em home."

Chapter Two

The car jerked to a halt in the driveway at 88 North Rutgers.

Alice swung herself out of the car and stood for a moment, face raised to the rain, looking down the mostly tree-lined street with its rows of tiny post-World War II tract houses. Home at last, she sighed. But it felt more like, *Free at last, free at last!* And thank God for it.

She moved toward the house, vaguely aware that Gabriel had set the first of his speakers on the front porch and returned to the car for the other. She mounted the steps and unlocked the door, thinking.

Corrupt cops, politicians on the take, murdered informants, drugs missing from police property rooms, "hits"— Gabriel had told her he'd been called out of a pair of cases going nowhere in New Jersey to investigate the lot.

Instead of distrusting her for attempting to turn the tables on him at the pawnshop, he'd taken her partway into his confidence, explaining what he hadn't been able to explain to her before. With growing horror, she'd listened to him tell her how he and his partner had been shot in the wooded park not far from Alice's house shortly before dawn this morning retrieving evidence—a computer printout and the gun—how he'd watched his partner go down, how there'd been nothing he could do for him but run until he'd collapsed. How he thought the evidence he'd hidden with his badge and his personal emergency fund in one of the speakers weeks ago, coupled with the gun and the printout, would tie this case into a tight neat bundle that would bring arrests within the week. If he could stay alive, that is.

To Alice, who'd been raised to balance life between the Ten Commandments and the West Point cadet code, and who read the newspapers with an eye entirely focused on what books to stock in the store and what movie titles to recommend, and not on police cases and politics, the story was unbelievable. Things like this didn't happen in her world. Her life was forever bounded by the petty and the sensible, honed by soapbox family drama and—

She stopped to push open the door and let herself in, then shut it, leaning against it as though to keep the world at bay, automatically slapping the dead bolt into place and securing the chain. Maybe her sister Sam had been right yesterday when she'd said Alice could use an attitude overhaul. Or, more appropriately, a life overhaul. Whichever, Alice would have to think about it later. Because, if what Gabriel said was true, then the entire county's judicial system was on the rocks—and she'd brought the evidence home with her for a shower, a shave and tea.

As if she needed this on top of worrying about her daughters, Grace's wedding, that damned stockbroker and all the seed pearls she had left to sew onto Grace's veil. And she'd thought *last* week was the worst of her life. Ha! But she supposed that only went to prove how relative *worst* could be. At least last week the "plethora of evil things," as her grandmother used to say, had only happened one a day, instead of one every five minutes. Just as soon as she could scare up the energy, she meant to have a serious talk with whoever dealt out lives and demand recompense for the past few days of hers. Surely in the heavenly scheme of things she was entitled to a reduction in purgatory time. If not for last week, then at least for today?

A clear conscience is payment enough, her mother whispered wisely to her thoughts, and Alice sighed. Wasn't that exactly what she'd been trying to teach Allyn and Rebecca for the past eighteen years? Wasn't conscience what she now prayed would carry them through their reckless rush to come of age? And wasn't conscience exactly what had landed her in the middle of this terrible, horrible day?

Nothing's black and white, Allie, her father's voice assured her. *Your mother forgot to tell you there are always shades of gray.*

Shades of gray, Alice humphed wryly. Shades of mud would be more like it. Mud-colored choices, mud-spattered conflicts, mud-murky days, mud-coated bodies—speaking of which . . .

She turned to the mud-coated body she'd assumed was right beside her, but the space was vacant. Her eyes lit. Maybe it had all been a dream. Maybe she'd never left the house this morning. Maybe between daily stress and her occasionally rabid imagination she was only in the midst of a PMS breakdown. What luck medication was available to take care of these things—

Someone kicked the wooden door behind her. Whispering a word she'd never used before Allyn and Rebecca had left home, Alice undid all the locks and yanked open the door.

Looking something like a drowned Big Foot, the being on her porch hefted one of his speakers and lifted a soggy hairy upper lip at her. "Fuller Brush Man," he said.

With a huff of irritation, Alice flung the door aside and grabbed a stack of newspaper from beneath the chair beside it. "Why can't you and my parents leave me alone?"

Gabriel stepped into the house and set the speaker on the floor, taking the non sequitur in stride. "Trouble with authority figures?" he asked.

"I—" Alice shut her mouth and took a breath, then gave him her mother's best I-am-not-going-to-rise-to-that-despite-untold-provocation face and opened newspaper sections, piling them on the carpet. "Drip on these."

Obligingly Gabriel stepped onto them "My mother used to say the same thing to me. Makes me feel right at home."

"Don't," Alice urged, and he grinned. Even through all that hair, he had a nice grin.

As if she should notice.

The fuzz on the small of her back rose, sent provocative messages helter-skelter through every nerve. For no appropriate reason at all, she suddenly felt connected to him, bound by something more than circumstance or the responsibility incumbent on saving his life. Her veins still tingled and her nerves rattled but, caught in his smile, she once again understood the legendary lure between schoolmarms and wounded desperadoes. She understood race-car drivers and the thrill of speed. She remembered what Allyn was looking for on the road to California.

And that scared her. And thrilled her. And intoxicated her.

She never remembered feeling so alive, so reckless. Not even when she'd given Matthew her virginity. *This is how Becky feels when Michael looks at her,* she thought, then stamped on the notion in shock. She shouldn't be able to imagine how her son-in-law made her daughter feel—especially not when she was looking at a man who'd held her at gunpoint, ruined her morning, then trusted her with a whole lot of information she didn't want to be trusted with at all.

Boy, had he rattled her cage.

"Look," she said uncomfortably, and he did. Looked her up and down, looked her patiently in the eye and dripped on the papers. Alice turned her back on him. It wasn't right to feel the way he made her feel. It wasn't *safe*.

"Let's get a few things straight," she tried again, but the phone rang. Surprised, she looked at Gabriel, turned to the wall where the phone hung, automatically pointing a finger to keep him in place. "Wait," she ordered.

He reached for her wrist, aiming at her attention, captured both. "Careful what you say," he cautioned. "I'll be right here."

Alice swallowed, aware of him as she'd never been aware of anyone. She nodded and answered the phone to hear her eldest daughter's absurdly pleased, slightly rebellious and more than a little nervous voice at the other end of the line. Forgetting Gabriel entirely, Alice-the-mother pressed a hand to her mouth in relief. "Lynnie? Where are you? Why haven't you called? It's been three days—I've been worried sick. You were supposed to call—collect." Frightened-Mother Gambit Number One: attack and impose guilt.

"Ah, Ma, get a life, will you? I'm fine. Jeez," Allyn snapped.

Alice shut her eyes at the automatic offense and swallowed Gambit Two. This was her child, her daughter, her...life. *She's grown up now, Allie,* she told herself. *It's time to let go.* "I'm sorry, Lyn. I'm sure you're fine. It's just..." She looked at Gabriel. He gave her half a smile and shrugged. "It's just been really hectic around here."

"Oh, man. Becky told you she was pregnant and married, didn't she? God, what a fool. I mean, I tried there, Mom, I did. I told her she should protect herself 'cause Mike wouldn't. I even went to the school dispensary to get her some condoms, but she wouldn't take 'em. Said Mike didn't think it was 'natural.' I told her I thought Mike was an immature jerk. I mean, it's her body. I said, use your brain, Beck, look what happened to Ma. But she said she wanted to be like you."

"Like me?" Something that felt like hysteria gurgled inside Alice. What was it her mother used to say about setting a good example and just wait till she had children of her own? Then the gist of Allyn's tirade registered. "You *knew?*"

Allyn made a sound of annoyance. "Who else was she going to tell?"

Alice felt like strangling someone. It didn't matter who, as long as she was an eighteen-year-old, hazel-eyed brunette named Meyers. "Me."

"Oh, right. Like, tell the person who'll have the biggest hissy-fit. Get real—"

"God bless it, Allyn! You don't always know how I'm going to react. Sometimes you've got to ask the questions before you give the answers. I'm concerned about Becky, period. Has she been to a doctor, is she really pregnant, is she taking vitamins, does she have morning sickness, does she need anything, is she all right, is Mike . . . is Mike good to her . . . ?"

"Ma—"

"I just don't want you girls to make my mistakes." Oh, good, now she was criticizing them for not having hindsight. Her mother had certainly trained her well. "Look, I know that's an awful thing to say. It's a burden, and I hated it when my mother said things like this to me, but—"

"Save the lecture, Ma. I'm up on the consequences of carelessness. I haven't needed 'em yet, but those were my condoms I was trying to get Becky to use."

"Allyn—"

"No. No. Let me go. Get your own life, Ma, and leave me mine."

"Allyn. Al—" The phone clicked hard in Alice's ear.

She hung up slowly, furious with herself for digging her heels into an argument with a daughter who was so far from home. Who did she think she was, anyway? Mother, rival, confidant, counselor—all and none in more or less equal amounts. They were too young to bear the crushing weight of daily life on their own, but she couldn't—shouldn't—protect them from it anymore. Alice punched the wall lightly with her fist. How was she supposed to let them go without dying a little inside, without wanting to smother and protect them from themselves and from each bent heart, broken trust, betrayed dream? She settled her fists on the dining-room table and made a sound somewhere between a sob and a whimper, hoping semisilent agony was what courage really was.

Without thinking, Gabriel touched her shoulder. "Can I help?"

"No." Alice shook her head. "All they want me to do is get my own life and let them start theirs and I'm not ready to. I don't know how." She moved around the table settling already settled chairs in place. "Even if you were a single parent with twin daughters exactly like mine, all you could do is commiserate with me for a while. I'd still have to deal with the worry on my own." She glanced at him suddenly. "You're not, are you? A parent with teenagers? I don't know why I assumed—"

"It's all right. Most people assume. And no, I don't have any kids—never been married." He gave her a story-of-my-life shrug. "An undercover cop can be tough to live with—one-track mind, makes up his own rules as he goes, gone for months at a time, character compatible with the scum of the earth..."

"Is that what you really think?" Alice swung on him abruptly, eyes flashing. "Is that what you want people to think? Because they will if you let them."

Surprised by both the passion and the challenge, Gabriel stood mute, watching her struggle with demons he could only imagine.

Alice looked at her hands. "I guess that wasn't my call to make, was it? Sorry. Your life, my life, cars on the expressway—they all look alike, don't they?" Uncomfortably she smoothed her wet skirt over her hips, eyed the filthy T-shirt sticking to his skin. "Oh, gee, look, some hostess, huh? Here I am keeping you standing around in wet clothes when what you really need to do is change your life—" She rubbed her forehead. "Sorry, Freudian slip, long morning. It's *my* life that needs to change. Um, look, let me get you some towels and, um, what, a razor, some sweatpants, sweatshirt..." She moved through the tiny house as she spoke, collecting items as she came to them. "I think I've got some 'fat' pants left from before my diet last year— yeah, here they are, these should do." She piled everything into Gabriel's arms. "Anything else? Scissors, shaving cream? If you don't mind the stuff I use for my legs there's some in—"

"Alice."

She ducked her head, not wanting him to see how close to folding she was. He saw, anyway. He was trained to see.

"If you give me your clothes, I have to do a load of dark laundry, anyway. I can just throw yours in—"

Reaction set in without warning. He'd seen it happen this way often—people strong through the most extraordinary circumstances falling apart afterward. His heart knotted. Her hands shook, and her lips trembled, but she was still in there pitching, still hanging in, striding forward with life despite the curves it had thrown her. From listening between the lines, he knew there was nothing as simple about her as he'd imagined. She had a life as complicated as his own, just on an entirely different scale. And here he was adding to it. He wanted to say something, offer her something, some kindness. Thank you. But he knew without being told that she was the kind of person who'd pull herself together best if he left her alone. As he would.

"That'd be great," he said. "I'd appreciate that. You said scissors and shaving cream were in the bathroom?"

Standing in the center of her too small kitchen, Alice shoved damp hair out of her eyes and pulled her old blue terry robe tighter. It had stood her in good stead over the years, kept her warm, caught her tears, weathered late nights full of panic while she waited for the girls. It somehow managed to give comfort when she needed it—a "blankie" for a grown-up who had no other sense of security to depend on. Everyone needed a security blanket once in a while. There was no shame in that. Except today it wasn't working. She'd put the robe on to find some sense of safety, lost this morning at the side of the road—or was it last week when she'd turned thirty-five, or been given notice on her job, or watched Allyn and Rebecca share the commencement address, or learned she was going to be a grandmother? When exactly didn't matter, she supposed, only that safety was gone and the old blue robe couldn't retrieve it for her anymore.

Instead she felt restless, frightened, unraveled, on the verge... confused. For eighteen years she'd known exactly who she was and what was important. She'd been mother, father, provider, drill sergeant and safety net, and Allyn and Rebecca had been everything. She hadn't had to think about herself, *for* herself. Everything had been about them, for them—and through them, somehow, for her. Somehow. Now they were gone, the bookstore was gone, there was a hairy, aqua-eyed fugitive in her bathroom, and she didn't know anything anymore.

Sighing, she surveyed the cream-and-slate portion of her domain, looking for answers where there didn't seem to be many. Something sticky made tacky noises underneath her slippered feet, and she reached across the counter for the damp rag hanging on the towel rack to clean it up. A bottle of light rum, two bags of nacho chips and the can of nuts she'd bought from one of her nieces at Easter caught the corner of her eye as she did so. Oh, rats, she'd forgotten. It was pre-wedding-and-Christmas-traditional "sisters, sisters" night here tomorrow. That meant no children, no mom, no men, just the seven original Brannigan girls, a pitcher of Bacardi and soda, a lot of pizza, the movie *White Christmas* and a command performance of the Rosemary Clooney/Vera-Ellen duet "Sisters" sung with heart.

Her lips twitched. Trust thinking about her sisters to put life in its proper perspective.

"Still feeling pretty martyred, aren't you, Allie?" she kidded herself aloud. "Better perk up, be positive—as corny as Kansas and as cockeyed as the optimist, or they'll take *White Christmas* out of the VCR and sing every song from *South Pacific* to you, and then go on to *The Sound of Music*. You don't want to sit through that, so buck up, girl!"

She turned, changing places with herself to make the conversation two-sided. "Oh, shut up," she told herself now. "I've been corny, I am cockeyed, and this is only temporary, so hop off and let me wallow in peace, hmm?"

"Can't do that, Alice." She switched places again. "You don't have time. Can't let you—"

She glanced around at a sound from the doorway. Gabriel cleared the chuckle from his throat. "Sorry," he said solemnly. "Didn't mean to interrupt your conversation. It was fascinating." He hitched her too-big gray sweatpants higher up his waist and finished wiping shaving cream off his cheek with the pink towel she'd given him for his shower. "Do go on."

Alice stared. Beardless, shirtless and clean, he hardly looked the same bedraggled biker she'd thought mostly dead less than three hours ago. Her cheeks pinked slightly. "Can't," she returned, trying to concentrate on what she was saying and not on admitting that Gabriel Lucas Book looked a darn sight better in her fat pants than she ever had. Or wanted to. "It was private." Sharply she warned her pulse to quit bouncing as if it belonged to someone younger and more foolish.

"Too bad."

Again he gave her that grin, the contradictory, not-quite-sly one that had somehow connected her to him before. The one that had let her see that appearances with him might not always be what they seemed. Oh, sweet heaven, just what she needed now, a schoolmarm crush on a desperado.

To distract herself she picked a piece of antique lace off the back of a kitchen chair and examined it critically and laid it down again. "I've got 200 seed pearls left to put on this before Saturday," she said abruptly, "and it makes me nervous having someone like you in the house, so I'd appreciate it if you'd quit grinning at me and just do what you came here to do."

"Not much I can do right now. Tonight I can make a phone call, but..." He paused, looking as though he had more to say, but thought better of it. He gestured awkwardly at the lace. "Is this what you do? Are you a seamstress?"

"No. Well, sometimes by necessity. This is just...my sister's veil. I offered, and..." She smiled slightly, shrugging, and the wealth of love and exasperation in the movement said it all. "You know family—they expect the world from you."

"Don't they just." Gabriel's chuckle of commiseration ended on a note of regret. "So do friends," he said sadly. Expected you to lie for them, turn a blind eye to what they're doing, cover up evidence... He dropped his gaze to the floor and fingered the medal sticking to his chest, suddenly more ashamed of than angry at the people he'd called friends.

Alice looked at him. Understanding struck without warning, an ice ball in the pit of her stomach. *Only three people knew where I was. One of them is dead and the other two are friends.* He'd said it in the car. He'd been called into this investigation by a friend, one who might expect more from him than he could give. A friend who had almost certainly ordered Gabriel and his partner killed.

Shock registered as quickly as awareness. Brown eyes met azure, read grief in the truth. "Oh, Gab—"

Gabriel shushed her with a shrug and a shake of his head, a desire not to believe it yet. "No proof."

"But the serial number on the gun—"

"Might prove everything or nothing."

"But how will you—"

"Tonight. I'll have to stick around here awhile yet, but I know someone—computer expert. I'll call tonight when he's at home and can't trace the call."

Alice viewed him with the helpless sense that things would never again be as simple as she'd like. "I'm sor—"

"So am I."

They regarded one another awkwardly, strangers with too much history between them, who knew too little and too much too quickly about one another for comfort. Gabriel turned away first, fingering the veil. The nubby texture reminded him of a tablecloth his grandmother had made; his mother had laid the table with it every Sunday he could remember of his childhood, no matter where they'd lived at the time—Thailand, New Guinea, Vietnam...

Packed away in a box in a rented storage shed with everything else that reminded him of who he'd been taught to be, the cloth was his now, a family heirloom to be passed on with Great-Aunt Esther's candlesticks and Great-Great Grandma's wedding ring to the wife he didn't have and never intended to have. He let the veil go. "Pretty," he commented vaguely. "You do nice work. Did you say your sister's getting married?"

"Saturday." Alice wandered into the kitchen, took down a cutting board and knife and reached for a loaf of bread. "I'm a bridesmaid. Again. That's four times in two years. I've made two wedding dresses, three veils and put the frou-

frou on one hat. My mother always said when we found the right guys we'd go down like dominoes. Unfortunately she was right. I wish they'd start to elope.''

"Sounds like a big family.''

"Seven of us—all girls.'' She shuddered and opened the refrigerator to contemplate its contents. "Do you have any idea what it's like to grow up with six sisters all younger and more in step with the world than you are? And my mother's the youngest of five girls—even the grandchildren are all girls. Family reunions are a nightmare. You never know exactly how many people are going to be there, because all the women in my family have always listed just a bit left of center and have absolutely no reverence for anything—and that includes an unfortunate tendency to exaggerate numbers. You have to cut every number they give you by at least eighty percent to even come close to the mark. Which is aggravating when you're the one giving the party.''

She paused for breath, then went on, "Then of course, once you get to the party, the husbands, who married these women thinking they were sane, are sort of forced to gather in a little bunch in the corner of the living room closest to the television and hope nobody's rented a copy of *Gone with the Wind* because there're more of us than there are of them, you see, and they've never actually learned how to handle Brannigan women in a group. The women, on the other hand, just gather serenely in the kitchen to trash political figures and movie stars, or to discuss how whichever sister who isn't in the room at the moment should straighten up her life. Then when she comes back they tell her what they've decided.''

She leaned over and opened a refrigerator drawer. "Their latest decision for me is that I should get heavily involved with some *stockbroker* who went to school with my sister. The selling points are that he's clean, intelligent, attractive and has a stuffed Blue Chip portfolio. He also thinks it's time to settle down and have two-point-three kids.'' She shivered and made a squeamish gesture with her hands. "Ugh! Frightening. Tact doesn't run in my family."

"Mmm." Trying not to laugh, Gabriel braced the wide doorway behind her. "You don't participate in the family, er, discussions?"

Alice measured him and his apparent lack of intelligence over the top of the refrigerator door. "I didn't say that. Are you kidding? I go to the bathroom before I leave home and don't drink anything once I get there so I don't have to leave the room for any reason. Then I lead the discussion so they have as little chance to talk about me as possible. No—" she shook her head "—they plan *my* life on the phone where they have to pay for the privilege. Are you hungry?"

Choking on a chuckle, he waved a hand at her. "Don't go to any trouble."

"No trouble. I'm starving." She collected sandwich fixings into a bundle and kneed the refrigerator door closed. "So," she said lightly, "I've never done this before. Are sandwiches appropriate for a hostage to feed her captor?"

As easily as it had come, laughter fled, leaving behind a yawning hole filled with anger and truth. Gabriel's eyes flashed and his face darkened; the violence that lately always seemed to lie just below the surface of his control turned his hands into fists. He tucked them tight into the pockets of the borrowed sweatpants. Her sweatpants. "You are not a hostage."

She glanced at him, startled, hearing the anger he fought to restrain. "I know. I let you use my shower, remember?"

"You're a Samaritan, Alice. I might have killed you this morning before I even opened my eyes and just because you wanted to help me. *You* remember that. People like me, we're hazardous to people like you. Don't think of it as a hobby and don't treat it like a game."

"I don't think of it as a game." Alice removed the twist tie from the bread bag, unsettled by his vehemence. "I'm a rotten loser, so I don't play games. Any games. Not even solitaire. Maybe particularly solitaire. There never seems to be much point." She tipped her head and took a quick inventory of his face, the fists bulging his pockets, the tension in the muscles along his throat and through his shoulders, and she reached for reassurance automatically.

"Gabriel," she said quietly, "when I saw you this morning, I was scared to death even before you pulled the gun. I know what you could have done to me and I know what you didn't do. I'm not so much afraid of you anymore, but I'm still afraid—I'm not sure of what. It could be of everything, it could be of nothing. Some people get high on being scared, but I don't. Fear kind of...paralyzes me. So I make jokes because the thing that scares me more than anything else is...if something happened and it was life and death and I was too afraid to move..." She grimaced. "I'm sorry. I'm explaining this badly. All I really mean is that I stopped this morning because, as scared as I was of you, I was more afraid of being too afraid to stop and try to do something *for* you. I don't like being too afraid. Do you understand?"

It took him a minute, but then he did understand, clearly and completely. Because the reason she'd stopped for him was exactly what drove him to do what he did for a living; fear haunted him regularly. Not fear for himself, not fear of reprisal from someone else, but fear of himself, of his conscience, of not being able to look himself in the eye. Of not doing the right thing. He'd watched too many people waste away in their own fear too afraid to open their doors, to notice a crime, to take the responsibility on themselves to turn in a thief, a dealer, an extortionist, an abusive husband or parent. Cops sworn to "serve and protect" too afraid of ouster by the blue brotherhood to turn in—or even notice—a dirty cop. Yeah, he understood.

"Understand?" he repeated. "Better than you know."

Recognition stirred, linked them unexpectedly in those last four simple words. Alice blinked and bundled the clutch of food in her arms onto the stove, glancing at Gabriel again and again as she did so. Not her physical ideal, she thought, but attractive in an I've-seen-better-days sort of way. Not like Matthew, the all-American blond all-State running back. No, this man was leaner, tougher, older, less open, less . . .

She searched for the word, couldn't find it and settled for a phrase: less full of himself. He was a man who knew he could be wrong—and had been. And admitted it.

She looked at her hands in consternation. What an odd thing to think.

Unable to help herself, she regarded him again from the corner of her eye. Dissecting him like this surprised her. Generally, she steered clear of the man-woman nonsense, the eyes-across-the-room foreplay of staring, sizing up, wondering. But then she'd never been in this situation before, either—one on one, life and death, every thought focused on the next instant, his next movement, her next response. It made her look at him again, twice, three times, led her to wonder . . . Led her to wonder what?

She tried to keep her attention on what she knew: slicing bread, carving turkey, peeling carrots.

Gabriel watched her, then retreated to the dining room to retrieve the scissors he'd carried out of the bathroom. He needed a haircut to finish transforming himself into someone new, and now seemed as good a time as any to do it. Also, distancing himself from her seemed the easiest way to retain his perspective, clear his head. She was not someone he'd struck up a conversation with in a bar or a grocery store, not someone to be attracted to first and consider later. She was someone whose life he was disrupting, at first accidentally and now on purpose, for reasons of his own. She was someone offering aid and comfort to an intruder who could, as far as she knew, be anyone, do anything. The last time he'd run across anyone like her he'd still been a Quaker, a conscientious objector, working as an orderly at the

Ninety-first Evac in Chu Lai, Vietnam. She'd been a rebellious Catholic nun working with the American Friends Service Committee Rehabilitation Center at Quang Ngai who'd reiterated his parents' belief that trust was the key to peace—and happiness. She'd given him the St. Jude medal as a reminder of the impossible causes she and his parents passively fought for, then died for her beliefs a few months later. It had been a long time since between Samaritans.

He returned to the kitchen with scissors in hand, and studied the blue robe on Alice's back as it tightened and relaxed with every movement of her arms. Eighteen, twenty years. Long time ago.

"Horseradish?" Alice asked hesitantly.

"Hmm—what?" His head throbbed.

"Horseradish on your sandwich," she repeated.

"No. Thanks." Then in afterthought, "Look, you've already done enough for me, but do you have someplace—" He held up the scissors. "I need somewhere to give myself a haircut."

Alice put down the knife and the slice of bread she'd been mayonnaising. "I'll do it for you," she offered without thinking. "You want it done before we eat?"

He looked at her face, her eyes, hearing the genuinely uncomplicated offer of someone who considered service to others a way of life, and he knew he shouldn't let her touch him. Not emotionally, not physically, but it was too late. She'd already brushed past him, returning in a moment with a sheet to spread on the floor. She settled a chair on top of the sheet and took the scissors from him. He didn't stop her—*couldn't* stop her—and straddled the chair at her direction and felt her fingers fluff through his hair. He shut his eyes to the shiver that ran down his spine and felt her shadow on him, circling.

"How short?"

He shook his head. "Doesn't matter so long as it's different."

"Hmm."

Alice combed his hair back, lifted a strand and cut it. The clipping tickled his shoulder on its way to the floor, but all he felt was Alice's fingers in his hair, the warmth of her body at his back and a dizzying, burning sensation that went deep down inside him. The scissors made loud clipping sounds in his ears, then paused.

"This won't be a professional cut, you know," she said suddenly.

"Alice." His voice was thick and unsteady. "I don't care what it's like. Just finish it."

Uncertainty made her pause with her hand laced deep in his hair. "Gabriel?" His name spilled off her tongue for the first time like the hushed sound of a waterfall suddenly springing up in the desert. He turned to her because he couldn't help himself. The emotion on his face was raw, stunning. Her fingers started to tremble and burn where they touched him. Her lungs swelled, but she forgot to breathe out. As though it had a life of its own, her hand lifted, stroked his hair into place. Then she got control and snatched her hand back to herself, and her lungs released the pent-up air.

Dangerous. Oh, God, he was so dangerous. Even when he didn't hold lethal weapons. She watched him catch hold of himself and turn away.

"Do you—" she began unsteadily, but was interrupted by a knock on the front door. She started and glanced at Gabriel uneasily, afraid for him. "Should I—should you... hide?"

Gabriel ran a hand through his half-cut hair. "No. Just give me a minute—and my boots."

Alice retrieved the filthy items from the kitchen landing where she'd set them to dry. "What do you need them f—" She stopped in the doorway on the top step, staring while Gabriel whisked a finger quickly across each eye, then wiped it on the paper napkin in his other hand. When he looked at Alice again, his eyes were brown.

"Colored extended-wear lenses," he said, crumpling the napkin around the contacts and dumping both in the kitchen basket. "Useful. There's a pair of glasses in a pocket in my left boot. Hand them to me, will you?"

After a moment's search, Alice found the carefully constructed pocket in the boot's seam and withdrew the light, silver-rimmed spectacles. Gabriel cleaned them with the soft cloth they'd been wrapped in, and put them on. Expressive chocolate eyes blinked and focused behind the circles of glass. "Recognize me?"

Alice shut her mouth and uncocked her head from its incredulous tilt without telling him she doubted her pulse would ever not recognize him again. "You need the rest of your hair cut," was all she said.

Gabriel laughed. "Anyone ever tell you you'll never make a poker player?"

Alice, the woman who thought she couldn't handle much of anything, especially flirting, collected herself and winked at him. "Only people who don't know me," she said. The smile she gave him was small and enigmatic, disturbing him in all the places she hadn't disturbed already—in ways he could become accustomed to if he wasn't careful. Dangerous. The kind of woman who could make a man stop and question who and what he was, who made a man feel—and emotions were a luxury he didn't have time for. She was definitely not a woman to be taken lightly, nor one to turn his back on.

"I'll get the door."

She turned and dropped his boots back down the steps, and Gabriel breathed as though released from a spell. "Give yourself a minute. Don't answer it blind. See who it is first."

Nodding, Alice moved across to the dining-room window and peered through the lace curtains at the front porch. Gabriel watched her do a double take, have a second look and blanch. He was at her side in a flash. A woman officer in rain-speckled green army dress stood at the door beside a curly-haired, fashionable man in a distinctly Armani-looking suit. Gabriel turned to Alice without comprehension. "It's all right, it's just—"

Shaking her head, Alice backed away from the curtains in horror. "You don't understand," she whispered. "That woman—you don't understand—you don't know— She went to the academy. She's real gung ho—she was one of the first women to ever graduate from West Point. She scares me to death. She scares everyone to death. She thinks up *scenarios* and then she...makes us—makes me—*do* things."

Gabriel viewed her with unadulterated disbelief. Not even *he* had scared her this much. "So don't answer the door. Pretend you're not home. Don't let her in."

"You don't understand," Alice repeated, retreating as far as possible into her bathrobe. "She wasn't supposed to be home till tomorrow. I haven't seen her in six months. I have to let her in. That's my sister, the major."

Chapter Three

"Who's that with her?"

"Oh, God, it must be the yuppie—the stockbroker." Alice struggled to keep the "ugh" out of her voice. "I mentioned him—he went to school with my sister—the one they've lined up to accompany me to the wedding and the rehearsal dinner. I don't know how weddings affect your family, but with mine it's, you know, weddings, romance, boy-girl-boy-girl, Noah's Ark—symmetry in numbers. They wanted me to go out with him before the wedding. I was supposed to meet him for brunch this morning, but I begged off—told them I had to look for a job. Oh, God, I don't want to *do* this—I'm not cut out for this. They're making me crazy, always trying to fix me up, pair me off, drag me along with this man or that—usually with some yuppie professional or career military man who needs a cute little homebody to arrange his life and be his hostess. Home and hearth, earth mama, that's me. Or so they think. Dammit."

Agitated, she retreated to the kitchen, putting another wall between herself and the door. "Oh, God, why do you do this to me? I've been good, I haven't done anything— lately. I hate it when they do this. I always wind up sitting in some little dark corner listening to sob stories and fending off advances because they think that since my *sisters* had to get me a date I'm either desperate or a real loser, and I'm *not*. I just . . . don't like strange men. I mean, really, don't they think I'd get my own dates if I wan—"

Inspiration struck in the middle of the word, and she swung around on Gabriel, eyes gleaming with it—and terror. "Look, I don't count favors or call markers or whatever it is they say on those cop shows, but I'm desperate, and I'm *not* going out on any date *she's* set me up for, and you owe me. You don't have to say anything, just let her think—"

Ever quick on the uptake—a trait that, along with his skill at improvisation, had saved his hide more than once—Gabriel kissed her. Thoroughly. With something that began in amusement and ended in surprise. Or rather, didn't want to end at all.

Shaken, he pulled away from her, touched a thumb to her lip in amazement, then loosened the belt on her robe just enough to make her look rushed.

Warmth thudded through Alice, raised the color in her cheeks, her throat, spread into the pale skin revealed by the gap in her robe. He raised a finger as though to brush away the flush, hesitated, then folded the lapels of her robe over it instead. Where the aquamarine contact lenses would have hidden his emotion, desire lay exposed in the true color of his eyes. He moved his hand, and Alice clutched the folds of her robe together at her throat. He cleared his.

"There," he whispered. "Now you look like you've been too . . . busy to answer the door."

Alice tasted the trace of him that lingered on her lips, and some long unreleased sigh shuddered through her. "I, uh, kind of feel like I've been too busy to answer the door."

She touched her mouth and offered him half a smile, and Gabriel's gut tightened; his jaw worked. It was no good, he'd known that from the start. She touched him and he wanted her in the most elemental way possible. She surprised him. Fearful, generous, enigmatic, childlike, uncomplicated and complex—all of it genuine, unlike him. He wanted to convince himself he'd kissed her partly out of gratitude and partly because lying to people, acting, setting a scene to make illusion look like truth was something he did well, was what he did for a living. Seventy-five percent of making a lie work lay in making himself believe in it. Ninety-five percent of doing his job right lay in never forgetting it was all a lie—that even while he manipulated the way someone else might feel, he himself was never supposed to feel.

A taste of rain blew in when Alice opened the front door, and he didn't have time for the sudden recurrent loathing he'd felt too often of late for both himself and his profession. *Show time,* he thought and detoured quickly through the living room toward the bedrooms at the back of the house, having decided even as he despised himself for it how he would play Alice's lover....

"Helen, how, um—"

"Come on, Allie, let us in. It's miserable out here. Where've you been? We've been out here for ages. C'mon, woman, move! Let's get cracking here. We've come to cheer you up, take you to dinner. By the way, this is Skip—" Helen wiggled one dark brow conspiratorially in a move stolen from their late father "—your date."

"Skip?" Alice shut her eyes instead of rolling them. The stockbroker looked even younger and less grandfatherly in person than she'd imagined. She hauled her robe firmly together and snugged the belt. "Helen," she said, "it was nice of you to think of me, but I'm . . . busy. I have—"

"That's all right, we have no plans." When Alice still failed to invite them in, Helen pulled the storm door wide and did the honors herself. "Skip met me at the airport and this is just a spur-of-the-moment thing. You're not dressed, you got a few things to do—we'll wait, we'll talk. We haven't talked for a long time. Come on in, Skip, have a seat."

"Helen, I don't think she—"

"Nonsense." Briskly Helen eased out of her jacket and carefully shook the rain out of it over the carpet in front of the door, then turned to hand it to Alice. "She probably—"

"Here, let me." Gabriel hitched up his floppy pants and took the jacket from her, hung it over the back of a dining-room chair and examined the green-eyed brunette with interest. Although the major was taller, heavier and more imposing than her sister, with higher cheekbones, even fairer skin and a glint of the devil in her eyes that Alice lacked on first glance, the family resemblance was unmistakable. He extended a hand. "You must be Helen. It's nice to finally meet one of Alice's sisters—we thought there might not be a chance before dinner Thursday. I'm Gabriel."

"Gabriel." Helen looked at him with astonishment, at her sister with uncertainty, at Skip-the-stockbroker with discomfort. "Alice?"

"I said I was . . . busy."

"Yeah, but I didn't think that meant—I mean you've never—that I know of—not since Matt . . ."

"Could we talk? Now." Alice grabbed her arm and started to drag her sister toward the kitchen, thought better of the lack of privacy it provided and in midmove switched directions and headed toward her bedroom, towing Helen behind her like a reckless speedboat towing a water skier. Gabriel and Skip eyed one another.

"Embarrassing," Gabriel said.

"A bit," Skip agreed.

Gabriel stuck out a hand. "Gabriel," he said. "I hear you're in stocks?"

"Skip. And no, it's gold investments, actually. They never get that right—"

Alice slammed the bedroom door. "Helen, what the hell are you doing here?"

"Oooh, Alice, swearing! Don't let Ma hear you. Gee—" she indicated the rumpled bed Alice distinctly remembered making this morning "—you have been occupied—"

"Helen! *What* are you doing here?"

"We came to take you to dinner."

"It's barely two o'clock."

"So we'll hit a movie, play some miniature golf—"

"Helen."

"Okay, all right. I'm on a mission from Ma."

"Aaauughh." Alice violently grabbed tufts of hair at the sides of her head and yanked them in frustration. Whoever had said no good deed went unpunished knew what he was talking about. "I knew it."

"She's worried about you. Said you haven't been out of the house since Lyn and Becky's commencement. Said you were pining for them. Felt like you were getting old."

"How would she know? I haven't talked to her since the commencement."

"She talked to Edith who talked to Grace—"

"Oh, God."

"—who obviously didn't know anything about Gabriel or she'd have said something. 'Course, the state she's been in since Ma told her Aunt Bethany invited another hundred—"

Ten or fifteen, Alice interpreted silently.

"—people to the wedding, she might not have noticed. But bod like that, you'd think he'd be hard to miss." Helen ran a hand through her unruly curls, a statement of disappointment about their youngest sister Grace's as yet underdeveloped sense of nosiness. "So—" she switched tacks abruptly "—what do you think of Skip?"

"What do I . . . ? Back off, Helen. What did you think? You'd come over and introduce me to the guy and I'd marry him? I've been married once. I didn't like it." Unable to stand still any longer, Alice turned to the bed, yanking rumpled sheets into place.

"Well, you know—" Helen shrugged and pulled down the sheets on the opposite side of the bed "—we really didn't think you'd go quite that fast, but Skip's a nice guy, and Ma's always said when we find the right guy we know."

"Well, forget it, he's not the right guy."

"What's wrong with him?"

"He's . . . he's . . ." Alice squashed a pillow in frustration looking for a mentionable reason. "He's *cute*. I mean, Skip. What kind of name is that for an adult? And the age difference—it's impossible."

"He's thirty-three and you're thirty-five. Big deal—he's less likely to die before you if he's a couple years younger than you."

"He's thirty-three going on ready-to-settle-down-and-raise-a-family, and at the moment I'm thirty-five going on gray hair and grandma-dom. Trust me, it won't work."

Helen fluffed her pillow and waited for Alice to pull up the quilt with her. "Well, at least come out with us for a while. He took a day off work and came all this way—"

"Helen." Alice snapped the comforter loudly into place. "Helen! In case you haven't noticed I've got company. *Male* company. He's wearing my fat pants, and I'm in the middle of cutting his hair. It's midafternoon, and we're making my bed. What does that say to you?"

"That you've mutated since last Friday. Did you protect yourself at least?"

With difficulty Alice strangled the scream welling in her throat. "Quit meddling in my life."

Helen blinked at her. "We only do it because we love you. You've done the same for us."

"I have never thrown men you don't want at you."

"I'm a career woman. I can take care of myself." She shrugged. "Besides, if you were a man, would you want to be thrown at an inflexible thirty-three-year-old army major who was a regiment commander at the Point and who thinks a good day's fun is a twenty-mile slog through the nearest swamp? Think about it. Not many men are up to the challenge—although, your Gabriel looks like he might be. How long did you say he's been around here?"

"I, uh—"

The door opened behind them and the *he* in question stepped into the room in time to answer for her. "Long enough to like what he sees and know what he wants." He swept Alice a slow intimate glance head to toe and brushed a strand of hair off her cheek with the tip of his finger. "Definitely knows what he wants," he repeated softly, as though for her alone, and Alice nearly forgot the scene was merely an act.

"Oh, yeah." Helen drew out the word on a sigh her staff would never have believed the major capable of. "Now I understand what it is about Skip. This one's a lot more dangerous."

"You don't know the half of it," Alice muttered, and Gabriel grinned. She quelled the grin with a look. "Did you come in here for a reason?"

He shrugged and shook his head. "Just wanted to rescue you—and tell you we could hear every word you said. And oh, by the way, there's another one of your sisters shuffling in the doorway." He eyed Helen and saw no reason not to be blunt. Enjoyed the prospect, in fact. "She didn't give me her name, but she turned white and nearly left when I told her you were here, Helen. Alice did the same thing when she saw you on the porch. Do you have that effect on everybody?"

Helen nodded sadly. "It's the curse we who are tactless, insensitive and decisive about everything have to bear. You are coming to the wedding and you will steal my heart and dance the night away with me, won't you—"

"Oh, hell," Alice said and left the room.

The baby of the family, just three years older than Alice's daughters, honey-haired hazel-eyed Grace, shuffled guiltily at her approach, reminding Alice of Allyn on the day she'd backed the car into the wall at school. She couldn't help it; suspicion settled immediately. "What's up?"

"Nothing." Grace spread her hands wide. "Mom said Helen said you were home so I just came to try on my veil. But you've got company, so I won't stay." She made a move to go, but Alice stopped her.

"Grace? Is something wrong? Do you..." She glanced at Gabriel and Helen behind her, at Skip looking as vacant as possible on the couch. "Do you want to talk?"

"Not really. It's just...Mom thought I should tell you..." Grace shuffled a little, glanced at Alice, at Helen, two of the legends and censors of her childhood, older sisters whose approval she needed to earn and whose expectations she had to live up to. Her waffling features firmed, her chin took on a stubborn tilt. "I think you should know Phil and I stood up for Becky at her wedding because Allyn wouldn't, and I thought they should have someone in the family support them."

She settled her hands defiantly on her hips and didn't say *so there,* but the room resounded with the sentiment, anyway. Skip squirmed on the couch looking as though he'd prefer to be anywhere else; Helen arched one brow incredulously for Alice's benefit, then slipped Grace a delighted grin and an unreserved thumbs-up behind Alice's back. Alice opened her mouth, shut it with a snap, then gaped at Grace unable to utter a word.

Gabriel laughed. He couldn't help himself. The urge bellied upward and burst from his lungs before he could stop it. The harder he tried to suppress it, the harder he laughed. His sides hurt and some of the humor he saw was a bit macabre—the parallels he recognized between Grace's betrayal of Alice's trust for the sake of Alice's daughter, and the possibility that he'd been set up for a hit by his oldest friend and mentor were painful—but it had been a long time since he'd been able to laugh at anything and, God help him, he didn't want to stop. It was the first remotely normal feeling he'd experienced in months.

"Shut up," Alice said.

"It's funny," Gabriel gasped.

"Maybe if it was your daughter it'd be funny, but it's *my* daughter and *my* sister. I've put 950 seed pearls on her veil so far, and she helps my eighteen-year-old get married *without me* behind my back. Why didn't one of them come to me? I might have tried to talk Becky out of it, but I'm not an ogre, I'm just a mother." She swung around at a strangled gurgle from Helen. "Don't say it," she ordered fiercely. "You know what I mean."

"Sure," Helen agreed. "You can't stand it that Becky ran away to get a parent-ectomy on her own the same way you did, and you're hurt that she felt she had to, the same way Ma and Dad and the rest of us were hurt when you cut the family out of helping you with your problems. Face it, Allie, we come from a long line of independent self-righteous granite-willed women, and the fruit just doesn't fall far from the tree."

For a heartbeat after Helen's pronouncement the silence was so absolute that even the refrigerator seemed to have stopped running on cue. Then it was as if everyone drew a collective breath and rushed to find the place they'd been before the disturbance began.

"Well, I've got to get to work." Grace said to no one in particular. "I just stopped to tell you I'm sorry if you're hurt, but I'm not sorry for being there for Becky."

"Yeah." Helen picked up her jacket, kissed each of her sisters. "Come on, Skip, we'd better go, too. Oh, Gabriel, as long as you're going to be at the wedding, anyway, you might as well meet Phil and get a tux. Way things are going, we'll need at least one more usher just to help with crowd control. Grace, see you tomorrow at eleven for our final fittings, and then sisters-sisters night here? Alice, you'll be there?"

"I'll be there. Grace?" Alice caught her youngest sister's hand before she could slip out the door in Helen's wake.

"Allie, look—"

"No," Alice shushed her. "It's all right. I just...I'm glad you were there for her—glad she trusted someone. I'm a little jealous, too, but I'll get over that. It's just...hard right now. And I wish—" she squeezed Grace's hand wistfully "—I wish you'd been old enough to stand up for me."

She hugged her sister quickly before Grace's natural inclination to run at the sight of emotional display got the better of her. And for a moment it was almost like having the chance to hold Becky and say all the things she'd never given her own mother the chance to say to *her* on her wedding day.

Almost.

She watched Grace descend the walk, and the tears ran before she knew they would come. She shut the front door in the face of the rain and pressed her forehead to the painted wood, trying to hold the tears back, trying not to sniffle. Trying to be a grown-up with company in the house instead of an exhausted adult whose world seemed to be falling apart around her. Trying to remember that the way things looked today would not be how they'd look tomorrow. Trying not to feel too sorry for herself.

The tears flowed, anyway. There were so many things she'd stored up to say to Allyn and Rebecca when the time came, things she'd say to them eventually, next week, next month, in a few years, but she'd wanted to say them now.

But the only things it really mattered that she hadn't said—hadn't been given—hadn't *taken* the time to say were: I love you. See you later. Take care. Call if, and I'll come. Take care, take care, take care....

She slapped the door with the side of her fist and didn't care that the tears flowed.

Gabriel watched her cry out a grief he wasn't sure he understood. Letting go was something other people did. He'd hung on to nothing and no one over the years; he remembered nothing about letting go. People came and went, that was how it was, nothing tearful about it. But maybe watching a child you'd raised, or a friend you'd blindly trusted walk away—grow away—run away from you was different, harder. At least for the time being. And if the gun at the back of the top shelf of Alice's closet turned out to be Markum's or Scully's ... He'd have to deal with that soon. But not now. He didn't want to handle it now.

He started when Alice pushed herself away from the door and dried her eyes on the sleeve of her robe. "I'm sorry," she sniffed. He handed her a napkin from the holder on the table and she blew her nose. "I don't know what happened. Something between my lies and their truth just snapped and I guess I just ... couldn't do it anymore. Can't handle it."

"Yes, you can." It was suddenly fiercely important to him to say something to her, to give her back a piece of what she might have lost today because of him. "You've handled tougher things today. Beside them, this is nothing."

"But I—"

"You don't give yourself enough credit," he said softly. "I heard you with your daughter on the phone. I watched you with your sisters. Things don't stop you because they're difficult or because you aren't sure what to do. Or because you find out that maybe what you were doing was the wrong thing. You handle what life throws at you." He touched her hand, and his voice roughened. "Because you break down once in a while doesn't mean you lack courage or can't handle it. It means you're human whether you want to be or not."

What was he saying? And who was he saying it to? Her, or to himself?

He touched her cheek and smiled at her because it seemed the natural thing to do. "You've got almost too much courage, lady. No one else would have done what you did for me this morning—not even the major. I still owe you for that."

His eyes were dark, deep, unending—too seeing, too close. In consternation, Alice looked at her hands. How many times had she needed to hear just those words, needed to be reassured in just this way that she wasn't merely run-of-the-mill, wasn't cowardly in the way she dealt with life? How many times had she wanted someone else simply to notice that she was more than she appeared to be? And now that someone had . . .

She shifted awkwardly, once again aware of him as she'd never been aware of anyone, aware of feelings and sensations roused by confusion and . . . excitement and anticipation. "I don't know any other way," she said, pulling herself from her thoughts. "I was taught people count, no matter what they are."

Gabriel smothered a grin and ignored the implication, nodding. "I was taught that, too, but I forget it sometimes."

They looked at one another and something passed between them, a measure of trust, a bond of understanding, a sense of intimacy that made them both uncomfortable. Recognition drew them apart immediately. While Alice blew her nose and fled to the kitchen doorway, Gabriel white-knuckled the back of a dining-room chair. From these safer vantage points they eyed one another again.

"I—I'll go down and get your jeans," Alice said. "They must be dry by now. Your shirt was kind of a wreck—I threw it out, but you can keep my sweatshirt, and there's some men's T-shirts the girls and I have slept in. I don't know about socks. We may have some men's winter ones and there's probably some boxer shorts left from when the girls were wearing them and—"

"It's fine, Alice, really. It's fine."

"But you'll need—"

"And I'll get, don't worry."

"Oh." She twisted her ear, unsure of what to say next, needing to say something. "Thank you for helping me with my sisters."

"My pleasure."

"And what Helen decided—you don't have to come to the wedding, let alone be in it. I'll just tell her you were a...fling."

"You don't have flings, Alice."

"How do you..." she began indignantly, then blushed. "No."

"I'll be at the wedding. I'd like to. It'll be a good place to hide in plain sight."

"You think—"

"I don't know."

Alice nodded thoughtfully. "Okay." Then she laughed. "You don't know what you're getting yourself into. My family, weddings... You've only met two of my sisters and you haven't survived my mother yet. Individually we all make great grown-ups, but you put us all together in a room full of hearts and flowers and—"

Gabriel smiled. "Will you be wearing full skirts?"

"Uh, yeah—"

"When the going gets tough, I'll hide behind 'em."

Alice laughed. "I don't think they're that full."

They shared a momentary grin, then Gabriel said seriously, "It'll be all right. No matter what happens, this won't come to the same end as a botched undercover might, so don't worry about it. I'm a survivor."

"Hmm," Alice muttered dubiously. "We'll see."

The afternoon passed companionably, accompanied by the staccato strains of rain on the roof. Alice finished cutting Gabriel's hair, carefully matter-of-fact about touching him, sensing that he was just as carefully matter-of-fact about feeling her touch, then put their interrupted lunch on the table.

She wasn't good at being uncomfortable around people. When her eyes cautiously strayed from her food and met Gabriel's cautiously straying from his for the tenth time, she laughed hard, suddenly finding the humor in the whole ridiculous situation. Unable to resist her laughter, Gabriel chuckled too, trading gibes across the table with her about the day, about the tangled web of lies they'd woven and about the situation they'd cornered themselves in, relaxing for the first time in years.

While Alice put a few more pearls on Grace's veil, Gabriel put a seal on the drippy faucet in the kitchen sink and told her a little more about his case, thinking aloud, trying to tie the ends of it together in a way that suited him, while feeling that all he'd managed to accomplish was buying a few seconds' peace in the eye of that particular storm.

The rain petered out toward evening.

Gabriel called his computer expert to find out about serial numbers and ballistics tests, and Alice sat in the living room with the veil trying not to listen to his side of the conversation, because it bothered her. She felt responsible for him, for his life. And...

Trying to convince herself that whatever happened to him now was out of her hands, she bound more pearls into the handmade lace, jabbing the needle in, through, out and around again and again, wanting to hypnotize herself with the movement so she wouldn't think. About anything. The ploy didn't work. However briefly, she had a stake in Gabriel's life now, and no matter what, she'd care what happened to him. She liked him.

Restlessly she opened another bag of pearls and thought about her girls in order to stop worrying about Gabriel. When those worries backed her into another corner she tried thinking only about Grace and her veil, but wound up imagining how Grace would look as a bride, and how she glowed whenever she looked at Phil, about the look that Phil gave her back, making Alice feel as though she should leave the room, leave them privacy in an emotion that was too uncomfortable for her to share.

She looked across the room at Gabriel, and the veil's magic worked on her, gave her the same fleeting sense of longing for a man of her own that holding her sister Twink's new baby gave her for a new infant of her own. The feeling never lasted. She always reminded herself of Matthew and his parents, of the negative side of caring for infant twins alone so that she'd stop wishing for what she didn't have— and couldn't bring herself to find.

The sun came out in time to go down.

Red and brilliant, it crowded the tiny house with shadow and illusion, fresh awareness and knowledge Alice didn't want to possess. Needle poised inside a seed pearl, she raised her head to study Gabriel again.

Unlike her first impression of him this morning, she now saw an innate peacefulness about him, something at odds with the violence of his profession, a quality he must have grown up with rather than one he'd developed later. Something—she chose the word helplessly—*good*, a sense of patience and repose, a quality to trust and rely on. A subtle man who, underneath an explosive surface, knew what was important in life and how to get it without grabbing.

Still waters, she warned herself silently. *Watch out for deep holes.* But she couldn't stop staring at him. Couldn't stop herself from wanting him to turn around and see her, cross the room to her, touch her....

As though he felt the weight of her eyes, her fantasy on him, Gabriel cradled the phone and turned. The patterned shadows hiding his eyes seemed to change, to darken, to intensify as he returned her study. Alice's lungs stopped working. She wanted him to kiss her.

Shocked, she dropped her eyes quickly, stabbing the needle through the lace rose between her fingers. His gaze on her forced her to look up at him again. She'd never felt in quite so much danger before—not from him, but from herself. Her nerves, her emotions were coated in excesses, jangled to the point of explosion. The passion and desire she remembered feeling for Matthew at sixteen and seventeen had never seemed more juvenile, more irrelevant. The way she felt now was different from that. Her longing was deeper, more mature.

More adult.

A stray orange strand of sunset crowded into the room. The slant of light made intimacy exist where it didn't seem to belong, made closeness imperative, made them translucent to one another. Bonded them with a knowledge that didn't come from knowing.

No move, no sound jarred the atmosphere. With both ears wide, Alice listened to the roar on the other side of silence. Goose bumps shivered up her arms, and she shook a little in the cool intangible breeze of decision. She wanted to kiss him and she wasn't going to.

Without caring how, Gabriel knew what she thought, what she wanted. What *he* wanted. It was printed plainly in the air between them, as readable as words.

I can't, he thought and moved anyway, slowly, lazily, toward her.

Undercover means different rules from the ones you grew up with, he imagined Markum saying over dinner one evening. *At the same time that you can't afford to forget who you are, or what you're doing, you can also never afford the truth, never forge ties with anyone. Compartmentalize everything. Your personal life can't bleed into your professional life. Your undercover life can't touch anything outside of it. Use your experiences, but never leave a frame of reference. In the long run what you'll learn to be is less than an echo in an empty room. Remember that.*

He stopped and swallowed, aware of the truth, aware of Alice, uncertain of whether he wanted to be aware of either.

As though pulled by some invisible connection, Alice dropped Grace's veil and took the last two steps across the room to meet him. And stopped.

She didn't want to do this. She couldn't trust herself. She'd been here before; she knew what came next. She'd fall in love, lose her mind and go to hell on good intentions. Think about it, she told herself. When it came right down to it, couldn't she trace every pickle she'd been in during the past eighteen or so years directly back to the first time she'd kissed Matthew, had sex with him?

Her breath caught on her own slipshod imitation of The Truth as her mother saw it. Not as she herself saw it. Not as she herself wanted to see it. As her mother, grandmother and great-grandmother envisioned The Truth and passed it on to her. As she'd passed it on to the girls.

She blinked in the deepening stillness, at the unquiet shadows, listening to the no-no's of generations echo around the room. Blinked at the disturbing buzz of her thoughts as her awareness of Gabriel increased with the beat of her pulse.

His tongue moved nervously between his teeth as he looked her up and down, found her eyes.

Her lungs constricted and her skin tingled, but she was cold.

Wasn't she?

She dropped her gaze, acutely conscious of her body and the war it waged against her. Chastity versus lust versus set-a-good-example versus...something else, something stronger, something terrifying and hopeful…and real. Her breath became a painful weight in her lungs.

The air hung heavy, seductive between them. With great care, Gabriel fitted a palm to her throat and tilted her chin up with his thumb. He held her with his eyes; his mouth descended deliberately until every breath he exhaled she breathed in. Anticipation fluttered in her stomach, raced through her veins. She wanted to pull away but didn't.

Silence drew them together. They were a hair's breadth from one another when he sensed her hesitation and lifted his head. Wounds, doubts, needs flitted openly through the shadows on her face and he recognized them for exactly what they were. If they touched one another now, there would be no going back. For either of them.

He slipped a hand into her hair, drew the strands gently through his fingers, let them drop away. She wasn't a woman he could bed once and leave; somewhere deep inside himself he knew that, recognized it, accepted it, and gathered himself back into the box he'd labeled self-control because of it. He felt Alice's sigh of regret, of relief, kiss his lips. Their breath mingled for an instant longer than their eyes held. And then they were apart, on opposite sides of the room, caged in their own emotions, imprisoned by the desire that clung to the air.

It was a long night.

Chapter Four

Unable to sleep, Alice restlessly prowled the darkness long after she'd shown Gabriel to bed in the girls' room. Convenient when the girls had been tiny and when they were older and out late and she could hear them from her bed, the room's proximity now fed a mood, an itch she found harder to ignore by the minute. She was an adult, she reminded herself. She didn't have to scratch all her itches, satisfy all her urges. She was an adult, a mother, not an eighteen-year-old obsessed with the newness of her body who couldn't see beyond the moment, and for whom every passion carried life or death weight. She was older. She had hindsight, she had history, she understood consequences. She had learned from experience.

But denial of its existence only made desire worse.

The creak of bedsprings unthinkingly drew her to the crack in the sliding door to Allyn's and Rebecca's bedroom. Guiltily she peered in at Gabriel, listening to him breathe as she watched him sleep. It was an old habit, one she'd developed months before Allyn and Rebecca were born. She'd loved watching Matthew sleep—sleep was full of promises and dreams, the hopes of tomorrow. Just as *they'd* been full of promises and dreams....

But they hadn't been married long enough to meet any promises, fulfill any dreams.

Though old, the memories of that time were still painful, still caused her to cringe every time she realized how blindly, gullibly, *romantically* in love she'd been. It had taken barely a month after she and Matt had eloped for his parents to find them in their fifty-dollar-a-week, one-room-over-a-garage apartment near the high school and get Alice's marriage to their son annulled. It had been easy to dissolve the union as though it had never been. She'd been slightly underage, and he'd been a university football recruiter's dream, his eyes full of stars, his legs all raw talent and potential. A lot of emotional weight had been carried into that brief hearing, a lot of names Alice had never dreamed anyone would call her.

She'd come out of the judge's chambers feeling dirtier than she'd ever felt, morally bankrupt, a corrupter of children, wishing she'd allowed her parents to accompany her. But Helen was right: they did come from a family of stubborn, overly independent women, and Alice remembered deciding at the time that, since she'd gone into marriage on her own, she'd come out on her own.

Her father had been there afterward, anyway, waiting in the hall with tears in his eyes and a quick shoulder squeeze, and Alice never remembered feeling quite so loved or quite so alone.

She pressed her fingers to her lips and eased away from the sliding door. Odd, the things you remembered, the times you remembered them.

Though probably a wise move in the long run, the end of her marriage had been devastating at the time. To give him credit, Matt had wanted to "do right by her," but he hadn't known how, hadn't been strong enough to buck his parents and their image of themselves—and him. It hadn't been enough to be told that she was a stronger person than he was. He'd been the same age as she, but emotionally much younger—the youngest of four where she was the eldest of seven. Where he'd grown up learning how to play, she'd grown up on the right hand of responsibility, counting heads at every family outing, keeping track of the little ones when her parents needed time for the older ones, time for themselves. If only she could make Becky understand how long it had taken her to forgive Matthew his age. Except she'd never really told either of the girls much about Matt.

She shut her eyes and took a deep breath. God, why did she have to think about all this now? The man sleeping in Rebecca's bed had nothing in common with Matthew except gender and seemed somehow safer at the same time as he was more dangerous. There was something infinitely seductive in the fact that someone like Gabriel chose to trust someone like her enough to sleep while she was awake. Seductive, and frightening, that is, because in order to be seduced, a person had to give up something of herself, like innocence, and allow herself to be led astray, tempted. Corrupted.

Momentarily, Matthew climbed back into her thoughts, and Alice swallowed. Seduction was such a lazy, powerful word. A woman should never allow herself to watch a man sleep; it made her too vulnerable to him. Because no matter what he was while awake, no matter how he treated her, asleep, he was pure potential and there was nothing more seductive to a woman than the illusion of what might be.

Unable to sleep, Gabriel listened to the rustle of her movements through the house. She moved with the soundless grace of a mother ever conscious of wakeful children nearby. He heard her because he was listening for her and so knew she was out there, beyond his door, disturbed by his presence in her house. As he was disturbed by her presence in his life. Even with his eyes closed he knew when she darkened the crack in the doorway to her daughters' room. He had the rather disturbing feeling that he'd always know when she was near, if not through the physical sense of sight, sound or scent, then through an extra sense, a warning sense—through the same tingling in the small of his back that alerted him to unseen dangers during an investigation.

He turned over in bed and listened to the darkness, trying to distract himself by thinking of something else. Thinking how much more tempting the double bed in Alice's room had looked, imagining how she would feel in it and beneath his hands, how she would look if he opened that damned robe....

With a dry and silent "Get your mind out of the gutter, Book," he flopped onto his back. He hadn't been this rattled by a woman since he'd been twenty. But then, maybe it wasn't really Alice at all who disturbed him; maybe she was only part of the circumstance.

His mind turned over to Scully and Markum. Innocent until proven guilty, he thought, and knew he'd hide behind that rationale as long as he could. Jack Scully, the FBI section chief who'd assigned him to the Oakland County undercover, a man Gabriel had worked for and trusted for almost ten years. Silas Markum, the Bureau legend, his instructor at the academy, his mentor. The man who'd asked him to be godfather to his youngest child twelve years ago. The man who'd personally requested Gabriel to handle this investigation. Because he trusted him, or so Gabriel had thought.

Letting someone else do his thinking for him was dangerous.

He twisted savagely in the bed again. He didn't want to think about it, didn't want to face the possibilities—didn't want to know how blind and naive he might have been. Shouldn't have been. Shouldn't be.

He threw his legs over the side of the bed and sat up wanting to run from the claustrophobic silence of his thoughts. Outside the open window above the bed a lone cricket sang, tumbling him unexpectedly backward into the two years he'd spent on Aunt Sarah's farm helping her with the orchards after Uncle Luke had died. He'd been sixteen, shy, obedient and ill at ease, and upstate New York had been a far cry from the Quaker mission in Vietnam his parents had sent him from.

Odd to think how sheltered and innocent, how little of the world he'd truly seen up to that point—given the countries he'd lived in and the wars he'd grown up witnessing. At sixteen he'd wanted nothing more than to grow up and carry on his parents' work, to share peace and understanding with people instead of violence, death and war. The thought of physical privation hadn't mattered—he'd grown up with nothing else. And the fear of dying violently in some guerrilla-torn backwoods... Well, fear was something his mother had assured him was best left to those without faith; fear was a killer, an implement of doubt. She hadn't told him that faith carried its own arrogance.

He pressed the heels of his hands against his eyes. It had been so simple to believe her before she and his father had sent him away.

But far from their protective thumb and out in the world beyond the missions for the first time, he found Aunt Sarah's to be a revelation—a parade of firsts, some but not all of them bad. First date—she was blond, he remembered; they'd shaken hands good night. First kiss—his memory of the moment, if not the girl, was hot, wet and stimulating. First fight—a battle of wills and beliefs, over what he couldn't remember now, that had begun as a sit-in protest in the school cafeteria and erupted into a melee the police had needed tear gas to quell. First killing...

Haunted, he struggled to keep himself from leaving Alice's daughters' room in search of escape elsewhere in the house. He owed Alice at least the privacy to roam her own home at night without intruding on her. But it was difficult. The room was barely the size of the stifling hut some North Vietnamese Regulars had imprisoned him in when he'd gone back to see his parents. The incarceration had been brief—three days, nothing. But long enough for him to find out what his imagination could do to him if he let it.

He stood at the window and sucked deeply of the night air. The humid Michigan summer darkness tasted nothing like Vietnam, just a little like Aunt Sarah's upstate New York. He shut his eyes and took refuge in the smell and taste of nighttime, forcing himself to finish out his thoughts.

He'd grown up a pacifist right down to his socks, belief so ingrained in him that even during his most volatile adolescent years he'd never defended himself—verbally or physically. He allowed himself to be beaten or humiliated instead by fascinated peers who couldn't understand his refusal to fight. He'd never even considered the possibility of taking a life—any life—for any reason. The killing at Aunt Sarah's had been a mercy thing, a calf in the west pasture with a crushed rib cage, a case of watch it labor its life painfully away or kill it quickly. He'd been with two other guys, classmates who sometimes tolerated him. They'd wanted to get the little animal up and moving, but it had been too weak. One of them had taken out a knife and the three of them had sat there knowing what had to be done, none of them wanting to do it.

In the end the other two had left the knife and run away, and Gabriel had slit the calf's throat and watched it die, horrified and fascinated at the same time by a power he'd never understood and now held in his hands—life and death, instinct and choice. Doing what you had to do, whether you wanted to do it or not. Who he was now had begun there in Aunt Sarah's pasture, her orchards, her house—at the small high school where he'd learned that standing tough in the courage of his convictions could make him very, very lonely.

Still made him very, very lonely.

He lifted his head, deliberately ending today's entry in his pitiless introspective diary. Back in Alice's house the room smelled of sweet rainy air and teenage girls, of powder and perfume and innocence; the sheets on the bed beside him held the scent of fabric softener and sunshine—and, somehow, of family love, faith and forgiveness. His family...

He crumpled night air like a tangible substance into his empty fists, feeling suddenly trapped in an emotion he'd prefer to ignore, feeling like an invader. Feeling the need to fill his lungs with air that didn't taste of hope, to clear his head of tangled memories he didn't know how to sort out. When he thought about what he'd become, he didn't thank Aunt Sarah for it, didn't thank Alice Meyers for reminding him of who he'd been. Of who he'd wanted to be. Because after nearly twenty years, his faith still haunted him, sometimes, in the night.

A sudden scraping outside the window sent him crouching for cover, reaching for something to use as a weapon. Carefully, he raised his head over the windowsill, peering into the grayness that night vision made of the dark.

The yard behind Alice's house was deep, narrow and fenced. Toward the center of it, three slim maples raised their branches skyward, and there was a quartet of smaller trees at the back of the yard he couldn't see well enough to identify. A long picnic table sat below the window, and the stray illumination from a neighbor's floodlight allowed him to distinguish a hammock slung between two of the maples. A bulky bi-level wooden structure stood in shadow off to one side. Gabriel thought he detected rings, ladders, tire swings, a fire pole and a sandbox attached to it. Childhood lying in wait, beckoning all comers. A stage of life the only child of missionaries knew next to nothing about.

A figure moved into his line of vision, and he eased himself higher in the window, eyes no longer straining to find enemies. As he'd known he would, he recognized her even before he saw her. *Alice.* Not a shallow beauty sheltered from life's rigors, he knew. Her battle scars, though faded, were evident. Beautiful because life had made her that way, because after she'd tried dodging its blows, she'd turned around and roared back at it. Simple beauty earned through experience with life's contradictions.

His mouth pulled tight over his teeth in a grin full of sudden self-derision. Man, he'd been out there too long; he was beginning to sound like a soldier facing his last battle, as poetic as a Colombian drug merchant waxing rhapsodic over arts and flowers in the same breath he used to sentence his opposition to death. Only he was neither. He was just...

A man looking for the "more" life had promised him as a child.

He watched Alice climb onto the lower floor of the play structure and stretch her arms to catch the third rung of the horizontal ladder jutting out from the upper floor. Hesitating, she hung suspended for a moment, then threw her feet forward, swung out an arm and caught the next rung, struggled to cross the next two and dropped to the ground, puffing, rubbing her hands.

"Oh, jeez."

He smiled, listening to her gasp as she talked to herself, knowing he shouldn't eavesdrop, doing it, anyway.

"I'm out of shape." She straightened. "Come on, kid," she urged herself breathlessly. "Try it again, one more time, you can do it." She sank against a wooden upright, holding her sides. "Oh, hell, what am I trying to prove? That I'm as good as I used to be on the jungle gym? Thirty-five years old I ought to be able to choose my battles better than that, don't you think? Ah, shoot."

Almost as though she were trying to get it done before she could think better of it, Alice threw herself onto the platform again and jumped for the bars, using momentum to swing herself, hand by hand, most of the way to the other end. On the last bar, her hands slipped and she dropped to the ground, air whistling painfully between her teeth as she looked at her palms.

"Aaauughh, that hurts! Alice, you jerk. That was stupid. What did you do that for? Now you're going to have dry cracked blisters on your hands for the wedding, and won't that be just peachy for anybody who has to dance with you?" She shook her hands hard, trying to get rid of the sting. "Don't you ever think ahead, dummy? When do you plan to learn anything? When will you—"

Gabriel's laughter carried easily through the night silence. She stiffened. "Who is it? Who's there?"

"Just me." God, laughing felt good. Had he ever known that? Maybe once . . . He leaned against the window, touching the screen with his nose. "Sorry, didn't mean to scare you."

"You didn't." She drew herself up. "I was just being careful."

Honesty came back to her, laughing, out of the night. "Liar."

"Well—" she lifted her shoulders in a grand shrug "—like I said, careful. Isn't that why you lie?"

She flung the question at him casually, without thought or expectation, and the unaimed dart struck home. *I have to trust you. Why did you lie to me?* He'd had to ask Scully that once. Scully had given him the same reply Gabriel himself now considered stock: *Lying's what I do.*

"Did you go to sleep?"

Her voice came from just outside the window now, and Gabriel, startled, felt his heart jump. "No. I'm still here." He breathed quietly, glad she couldn't see his face. "What are you doing out there?"

"Getting away from you." It surprised her to hear herself say it. The night was full of honesty. "I'm sorry. I wish I didn't mean that the way it sounds. Oh, God." Alice covered her face with her hands, and Gabriel grinned in spite of himself. "There it is again. I'm sorry. I don't know what's gotten into my tongue tonight. It's probably my sisters. I get around them, and suddenly there it is, full-frontal bluntness and no brain censors left to blip it out."

His laughter was almost painful by now, held down out of respect for the hour, but full throated, using muscles he'd forgotten he had. "Where did you come from?" he gasped finally. "Who sent you out to find me this morning?"

"Your guardian angel, apparently." She grinned when he choked on a new wave of laughter, liking the sound. Laughter was a restorative, a joiner, a gift too many people threw away. "No, really, it was my family's fault. They wanted me to come to brunch—on a *Monday,* mind—with them and my sister's fiancé's family. Phil has five elder brothers, two of whom are single. I couldn't bear the thought of another meal where the undercurrent went something like nudge-nudge, wink-wink, what-do-you-think-of-Alice-and-what's-his-name?-wouldn't-they-make-a-cute-couple?-why-don't-we-fix-'em-up? So I told them I had a couple of job interviews to get to and couldn't possibly make it. Aren't you glad?"

"I'm beginning to wonder." Gabriel's chuckle subsided slowly. "Did you have job interviews? Is that what I kept you from?"

"Sort of." Alice slid onto the top of the picnic table and crossed her legs. "Actually, I was going to go up to the Yogurt Palace and apply for a job as a sparkling-water jerk, then maybe over to a fast-food place and see if they'd like to send me to Hamburger College or something." She paused thoughtfully. "Got offered a job with an ophthalmologist, but he wanted me to lose twenty pounds because his office was too small to work four girls comfortably if they wore anything larger than a size eight. I told him I was perfectly comfortable as a non-anorexic size ten and turned down the job. Thought about trying some business courses at night school, but..." As though all at once realizing how much she'd told him about herself without learning anything in return, she turned her face up to him suddenly. "Well, that's me. What about you? Who are you, really?"

"I'm—" he began and stopped, stumped. He had nothing to give her. He was a liar, a thief, a spy. Judas with thirty pieces of silver rattling around in his pocket. He was Gabriel, like the archangel, one of God's avenging forces. He was Lucas, as in Luke, as in the Gospel according to. He was an actor without a script, a lump of clay waiting for the sculptor. An expanse of empty road going nowhere. A man looking for a way *out* of everything, whose mind had lately begun to take some dangerous trips down some very dark alleys. "What you see..." he offered lamely.

Alice slapped at an insect on her arm, staring up at the bedroom screen, glad there was an entire house between them so she couldn't reach out unconsciously and touch him. He needed, she'd give. For better or worse, that's what she did. "It's dark," she said softly. "I can't see very much."

"Not much to see."

"I don't believe you."

A chuckle, harsh and guttural, burst from Gabriel. "It's true."

Her voice was like a cool breeze in the desert, soft and intense. Brief. "So you want to think. Where were you born?"

"Port Moresby. New Guinea." A name, a place among all the other places he couldn't quite remember.

"Really?" She was surprised. Shouldn't be, but was. "Were you there long? Is that where your family's from? What was it like? When I was a kid I always wanted to go there, emigrate to Australia, New Zealand—you know, wagon trains and pioneers on the last great frontiers."

Her eagerness overwhelmed him; there was a thirst in it he didn't think he could satisfy. It had been a long time since he'd told anyone anything that resembled the truth about himself. Didn't know if he should now, but he wanted to, anyway. What the hell. The truth was only a simplified version of the lie he lived, and it wasn't often that he could afford to indulge his conscience with candor.

He turned from the window, pressing his back into the cool, painted wall, and stared into the grayness of the room where his eyes couldn't trick him into seeing her. Wanting her. "It was hot. I don't remember it. We moved before I was three. Pulau Ambon. Bintulu. Bangkok. Da Nang, Quang Ngai." He didn't mean to sound bitter; he hadn't known he was. "My family's actually from Iowa. Friends—Quakers. Missionaries."

Darkness placed a seal around them, bound them in an acute awareness of mood and emotion shared only by strangers stranded in the same storm, feeling their way toward one another out of necessity. Alice tipped her face to the sky, letting Gabriel's loneliness wash over and mingle with her own before it cascaded away. "My mother sent her engagement ring to the missions." She shared carefully, not yet knowing where to tread. Talking about families wasn't the same as talking about the weather. "I think she's always wanted to be a missionary. Meeting my dad and having kids sort of sidetracked her for a few years, but maybe now that she won't have to think about Grace being alone anymore..." She shrugged and let the "maybe" hang. "Where's your family now?"

"Don't know for sure. Haven't heard from them in about ten years. Different hemispheres, different lives, different beliefs... You fight, grow apart, lose contact. Forget." Thinking about his estrangement from his parents made him restless as it always did; made him remember how uncomfortable he was with some of his adopted attitudes and beliefs. He elbowed himself away from the wall. "You know how it is—family's tough to live with sometimes. Strangers are easier."

"I hear that," Alice agreed softly, laughing and vehement at once.

Her amusement was contagious. It touched him in spite of himself, invited him to chuckle with her, at himself, at the grand and petty wonders of the universe. It felt good, released him. He listened to Alice's laughter trail into a comfortable sigh.

"For a man who doesn't like himself much you're pretty funny," she said.

"For a woman who seems to think she's nothing special," he retorted, "you're something else." He peered around the corner of the window at her shape in the darkness and thought he could almost see the color rise along her throat and up into her cheeks. Her face would be warm, soft to touch, the bones of her jaw firm, her chin stubborn, her mouth...

He shut his eyes and tasted it again in his imagination. Her mouth would never leave a man wanting.

"Don't." He felt rather than heard her say it, thickly, and with a shudder. "It's the night, nothing else. It's only the night."

He opened his eyes and knew she was pale now, tense. "What is?"

"Your imagination. Mine. Don't imagine me—us. Don't—" she stopped and he heard her swallow "—feel. Let it go. I don't—I can't let imagination run away...."

"Imagination isn't real, Alice." It didn't even occur to him to find it unusual that she somehow knew what he'd been thinking.

"Yes," she whispered positively, "it is. Didn't think so, either, before this morning, but now I know. Anything I can imagine might come real, and I can't let you—"

"It'll only be real if we do something about it, Alice. And that's not in the plan."

"We're talking. We've already *done*. Oh, you don't understand." She slid off the picnic table and turned her back on him, fists tight at her sides. "How could you. Nobody explained it to you, either."

"Explained what to me?" He didn't know what else to say, but he wondered if statisticians might find confusion an effective weapon in the war on overpopulation and sexually transmitted diseases. Or at least a distracting one. "Tell me what I don't understand."

Alice faced the window. "I'm sorry, it probably sounds stupid, but do you see? You, Skip, my family—my daughters... I mean, they've been my life. That's the way it is and I don't mind, but now..." She laughed. "I'm not doing this very well, am I? But it's... See, my father had his first heart attack the morning I turned fourteen. The doctors didn't think he'd live long, even if he recovered, but he had a goal. He wanted to see all seven of his daughters get through school, maybe settled. He died two months before Grace graduated."

She gestured passionately, inadequately at him. "Last week, I saw my daughters graduate, and it's not enough. I'm not ready to die now. I want more. I've been living for someone else since my junior year in high school. *My* life is finally beginning. I want to stay alive and see what I can make of it on my own. Find out what happens next. You, you're like a shock to the system. This morning, you were mortality knocking. Tonight, flirting with you is exciting and scary and kind of fun and *temporary*. I don't want to risk what I haven't done yet on a game. Do you see?"

Oddly enough he did. Not in words, but in some deeper part of himself where memory and experience counted more, he understood completely. "Yes." He nodded. "You've let a lot of your life happen to you by accident and you don't want to do that anymore. *You* want to be in charge of it now. *You* want to take control. You want to choose what happens next."

"Yes." She was positive. "That's it."

It was too easy, but he couldn't quite resist trying to skewer her as she'd skewered him before. "So what happens next?" he asked quietly. "What do you choose?"

She was better equipped to handle the question than he'd thought. "If I figure it out before you leave, you'll be the second to know."

He heard the grin in her voice and he grinned back. "Gee, thanks. Just what I've always wanted to be, second."

"Beats being third."

"Or fourth."

Alice moved toward the side of the house. "G'night, Gabriel."

"Hey, listen. If you come with an operator's manual, would you mind dropping a copy of it outside my door?"

No answer. Down along the side of the house, he heard a door slam, then the click of her bedroom door. His ears strained to hear her movements as she got ready for bed, for the creak of her bedsprings as she settled into the cozy spot where she would sleep.

"Good night, Alice," he said softly and climbed back into his own bed, where he lay awake for a long time smiling.

She wasn't ready for morning when it got there.

Sleep clung to her eyes, refusing to release her, instead pulling her just beneath its surface again and again to the place where dreams lay in wait. Just below consciousness, her hands clenched and released to the sting of night sweat and salt in her blistered palms. In the clinging shadows of repose where she couldn't control what happened, *he* lay beside her, touched her skin, slid a hand over the soft cotton nightshirt covering her breasts, slipped his fingers between the open buttons....

Restlessly she struggled with the vision, the sensations, turning over and twisting herself in the sheets, knocking her pillow aside. *He* turned with her, refusing to dissolve; his mouth tasted where she moved, tormented and roused and claimed. She flung the covers aside to escape him, to get nearer—it was hard to tell which. His breath was warm and gentle; his hands knew all of her. He raised himself to look down at her. His eyes were shadowed at first, then light claimed them, showed them to her. One was aqua, cold, intense, impersonal and unreal. The other was brown, warm and revealing, fathomless and real.

He tipped his head one way, and she was frightened, empty, lost; then the other way, and she was safe, whole, home. It was like looking at two men in one face; at two faces on one man. Unnerving. She scrunched herself into a ball and bit down hard on a knuckle hoping pain would wake her, bring escape.

The muted clang of aluminum pans, the smell of fresh coffee, warm yeast and cinnamon permeated the house. Disconcerted, Alice woke to sound and smell slowly, dragging her fingers across her eyes and down her cheeks, trying to remember what it was about yesterday, last night, the dreams from this morning, that she seemed to have forgotten. A confusing sense of unease, and paradoxically of accomplishment, lurked underneath her waking memory when she sat up and looked at her pulled-apart bed. She was not a fretful sleeper by nature—not even when she dreamed.

She sat on the edge of the bed, yawning, clutching blessed fog around her for security.

Rising finally, she dressed for her sisters and the bridal-boutique fitters, presentably conservative but comfortable, then stumbled through the house to the kitchen. Gabriel gave her an uncertain smile and dried a mixing bowl, then put it away in the cupboard above the refrigerator. Alice stared at him, recognizing the brown-eyed face of the man of her dreams. She colored slightly—now she remembered. Talking to him, listening to him, feeling for him. Bringing him home. Knowing him.

Self-consciously she straightened her peach sweatshirt, watching him take her in and assess her by daylight, nonplussed by those truth-telling brown, brown eyes in the impassive high-boned face. The mental picture of those eyes was the one she'd willingly gone to bed with, slept with, but the startling aqua contacts fit her daylight image of him better. Aqua went with the brazen arrogance she imagined undercover agents had to be born with; brown eyes did not. Aqua eyes belonged in a book: *You wear a red carnation in your lapel, I'll be the one with the turquoise eyes* . . .

Brown eyes belonged in front of a crackling fire with a bottle of wine and zip-together sleeping bags.

She bit down on the inside of her lip and ducked away from Gabriel's gaze, half-embarrassed, half-amused by the thought.

Recklessly, her eyes slipped his way again, surprising him in what must have been a similar unguarded thought. She'd said things to him, she remembered, implied things, revealing things about herself, about the physical wants of her body, the deliberate inhibition of her thoughts. He'd been more reticent, less verbal, yet equally informative about himself, equally expressive, equally lustful.

They studied one another awkwardly for a moment, caught between who they'd been last night, who they'd told themselves to be by day, wondering if the base they'd begun to establish between themselves could bear the weight of light. The air vibrated with embarrassment and desire, words they wanted to snatch back from the night and bury where no one would find them. Gabriel turned away first and lifted a "Mom" mug from one of the hooks beneath the dish cupboards, poured her a cup of coffee and handed it to her with verbal amenities.

"Good morning," he said. "Sleep well? Have a seat. Cinnamon rolls will be out of the oven in three minutes. It's an old family recipe, passed down for generations and baked only for special occasions. I hope you like raisins?"

"Not really. You catch crooks and bake, too?" Lifted from reverie, Alice stared around the normally less-spotless kitchen, feeling disadvantaged in her own home. Only the impolite guest rose and snooped through unfamiliar terrain to make breakfast before the host had a chance to get her bearings. But then, she reminded herself, he wasn't really a guest, was he? No, he was her—

"Your mother called."

—lover. Alice choked, and scalding coffee went down the wrong pipes with the thought and Gabriel's statement. A bout of uncontrolled coughing brought the coffee misting back up again to spray the kitchen floor and dribble down the front of her pale peach sweatshirt with the picture of the pale porcelain clown that, until this moment, had looked fairly nice with her pale peach rose-shaped coral earrings that the girls had given her for her birthday. Gabriel gave her one hard *thwack* in the middle of her back, grabbed a towel and began mopping her up.

"You okay?"

"My—" Glaring at him, Alice snatched the towel and cleared her throat to find her voice. Who was it had said no good deed went unpunished? "My mother called?" she whispered hoarsely, mortified at being caught like a teenager with a boy in the living room. "You answered the phone?"

Gabriel forced back a grin. Alice was thirty-five years old and still guilty as hell about sins she'd barely thought about committing. "You were asleep. I didn't want to wake you." Didn't trust himself to wake her would have been closer to the truth. "She asked if I came with references, welcomed me to the family and said there's a problem with—" he picked a red sticky note off one of the cupboards and looked at it "—Aunt Kate and Uncle Delbert. Their hotel reservations were canceled and they need a place to—"

"No. Absolutely not."

"—stay until Sunday."

"She's sending them to chaperone me."

"She also said she regrets inconveniencing us, but that they'll need your bed and a board under the mattress because of their bad backs." His mouth continued its losing battle with a grin. "If it helps, I think I understand you better now that I've, er, met your mother."

"It doesn't help." Alice threw the towel at the sink and turned her back on him, muttering, "They told her you were here and she called— No, no, *Helen* called the hotel, I'd bet my firstborn on it. Unbelievable. I've got to think about this."

She tapped her foot thoughtfully for a moment, then shook her head incredulously. "I can't *believe* this. We're eight grown women, but here I am trying to think up ways to outdo them because they've decided to tease me over a man I'm pretending to sleep with. Just wait. I'll get to that fitting today, and they'll have something set up." Her fingers drummed her thigh. "What will it be? Potty-chair photographs? Embarrassing stories—"

"Your parents took a picture of you on a potty chair?"

"No, I think that was Meg. I was standing behind her."

"Naked?"

"I was wearing a bathrobe. And pajamas. Meg was wearing Mickey Mouse ears."

"I'm sorry I asked."

Alice flipped an impatient hand at him. "No problem. Apology accepted. It's them there's no excuse for. Practically throw me into the future with a guy named Skip, then can't leave me alone when I actually bring home a guy on my own." She looked at Gabriel earnestly. "What do they want?"

"Your happiness?"

Alice snorted. "Interesting theory, but people who really have your happiness and best interests at heart usually ask you which of your interests will make you happy before they go off to meddle in them for you, don't they? They don't just assume they know what's best for you and then try to cram it down your throat when you tell them pretty specifically you don't want it, do they?''

"Ah..."

Happily, the timer on the stove buzzed before he had to think of an answer, and Gabriel grabbed a pair of pot holders and opened the oven door. Alice considerately found a cooling rack and slid it under the pan as he set it on the counter. Warned by a male survival instinct too ancient for its origins to be recorded, Gabriel put the pan and the pot holders down and gave Alice his full guarded attention.

"You know," she mused, chewing the tip of one fingernail meditatively, "I know they love me. I can't really fault that, can I? I love them, too. And I guess, when you love people, you try to make them happy whether they want to be or not. It's just that, well, this has really started to bug me, and maybe it's time to be blunt. Hmm..." She tapped her teeth. "I guess I actually should have dealt with it once and for all when I was twenty-six, but you know how it is. Whenever I thought about it I was in the middle of somebody's 4-H fair or soccer practice or something and didn't have time." She folded her hands angelically, and used them to prop up her chin. "I've never had time *before*," she added dreamily.

Chapter Five

Gabriel dumped the cinnamon rolls onto the counter, oblivious to flying raisins and dripping sugar. Long ago, when he'd been just any other Bureau rookie, he remembered the look Alice was wearing as a danger sign that had invariably brought him unfavorable notice from people whose displeasure he'd rather have avoided. Older and wiser now than he'd been at twenty-five, he wanted no part of that look or anything that went with it. Not even if he did "owe" her. Hell, he didn't believe in counting markers or trading favors, either. Not usually.

Hastily he cut two cinnamon rolls, slid them onto a plate and plunked them on the dining-room table. Relieving Alice of her coffee mug, he guided her to the table and seated her unceremoniously in front of the rolls. "Eat," he ordered. "Enjoy. They're best hot. I'll bring you more coffee."

"With milk? Poured in before the coffee."

"Naturally." Gabriel sloshed the coffeepot back onto its burner, then rummaged in the fridge for milk. "You're out."

"I think there's some Cool Whip in the freezer. That'll do."

"In your coffee?" Gabriel shuddered, poured it black and set it in front of her. "No whipped topping. It's better for you this way."

"What is?" Absently Alice tore off a piece of cinnamon bun, dunked it in her cup and nibbled on it thoughtfully. "You know—" she ran an appraising eye over him, from bare feet to brown cords to bare chest "—we really ought to go shopping before we go to the fitting—spiff you up a little, you know? Not," she continued, wondering if she sounded as manic as she felt, "that you aren't spiffy now, just that maybe we ought to make you spiffier so there aren't too many questions." She regarded the left side of his forehead where the cut in his temple looked hair-matted and oozy. "And you need a big Band-Aid and some antiseptic on that. If we let it go and it gets infected... It's awfully close to the brain. And besides, Helen might not have noticed it, but Helen never pays attention to that sort of thing, and the fact of the matter is that Edith's a nurse and—"

"Clothes and a Band-Aid," Gabriel agreed. "We redesign me to fit you. No problem. Do you have a story for me, too?"

"What?" Alice sat up, taken aback. All she'd been interested in was sidetracking her disquieting desire for Gabriel while doing something to make a point with her family. The means to that end hadn't really occurred to her. But now... "I didn't mean we should *lie*. Skirt the truth a little, maybe evade it, *delay* it, but I'm no good at lying."

Gabriel looked her over, the woman who'd grabbed his heart and forced his honesty by dark, suggesting deceit by day. Who we are, he thought, is almost never who we seem to be. "I am."

He made the statement flat, and Alice looked at him hard, concentrating all her attention on him. The ragged edge she'd heard in him last night was back full force. Time to tread carefully. "I don't want you to lie for me."

"Then what is it you *do* want, Alice? Besides a back to hide behind."

"Nothing. That's all." Defensive. Stubborn. Rebellious. Defiant. Emotions that had gotten her through the comments made at school when her pregnancy had started to show. The state of grace that had kept her tough enough to finish out the credits she needed to graduate from high school early, at the end of the January term, when she was eight months pregnant. It had been a long time since she'd felt any of those emotions.

Having the twins when she did had forced her to rise to the occasion, to take charge of her own life before she might have otherwise. If she hadn't been so dead set on keeping her babies, she'd never have had the courage to do many of the things she'd done. Not having the girls to propel her through anymore frightened her, made her afraid she'd get lazy, no longer choose to rise to the occasion because there'd be no one pushing her forward, no one holding her back. She was on her own. *Freedom,* she realized with a start, was a terrifyingly responsible word. She lifted her chin.

"Do what you have to do for you," she said softly, "but leave me out of it. I don't need anything from you."

Or anyone, her tone implied. For some reason her autonomy angered him. She got to him, her directness, her innocence, her expectations. And the lack of them. "You got it, babe," he agreed scornfully, "just as soon as you give me something to work with. Tell me, if you were really going to live in sin with someone, who would he be? Who's your dream man, Alice?"

"I don't know. I thought I did once, but he turned out to be a shadow on the wall—all looks, no substance."

"How old was he, seventeen, eighteen?" He was treading thin ice and didn't care. Or *did* care and didn't want to. He'd been that boy once, all hormones, no soul. "What kind of time had he had to develop any substance?"

"Almost a year more than I had."

They were talking to one another in riddles, he realized, as though they'd known one another forever and could assume understanding. The intimacy of the bond might have worried him if they hadn't been so busy accusing one another of things someone else had done. "And that's what you judged him on. How old he was compared to you?"

"No, I judged him on how he let other people treat me and make his decisions for him. On how he made me see myself. Judge myself." Her eyes focused on the dining-room window, looking at things he couldn't see. Life was too busy to spend much of it chasing her tail around sore memories all the time, she knew, but there were moments...

She firmly shoved yesterday behind her where it belonged. One thing Alice Meyers-née-Brannigan did well was to push herself forward all the time, no matter what, without ever turning around to peer backward with regret. In fact, she reminded herself, the only time she did look back was when she wanted to remember who she didn't want to be anymore. And, maybe, who she could be now.

She took in Gabriel's face, the planes and angles, the bruises and the tired brown eyes, the remnants of a yesterday that made her shake. "Why are you defending him like you knew him?"

"I was him. Oh, not—" he waved a coffee mug in a gesture of denial "—anybody's father, I don't mean that, but I've given in to peer pressure, let other people influence me, make decisions for me." He turned his face from her, thinking of Scully and Markum and their dangerous hidden agendas, then eyed her directly. "I let people use me."

"Like I'm using you?"

"And I'm using you. It's mutual. We made a deal. Agreed to it." He shrugged acceptance of a suddenly unpleasant fait accompli. "Chose it as the lesser of available evils."

She didn't like the picture he was putting together. It wasn't pretty. It wasn't fun.

She tried to look away from him, but his face, his eyes, his acceptance and awareness of the little sins that diminished people held her. Last night he'd touched her heart, yesterday evening her fantasies, today the hidden places inside her, the places she didn't want to see, acknowledge, hear from. "I don't think I like you very much."

"We don't have to like each other to work together, Alice."

He regretted it the moment he said it. As he had occasion to know, words wounded more easily than shrapnel, did more damage, were harder to remove. He watched Alice's eyes grow hooded, her face aloof as though she'd dealt once too often with disapproval and knew exactly how to numb herself to it. He looked away from her. "I'm sorry. I didn't mean— You've been kind. I shouldn't . . ."

Alice shook her head sadly. "Yes, you meant, and so did I. We don't always say what we should in awkward situations. People are so contradictory, don't you think? One way at night, another by day. It's hard to remember where you stand, what rights you have, how well you know someone after only twenty-four hours in their company."

Just like that her directness caught him again, made him feel good, made him like her. Made him grin. "You're good," he said with admiration. "You sure you don't come with an operator's manual?"

"Sorry, burned it. Makes life more interesting. Or so my kids tell me."

"Too bad. I wanted to see what it had to say about mood swings and character traits."

"Oh, I can tell you *that*." Alice bunched her face into a reflective attitude. "It said, and I quote 'Handle with care. Mood and character subject to change without notice.'"

Gabriel chuckled. "Somehow I knew that." He eyed her, and connection stirred between them again, took firmer root. "So, philosophies aside, we are dealing with your family and I do need to know who I am today. Helen and Grace have already met me, but what they really saw..." He shrugged. "Could be a mistake. I can still change anything to be... whoever would suit you best. What color eyes do I have, what clothing do I wear, how do I appear? Am I rich, submissive, cocky—"

"'Rich man, poor man, beggar man, thief,'" Alice quoted the child's rhyme gently. "'Eeny, meeny, miney, moe...' You choose. I told you I wasn't any good at games. Ask my sisters— I'm a poor loser. Just be yourself—that's who they'll expect." She stuck her tongue in her cheek, grinned at him. "I mean, if I wanted to know you, that's who I'd want to know."

"Thanks. And if I don't know me?"

Alice's smile widened, and all at once he knew how Daniel had felt girding himself for the lion's den. No matter what happened while he waited out the time until the serial number on the gun Nicky had died for was identified, ballistics checked, the computer printout verified, Alice Meyers wouldn't give him any ground. He understood that now. He could force her to look at herself all he wanted, but in the end the tactic would backfire on him. However much she hemmed and hawed, when it came right down to it, she'd give him flat truth without excuses, would make him see reflections of himself in the questions he put to her. A no-nonsense woman. Gave none, expected none. And whether he wanted to or not, he could identify with that.

The smile he gave her was genuine. "Let's go shopping," he said.

* * *

Alice approached shopping the way a four-star general approached military maneuvers: with calculation and an eye to getting everything she could out of the battle while sustaining the minimum number of casualties. That there would be casualties went without saying.

While Gabriel tapped his feet impatiently, she went through the ads in the previous night's paper. She needed, she told him, a few groceries, and the shoe store across the street from the Meijers Thrifty Acres megastore was having a sale on brand-name tennis shoes and dress boots. Since he needed clothing basics as well as one or two dress extras, they'd go to Meijers first, get groceries, underwear, jeans and shirts, drive across the street for shoes, then stop at the mall to find him a pair of dress slacks and a summer-weight sweater. Unless, she amended belatedly, he had other ideas?

"What time are we supposed to meet the family?" Gabriel asked, amused, but trying to hurry her along.

"Eleven."

"It's ten-thirty now."

Alice grabbed her purse and the ads, glanced over her shoulder at him on her way out the door. "So we'll be late," she said.

Gabriel grinned and followed her, letting the possible implications fall where they may.

It was amazing how intimate and revealing shopping was. Something as mundane as buying skivvies took on a whole new meaning when tackled by a woman used to purchasing necessities for children and a man who shopped only when he absolutely couldn't avoid it.

"What do you like?" Alice asked without embarrassment, reading the information on the racks of packages in front of her. "High-rise, low-rise, string bikini, cotton, poyester, nylon, fly-front or no-fly... What size are you, anyway?"

"I've never had any complaints."

"Huh?"

Ah, good, she hadn't been listening. Relieved, he selected a three-pack of medium low-rise briefs and dropped them into the cart Alice pushed. "These'll do."

Alice selected a second package of the same brand in brighter colors. "Better get two because you never know. It's always best to have enough underwear for a week."

"What is that, a rule?"

"No, it's practical." The always serious, ever responsible Alice eyed him strangely, then with a flash of insight. Her pushiness and newly laid-back attitude toward missing appointments were getting to him. Interesting.

She tilted her head to view him from a better angle. Hmm. It was intriguing to see someone who took his sense of responsibility for the world even more seriously than she did, to all at once understand what her sisters meant when they told her that she'd lost her sense of humor and forgotten how to play, to get a taste of what it must be like for her family to be around her. To understand why they teased her. She always took their bait, and it was fun.

She ran her tongue around her teeth wondering how far Gabriel would let his patience be tried. She decided to find out. "Didn't your mother teach you about buying underwear? You buy one package, that means you've got underwear for only three more days. It's five days till the wedding. If I don't do laundry between now and then, what will you wear?"

"I'll do what women do, I'll rinse out a pair in the bathroom sink and hang them on the rod to dry."

"Where Aunt Kate, Uncle Delbert and probably my mother will see them? I don't think so."

Patience bordering on exasperation, Gabriel glared at her. This was the most ridiculous debate he'd ever participated in, a far cry from the deadly meaningful conversations that were part of his norm before he'd met her. He was out of his element. He didn't give a fig about the details concerning how much underwear he bought, but she had a point. He opened his mouth to tell her so, but she'd moved on to socks.

He needed, she suggested, black dress socks for the wedding—he vetoed garters when she asked—and sweat socks for everything else. Did he prefer cushion foot or regular, calf-height, ankle-height or crew, white or gray-with-colored bands? If he'd been by himself, Gabriel would have grabbed the first package he came across, but Alice explored the display thoroughly, comparing styles, fibers and durability. Finished, she offered him an informed analysis of what was available for him to choose from.

In T-shirts she breezily ventured the opinion that, except for buying one hot pink surfer T-shirt that would do wonders for his complexion, he might color-coordinate the rest with his briefs. By the time they got to shirts and blue jeans in Men's Casual Wear, Gabriel was gritting his teeth and firmly suggesting that they would save time and tempers if Alice would simply go get her groceries from the other side of the store while he selected his own clothes, and thank you very much, but he would meet her at checkout twenty-seven in fifteen minutes. Alice's mouth and chin quivered at the tone of his voice. She shut her eyes and bit her lips, trying to hang on to her emotions. And failing.

Sound burbled into her throat, refusing to stay where it didn't belong. Air gasped between her lips, came out in a sob. Unprepared for this reaction, Gabriel stared at her in amazement. He hadn't intended to make her cry. He patted her shoulder awkwardly. Alice covered her face with one hand, shoulders shaking.

"Alice? I'm sorry, Alice. I didn't mean to criticize. It's—I'm not used to— No one's ever bought—we used whatever was sent at the mission, and since then I buy my own, and you—and I couldn't—"

"Take it anymore?" Alice supplied. Tears stood in her eyes when she looked up at him, and her throat struggled to suppress more laughter. Oh, dear, he looked so sincere, so repentant, so crushed. She couldn't laugh at him. Not in public. Really shouldn't. But she laughed at him, anyway. Giggled, chuckled, roared.

"Oh, hell." Gabriel shut his eyes and shook his head, disgusted with himself for letting her take him in.

Alice squeezed his arm, eyes bright. "Gotcha."

"Well and truly." He nodded, grinning reluctantly.

Alice wiped her face with the edge of her hand. "God, that felt good. My daughters keep telling me I should cut loose once in a while. I'm glad you stopped me before I had you try on every pair of jeans in the store."

Without thinking, Gabriel cupped her head, helped her smear the tears from her cheeks. It felt like the most natural thing in the world to do. "It wouldn't have gone that far. I'd have strangled you by pair number three."

Alice rested a hand on his wrist, smiling up at him. "Naw, you wouldn't."

Gabriel brushed the end of her nose with the tip of one finger. "'Fraid I would."

"Uh-uh. Too many witnesses. You'd have waited till we got back to the car."

Her hair was soft, skin smooth, her eyes trusted him. His lungs suddenly stopped working; feeling whooshed through him, saturated every nerve. "Well, maybe." God, he needed to kiss her. Not wanted to, nor even lusted to. *Needed* to. Because if he didn't, he'd be like the drowning man who'd fought his way to the surface of the water and gone back under without taking the breath of air that might have saved his life.

With conscious effort he opened his fingers and released her, turned to the rack of jeans beside him. Found a pair of prewashed button-flys in his size. Put them in the cart. Took a breath and looked at her again.

There was a breathless quality about her, something flushed and expectant that, if asked, he wouldn't have known quite how to describe. She wasn't waiting for him to *do* something, exactly. She wasn't exactly looking at him at all. It was something in the way she kept glancing at him and smiling as though she'd unexpectedly discovered something wonderful. In him.

Again he looked away, blindly reaching for the rack of shirts and sliding hanger after hanger aside until his fingers encountered the smooth-rough familiar texture of oxford cloth and paused. He held the light blue shirt up to check the size, glancing at Alice for approval. Odd. He didn't remember it ever mattering before whether or not he pleased someone else with his decisions.

He finished shopping uneasily, paying for his purchases and Alice's groceries, too, handing her back the money she'd lent him yesterday in the pawnshop. He didn't want to owe her anything, either in money or emotions. He had to keep track of everything, hold on to receipts, keep reality separate from fiction, the same as on any case.

Stick to business. Don't make emotional transactions, Markum had advised. Or had it been Scully?

But when they stopped to get him running shoes and walking boots, Alice made him laugh and Gabriel once again forgot to remember who he was.

It was nearly one o'clock before they arrived at the huge center that specialized in providing space rental, clothing and catering needs for banquets, balls and wedding receptions. Bunched accusingly together, five of Alice's sisters sat waiting for them at the edge of the decorative fountain in the lobby. Alice's courage quailed at the sight of them. At the edges of her mind, she could almost hear them grilling Helen about her, about Gabriel:

Who is this guy?
Where did he come from?
What does he do?
Where did she meet him?

When did she meet him?

She was dressed how?

You said she was cutting his hair?

What's his last name?

Nice butt.

Rest of him's not bad, either.

I'll bet they didn't do anything.

Nah, you're probably right. She was probably just trying to get out of dating Skip.

You think?

Sure. He's not really her type. Too nice.

"Oh, God." Alice stopped dead, turning to Gabriel for support. He cupped her shoulders instinctively.

"What's the matter?"

"They've been talking about me."

"That surprises you?"

"No, it's just . . . I don't think I can do this." She fiddled unconsciously with the buttons of the new shirt he'd put on during their last stop, tilted an anxious face to him. He felt and looked good, warm, sexy. Familiar. The tip of her tongue flicked out to taste her upper lip. "I told you I'm not good at this, Gabriel."

He touched her face, smoothed her hair back over her ear, liking the way she turned to him. The way it felt to hold her. Reassure her. "I'm right beside you. You'll do fine."

Alice crushed his shirt in her hand. "But—"

"Shh." Gabriel put a finger to her lips, shutting out the world for an instant, intent only on her. "Don't think so much, it gets in the way." He drew a long breath and stooped without warning, kissing her hard. Her lips parted slightly, asking to linger with his, but he pulled himself up sharply, shying away from the danger zone her mouth represented. "Just stick by me," he whispered, "and we'll both be fine."

He held her an instant longer than it took her to square her shoulders, then released her. Her eyes were on him, soft, self-conscious, wary, full of *maybe*. He tried to repress the surge of heat her *maybe* made him feel, and failed. His palms on her shoulders felt damp. "Ready?"

Not for you, Alice thought, and kept the hand that wanted to touch the kiss he'd left on her mouth folded tightly at her side. "It might be better for you if you just wait here and I do this first part alone."

Gabriel grinned. "Easier maybe, not better."

"Sure?" Alice asked. "I'll be all right if you want to duck off to the men's shop and see about your tux—"

"United we stand." He laughed and offered her his hand, wanting hers for support. "Besides, what else are friends for?"

"Well—" Alice's smile was small and crooked "—if you're sure."

Without a word Gabriel drew her hand through the crook of his arm and together they walked across the lobby. Friends.

With potential.

"You're late," they accused Alice, while their eyes pinned, examined and dissected Gabriel. "No one answered your phone—we've been calling for over an hour. You should have called. We were worried about you."

"Sorry," Alice apologized. "We made a couple stops. Gabriel needed a few things."

A likely story, their eyes said.

Alice sucked in air. If they refused to believe the truth when she told it . . . Why did she feel guilty about telling it? "So," she said into the stony silence, "anyway, we're here." She waved a hand at Gabriel. "I'm sure you all know who this is. Gabriel, these are my sisters—Helen you met yesterday, Meg . . ."

She began with the petite redheaded management consultant in jeans and the company T-shirt, indicating each sister in turn. Edith, the nurse, was a tall slim brunette with

an olive complexion and green eyes; Twink, another brunette slightly shorter than Edith, wearing a fluorescent green
sundress, managed a law office; Sam-the-paramedic-
volunteer-fireman was the one in the denim miniskirt and
yellow polo shirt; and Grace— "Where's Grace?" Alice
asked.

"Not here," Twink said helpfully.

"Nobody's seen her since yesterday," Edith breathed.
"Not since Ma said she came home and took a shower and
left."

"I called Phil," Meg put in. "But no one's seen him,
either."

"We figure they've gone off somewhere and eloped,"
Sam said, "and left us to deal with the relatives while they
have a bang-up time. I *told* certain people—" she looked at
Helen, who ignored her "—this thing was getting too big."

"Don't worry." Twink winked broadly. "If they've
eloped, we'll get 'em. I called a friend of mine with the state
police and asked if they'd keep an eye out for Grace's car.
They'll bring 'em back." She smiled gently. "I told him to
feel free to use handcuffs."

Gabriel raised an eyebrow at this pronouncement, but
wisely remained silent. Helen gave Twink a withering look
and linked arms with Gabriel, tugging him to one side to
impart dark secrets.

"Y'see," she murmured, "there's something you ought
to know about before you get any more involved with one
of us than you already are. We have a—" she made an expressive circling gesture with one hand "—little problem in
this family that nobody talks about. It's called communi-
cation. Nobody does. Not even—" she eyed Alice pointedly "—those of us with teenagers to preach at who really
ought to know better."

"Those of us who live in stone houses," Alice suggested
meaningfully back, "really shouldn't throw glass."

"You always say that," Helen complained. "What does it mean?"

"It means," Meg said, "that if the shoe fits your foot you ought to take it out of your mouth and put it there."

"What? Me?" Helen put a dramatic hand to her heart. "I'm the only one of us who communicates with anyone. Don't you get my memos? Aren't they clearly stated? Don't I always tell you who's doing what with whom and when?"

"Telling." Edith stabbed an aggrieved finger at her. "You're always *telling* people to do things. You never ask, you never suggest, you never *listen*."

"But I'm a major," Helen said, surprised. "That's what majors do."

"Not in this family," Sam said hotly, "'cause I'll tell you, Major, if I'd wanted someone to tell me what to do all the time, I'd have joined the army myself to save you the trouble. I mean, you're not even the *eldest*."

"Yeah!" Twink nodded. "That's right. Alice and Meg are both older—"

Gabriel drew Alice aside. "How long does this go on?"

"Until you stop it," she murmured. "It's a test to see if you've got what it takes to handle Brannigans. I tried to warn you."

"I thought you were a Meyers."

She cocked her head, surprised. Surely, she'd told him... No. They'd said a lot about themselves, one another, without sharing the details. The things he seemed instinctively to know about her, like the things she knew about him, came from somewhere else, from some deeper timeless knowledge.

Heart to heart, she whispered to herself, then immediately shunned the thought. Even a wide-open all-seeing heart needed time, and hers was neither.

"I was married to a Meyers for about a month," she said. "I kept his name for the girls. Pretense of respectability, you know?"

"I'm sorry."

"Don't be. It's old."

Again something passed between them, some intense deep-seated understanding, that curious sensation of fullness and not being alone that strangers could share because they didn't have to worry about what secrets they knew about one another—or didn't know.

Except they weren't exactly strangers anymore. And they'd begun to share secrets.

In the instant of recognition, their eyes slunk away from one another like thieves after a job.

"So," Gabriel said, "how do you suggest I handle your sisters?"

Alice shrugged. "Ignore them—they hate that. It always gets their attention."

Gabriel nodded. "Meet you here after I pick up a tux?"

"Or across the hall at Camille's Bridal Boutique."

"See you in a few." He brushed her mouth with a brief goodbye and started away, then turned back. "What name?"

"Witoczynsk—"

"Brannigan," Meg, Helen, Edith, Twink and Sam shouted after him. "Phil's marrying a Brannigan."

"Of course," Gabriel muttered and disappeared.

The minute he was out of sight, Alice's sisters dragged her into the bridal boutique changing room and pounced on her.

"Where did you find him?"

"At the side of the road."

"How long have you known him?"

"A ... while."

"Are you going to keep him?"

"He's not a stray dog."

"Are you living together?"

"For now."

"What are you going to do with him tonight while we're there?"

Tonight? Phooey. She'd forgotten about tonight. Too bad they hadn't. "Nothing in front of you, but he'll be there."

"Ah-ah, Alice." Twink brushed one index finger over the other, shaming. "No kids under eighteen and no men of any age. You made the rules."

"So, I'm changing the rules. Big deal." She bit down on the automatic defensiveness, ignoring her sisters' further comments by concentrating her attention on the brilliant teal, dark green, electric blue, violet and bright pink tealength dresses Edith, Sam, Meg, Helen and Twink wore respectively. Then she smoothed down the bodice of her own deep red scooped-neck cap-sleeved gown. The satin was smooth and cool to touch, easily the prettiest thing she'd ever worn. And even she of the self-deprecating attitude was willing to admit the color brought out the best in her. She should have known better than to distrust the artist in Grace.

She turned, posing in front of the mirror while the boutique's seamstress tucked and poked at the fabric. The one thing Grace had refused to quibble about were the bridesmaids' dresses. She'd refused any suggestion that summer was the time for pretty pastels, insisting instead that her sisters be outfitted in real colors that not only suited their personalities and complexions, but also in colors that didn't look as if they'd wash out in the rain. An overall theme of everlasting commitment was what she was looking for, she'd said, reflected by colors that looked as if they were committed to something besides a single afternoon's wear and a plastic bag in the back of the closet. Grace had chosen colors that looked as though they'd last forever, which was precisely how long she wanted her marriage to last.

Alice watched her sisters turn, preen and laugh, each beautiful in her own vivid hue. She wished she'd been as certain as Grace was about what she'd wanted for her own wedding—and marriage. But then, she wasn't Grace, or any of her other sisters, either. She was just plain old waffling never-knew-what-she-wanted Alice, who'd always thought that life should come equipped with rules—something numbered and printed on a little card she could carry around in her purse like a restaurant tip table to review whenever she couldn't figure out what to do next.

With a wry smile, Alice stepped out of her dress and handed it to the waiting salesclerk, who promised to box it up and have it at the front of the shop for her when Alice was ready. Not knowing what to do next seemed to be the flaw of her generation. They'd made every effort to do things better than their parents, but every time they thought they had it all figured out, some study came along and proved them wrong. Stupid, but true. In a day and age of ever available expert analyses, the only thing you could trust to tell you right from wrong was your conscience and your heart. And if your conscience lied and your heart had been wrong once too many times in the past, what did you have left?

Someday, Alice promised herself tartly. Like Dad used to say, you've always got Someday.

"But how do you know when it's Someday, Mom?" Alice could still hear the aggrieved note in Allyn's voice when her daughter had been eight and wondering when they could take a vacation to Disneyland, when she could get a horse, when they could buy a new house. The answer had always been "Someday." But how do you know when it's Someday, Mom?...

"You'll know," Alice heard herself assure Allyn, "when you're old enough to reach out and grab it."

"But what if I don't, Mom? What if I don't?"

"Don't worry," Alice promised, stroking her hair. "You'll know, my darling, you'll know."

But maybe Allyn hadn't really been worried about *how* she'd know when Someday was here, after all. Maybe what she'd really been worried about was what would happen if she didn't reach out and grab it.

Nothing, Alice thought, bending down and yanking the laces of her tennis shoes too tight for comfort as she felt the swell of the familiar unnamed anger and frustration. If you didn't grab for Someday when you had a chance, absolutely nothing happened.

She straightened, jaw set. The girls were grown and out grabbing handfuls of their own Somedays. They didn't need her, not today, and maybe not tomorrow, either. She was out of a job, but maybe that wasn't so bad. Maybe that was just Someday's Opportunity knocking, looking for her, challenging her. After the wedding, after she finished up her commitments to Grace, maybe she could take some time to find herself, too, travel like Allyn, go to college, take risks....

She stepped purposefully out of the dressing room, accepted her dress box from the woman at the counter and followed her sisters out of the shop. Gabriel was slouched against the wall beside the boutique, plastic-wrapped tuxedo over one shoulder. He straightened gladly when he saw her, and Alice felt a flicker of warmth ignite in her veins at the same time she felt her resolve drain. So much for Someday, she thought. Because if he kissed her hello, she damned well knew that, whether she intended to or not, she'd go to hell kissing him back.

Chapter Six

"Hi," she said.

"Hi." He reached for her box and fell naturally into step beside her, smiling, glad to see her. Enjoying himself, when from all past experience, he should not. "I ran into Skip at the tux shop," he murmured softly. "We had a long talk. I invited him to lunch."

"Yeah?" His breath in her ear made her senses buzz. She wanted to touch him; she wanted to run. There was a piece of thread on the sleeve of his shirt. She reached over and picked it off. "What about?"

"Seems the man has had quite a crush on the major since high school to the point where he—no offense, he says—was willing to go out with you to please her. And I think," he said conspiratorially, "if you're interested, I know what we can do about the major."

"Really?" She liked the twinkle in his eye, the sound of the chuckle he shared only with her. "That sounds evil but promising."

Gabriel nodded.

"Funny," Alice mused aloud, "I didn't picture opportunity wearing a Band-Aid when it knocked."

"Oh, honey, I haven't been called 'opportunity' for a long, long time." Acrimony was faint but evident. He covered it quickly, asking, "How should opportunity dress?"

"Sirens, bells, flashing lights."

Gabriel grinned. "Is that another way of saying 'I don't know what it looks like but I don't want to miss it when it comes'?"

"You got it." She colored slightly when he lifted a brow at her vehemence. "I've just..." She hunched one shoulder. "I've just been waiting for an opportunity to do something about Helen for years."

"I see," was all he said, but his eyes laughed at her, called her liar.

"I have," she insisted to them.

"Uh-huh." He nodded, teasing. "Sure."

Alice yanked open the outside door, furious. "Shut up," she hissed. "What do you know?"

"I know—" he stepped outside and faced her, barring her path "—that if I dropped everything and kissed you right now the way a real lover would, you'd kiss me back into oblivion and run."

Alice gazed up at him, breath shortened, heart bumping fast against her ribs. Gabriel's face was calm; his eyes were not. They challenged; they desired. They were uncertain. Alice gripped the handle of the door. This was crazy; it was nuts. She'd never been adept at dating, nor allowed herself much curiosity about bedroom gymnastics on the whole. Since the girls had been born, she'd avoided the former at most costs and had never felt she could afford the latter. But she wasn't a schoolgirl either. She shouldn't feel like one, behave like one.

Her tongue flicked around the inside of her teeth, her eyes dropped to his mouth, couldn't seem to leave it. She had so much to confront about sex and sexuality, things to understand, things to accept—about herself. Why she thought it was wrong to feel the way she felt. Why she denied desire existed, or joked crassly with her sisters to cover up her fears of it. The things she couldn't reconcile with herself. Like the very idea of love and marriage.

Like why she quite definitely, quite decidedly, wanted Gabriel.

She watched his lips bow and constrict, thin then part. Deliberately she shut her eyes, shut out Gabriel, shut out the curl of heat at the base of her spine. Her body and her emotions didn't control her anymore. She didn't let them use her; she knew how to ignore them. She was in charge.

She lifted her chin and opened her eyes, meeting Gabriel's unspoken dare with one of her own. "Move," she said, shoving him aside. "I'm hungry. I want some lunch. And I want to do something about Helen before the wedding."

The Irish-Mexican restaurant across the street from the Banquets 'n More catering service was packed. Alice and Gabriel threaded their way past tables decorated with shamrocks and shillelaghs, beneath bright piñatas, around waiters and waitresses wearing green Irish bowlers and bright Mexican frills, to the arrangement of tables at the back where Alice's sisters were already ensconced. Helen patted the empty chair beside her.

"Sit, Gabriel," she invited. "Is that what they call you? Gabriel? Not Gabe or Gabby?"

Twink snorted indelicately. "Leave him alone, Helen. Would you want to be called Gabby? Besides, it doesn't suit him. Neither does Gabe. He's more of a—" she screwed up her face thoughtfully "—Dane."

"Based on what?" Sam asked. "That he's mostly blond, with Alice and because Matt's middle name was Dane? Oops." She put a hand to her mouth and glanced contritely at Alice when Meg slapped her arm. "Sorry, I didn't mean—it just came out."

Alice flipped the remark aside with a hand, but not before Gabriel caught a flash of some involuntary deep-rooted pain mixed with self-disgust. "It's all right. Don't worry about it." She glanced around at Gabriel when he slid a gentle palm across her back and pulled out her chair for her. "I told him about Matt."

"And a lot of other things." His eyes on Alice were intense and warm, seeing. "We don't keep secrets."

He slipped into the seat between her and Helen and angled his chair closer to slide an arm across the back of Alice's. His fingers slid into the hair at the base of her neck, slid down again, massaging. She didn't want to be aware of him, not when he was performing. But she *was* aware of him, couldn't help it, couldn't—

"So, Gabriel," Helen asked, "what do you do?"

Gabriel's hand tensed on Alice's neck, then relaxed. "I'm in insurance—an investigator." Not quite the truth, not completely a lie. "What do you do?"

"Same general line of work—Military Claims Investigations." Helen grinned. "I'm a negotiations expediter. When all else fails, they bring me in to unravel the red tape. You?"

"No." Gabriel shook his head. "No red tape. I just try to make a difference."

"Do you succeed?"

Gabriel's grip on the back of Alice's neck grew painful; his eyes were blank. "Not always."

Something about the way he said it drew their eyes and their silence. Alice had the sudden fierce urge to protect him from that silence. She reached over and squeezed his thigh, leaned into the table confidingly, drawing her sisters' attention. "He's just come off a rough case—family dispute. It didn't go well." She settled back, nodded at an approaching waitress and opened her menu. "Everybody know what they want for lunch? Oh, look, there's Skip. Helen, move over, we'll get another chair and ask him to join us.''

From there, lunch turned into a round of pleasant family bickering and teasing, which included Gabriel and in which he participated; made him unconsciously feel as if he belonged. Mixed in amongst the banter were notes about the wedding preparations—who was in charge of which disasters—and the current state of the sisters' extra-family lives. Rebecca and Allyn were discussed by aunts who thought it was pretty funny that Alice, the big sister who had advised all of them about growing up, should now be so confused by her own children doing the same. Sam's newly announced pregnancy was congratulated, horror stories about labor rooms and breast feeding were shared—much to Skip's embarrassment and Gabriel's amusement. Then Twink, whose infant was barely two months old, and Edith, whose children were already nine and eleven, and Meg, who'd been married almost two years and showed no inclination toward having babies, were laughingly ordered to get busy and produce.

After a pair of margaritas, Helen lamented the fact that now only she, Alice and Ma were still unmarried and it didn't look as if Alice would be on the market much longer. Alice, ignoring Gabriel's restraining hand, advised Helen smartly that the major had better stay out of her sister's business and look to her own, where she might, if it was possible for Helen to see what was beneath her own nose— meaning Skip—discover the direction of her own future. Helen countered by asking sweetly whether or not Alice had put the board under her mattress yet, since Aunt Kate and Uncle Delbert would be arriving tomorrow. Twink pointedly advised them both that if they would each shut up and stop considering every possible angle before making a commitment to anything that they might both wind up happier.

Meg left the table several times to make phone calls, trying to find Grace. Skip offered to chauffeur Helen anywhere she wanted to go—and would she perhaps like to go to dinner and a concert if her schedule permitted? Edith, ever quick to spot a potential for disaster, invited Skip to join them all at Alice's for sisters-sisters night, since Gabriel, it appeared, was already going to be there. Gabriel raised a questioning brow at Alice over the suggestion, and Alice shut her eyes and shook her head; he didn't want to know. Sam's beeper went off toward the end of the meal and she left thinking she'd have to go to a fire, and returned to announce that Grace had been stopped by the state police while on a pizza-delivery run, had been late delivering the pizza and, to put it mildly, had been quite specific about where Sam and the rest of her sisters could stick their meddling overprotective concern for her.

Hearing the news, Alice surprised both herself and Gabriel by pressing her face into his shoulder with a whispered prayer of thanks. And it was with some astonishment that Gabriel discovered from the general giggles of relief, exchanged glances, hand gestures and quick little indrawn breaths exactly how apprehensive Grace's sisters had been about her. They'd barely spoken about her absence, but apparently overt demonstration and knock-down-drag-out-arguments had nothing to do with love in the Brannigan family. The bond was simply something that they all took for granted, and would remain a constant channel marker in an ever shifting sea—regardless of sunshine or hellfire—forever.

He stepped unconsciously away from them as they said goodbye to one another in the parking lot, his heart beating fast, blood leapfrogging in his veins. This was the way the world ought to be. This was the reason he'd picked up a badge and a gun in the first place. Here was hope. He'd forgotten what that was like. His job had pushed him so far underground that he'd forgotten what it was like to be trusted—or trusting. To be accepted at face value.

Alice's family—much like Alice herself—was from another planet, another time zone, and in some strange and indeterminate way they frightened him more than any undercover job he'd ever walked into. They did something that could prove dangerous to him. They drew him in, accepted him at face value, included him in their teasing, concern and relief merely because he was with Alice and they loved Alice.

"You have a very nice family," he said as he and Alice walked from the restaurant to her car.

Alice snorted. "Much you know." She peeked at him from the corner of her eye, wondering which worry puzzled him now. "They like you, too, but you've been accepted by a mob of lunatics. Don't you wonder what that makes you?"

Gabriel lined his arm through hers. "A lunatic's apprentice?"

"You're cute, Book, I'll give you that." They reached the car, and Alice paused to unlock it. "I should have known you'd fit right in with them."

Gabriel slid into the car, leaned across to open her door for her. "I take it that's not a compliment?"

Alice shrugged. "Depends on what they've done to— *for*—me lately."

"But they love you."

"Of course they love me. They have to. I'm their sister." Alice backed the car out of its parking space. "I love them, too, but the pressure gets to me sometimes." She paused thoughtfully, glanced keenly at him before she guided the car into the traffic. "No, that's not right," she said. "It's really not the love that gets to me. It's living up to it—their regard, their expectations." She made a sound of regret behind her teeth. "That gets rough sometimes."

Gabriel waited, silently watching her struggle with her thoughts, very aware that he wanted her to tell him about herself. For the first time in a long time he wanted to know someone else on a personal level, wanted to trade secrets he instinctively understood she would keep, tell her things about himself he hadn't thought about in years.

When he'd almost decided she wasn't going to live up to his hope, Alice turned the car onto a rutted dirt road that ran around behind a small private school. She brought the car to a halt near a tangled stand of elderly blackberry bushes and trees that broke the landscape between the school and a new subdivision under development, and rolled down her window. Yesterday's downpour had left everything looking shiny, matted and damp. The air smelled of sunshine and rain.

"Do you mind if we walk a bit?" she asked. "It's so beautiful out and once tonight hits, there won't be time to breathe again before Sunday and I need—"

Gabriel put a finger to her mouth. "Let's walk," he said.

They left the car in the shade and strolled across the school playground. A few fluffy cumulus clouds dotted the otherwise clean blue sky, and Alice dropped her head back and closed her eyes, lifting her face to the sun, feeling summer on her skin. "I used to bring Allyn and Becky here for picnics when they were little," she said. "I've always liked this place. Matt and I used to cut class and come here sometimes. This school was closed then, and what with two big families and all, it was the one place we really had to be alone."

There was nostalgia instead of regret in her voice, which surprised Gabriel. His experience was that people hid their sins in closets full of shame, bringing them out only when forced to do so in order to protect themselves in front of a judge. He rolled up his sleeves and pocketed his hands, waiting, watching Alice, drawn to the beauty that lay beneath the unadorned surface. He doubted he'd ever been more uncertain about what would happen next in his life. Doubted he'd ever been less sure of what he wanted to happen. Knew absolutely what shouldn't happen here, and couldn't guarantee that he'd stop it if it did. Didn't think he'd be able to, anyway.

"Don't get me wrong—there were a lot of things I didn't like about my family when I was growing up," she said now. "Few things that could still use some work, but when I'd see my friends with *their* parents, or listen to them talk about *their* families, I always remember being glad that I wasn't them and that it was *my* parents who'd had me." Puzzled she peered up at him. He looked like everything strong and sure in the world—relaxed, attentive, whole, secure. And yet... "I don't know why I'm telling you this," she said softly. "I don't usually attack people and show off my life, but there was something in your face back in the parking lot—like maybe there's something you need to hear. Or I need to let go of." She studied the ground at her feet, kicked up an old golf ball buried deep in the wet green-and-brown grass. "I don't know, maybe I'm crazy. Maybe—"

"Alice."

He caught her whole attention just by saying her name. His eyes were darker than ever, shaded from the sun. Her tongue flicked nervously between her teeth, then retreated. Gabriel waited, not forcing her to continue the way he wanted to. Not offering her support the way he also wanted to. Not touching her at all. And God help him, whether he should or not, he wanted to.

"You haven't minced words so far," he said gently. "Don't start now. It doesn't suit you. I'm part of your life for now by default. There are—" he grinned "—things I need to know in order to survive in it. Your sisters, for instance. They've never seen me before and for all they know I could be Attila the Hun, yet within ten minutes of meeting two of them, I'm an usher for Grace's wedding. You answer the door in your bathrobe with a half-naked man at your back—anyone else would leave in embarrassment, maybe file the scene away for extortion purposes in the future, but your sisters stay and ask you if you had responsible sex. Now—'' his jaw worked around a disbelieving laugh ''—being an only child, I don't know too much about siblings, but doesn't this all strike you as odd?''

"No." Alice shook her head. "I am the one who stopped for you, remember?"

"True."

"And we've always been a very . . . open family."

"Okay."

"And like my father always said, when you already have seven kids, what's two or three more?"

"That doesn't explain yesterday."

"No. Yesterday—'' her mouth curved ''—that was just my family. One of the first things we were ever taught was, 'Don't be afraid to ask questions—it's the only way to learn.' We were also taught that whether we agreed with one another or not, family was always there.''

She gestured inadequately, misinterpreting his expression. "I don't mean hiding fugitives from the law, or anything like that, but emotionally, supportively, *there*." She started walking again, searching for words. "It's . . . like when I got pregnant and ran away and got married, my family wasn't crazy about it, but they stood behind me, anyway. When Matt's family found us and convinced him to let them get us annulled, I felt like I'd failed my family somehow. It didn't make sense then, and it doesn't now, but I felt like I'd thrown away something, disillusioned them, because I'd always sort of thought they saw me as a kind of saint—which I'd never been. I even used to wonder if I didn't use Matt, if I didn't get pregnant just so my family would stop looking at me that way, so I could stop having to live up to their expectations. So they'd know once and for all that I wasn't perfect like they thought."

She shook her head, laughed at the idea. "'Course the funny thing is, I found out by getting pregnant that they'd known all along I wasn't flawless. They'd lived with me for seventeen years and I hadn't fooled them about anything.

And when I was feeling sorry for myself and thinking how unfair it was that they thought I'd hurt them, they really only hurt *for* me, not because of me. They didn't like what I'd done, but they didn't judge me for it, and they weren't ashamed of me. They didn't try to hide me in some closet where people couldn't see me. And they welcomed Matt into the family and said they'd do whatever they could..." She looked at Gabriel. "Sometimes I feel like I still owe them for that. I've done so many stupid things and they've always been there. It's kind of...daunting to have people go on loving you no matter what you do."

"But you said it, they're not perfect, either, Alice." Gabriel's face was hooded, drawn, emotion brewing beneath the surface.

"I know. That's not the point." Alice read the danger signals with a thrill of excitement. She was shooting in the dark and she was hitting things. Why that was so important to her, she didn't know, but whatever she had seen hidden beneath his surface back in the parking lot, she was touching that part of him now, the heart of him. The only part that mattered. "It's just the way I feel sometimes. I forget that they trust me to be there for them, too, no matter what. I forget that I'm not the only one who does stupid things." She stopped and turned on him with sudden passion. "Neither are you."

He was silent, angry, not sure how to respond. Last night she'd exhibited an uncanny knack for reading between lines he didn't even speak. The ease with which they communicated was something that both intrigued and disquieted him. He didn't pretend not to know what she was talking about; that was the easy part. He'd told her about his job, about his findings. About how the people he had to trust were the ones he also had to suspect of hanging him out to dry. She was sharp enough to come up with the rest on her own. But he hadn't told her about his family, about his guilt over them.

With an unaccustomed sense of resentment, he wondered how Alice seemed to know what he was thinking all the time, how she was able to pinpoint with such accuracy where her life paralleled his—and why she seemed to know exactly who he was. He eyed her the way one poker player eyes another, watching for a tipped hand.

"My family, my life—they're not like yours, Alice. The mistakes I make are not as simply forgiven. When I do stupid things—misjudge a situation, trust the wrong people— it affects more than just me and my emotional life."

"Are you talking about the mistakes you make as an officer of the law, as a man, or as somebody's son?"

Her voice was gentle. Her question was as insistent as his mother's last letter—and as unsettling. But he couldn't ignore Alice the way he could ignore his mail. "I'm talking about all of it, Alice. Which is more than you have a right to know."

He turned his back on her, striding across the drive they'd come in on and forcing his way into the jumble of brush and trees on the other side. Branches scratched his face, and he shoved them aside. Rain puddled in leaves poured down his back, soaking his shirt. Unconnected snatches of memory stirred his conscience, blurred in and out of focus. Two days ago, Sunday night, a dark dirt road, raucous voices, firelight shuddering in an empty oil drum. The weight of a killer's gun pressed into his hand and the feel of it tucked against his back. A deafening explosion beside his ear, a grunt of surprise, the sound of a body falling. He felt rather than remembered the out-of-control sound of two more jarring reports, the accompanying sensation of blind panic, of blood in his eyes, of slipping and scrambling to get away.

Blindly he pushed the brambles aside, but memory could not be coerced so easily. Twenty years ago, give or take a millennium, he was back in Vietnam by *his* choice, a conscientious objector-turned-medic who didn't believe in killing, but who arrogantly thought he could make a contribution and save a few lives. A patrol unit had brought a pair of wounded Vietcong prisoners into the hospital for treatment. One had taken a young soldier by surprise, grabbing his weapon and shooting another soldier whose rifle had fallen near Gabriel. Gabriel had picked up the gun instinctively, ready to fire it. And hadn't. Not at the urgings of his head, nor those from the soldiers around him. A nurse had echoed the voice of his conscience with her pleading *don't*.

It was the first time he'd ever picked up a gun; the first time he'd ever doubted the pure pacifism his parents had taught him to believe in. The first time he'd truly understood the impotence and violence of rage.

He picked up a dead branch and swung it against a fallen tree, seeking to jar himself off the path his thoughts had taken. But they refused to be sidetracked, instead leaving him with one more deliberately forgotten vision. Fifteen years ago, academy graduation. His parents had attended the ceremony. They didn't understand why he'd had to become a cop, didn't understand what he'd meant when he tried to tell them he couldn't sit by any longer and watch death happen around him as he'd had to at the evac hospital and not try to do something to prevent it. Try to make a difference. And if that meant he had to carry a gun, then he'd carry a gun and learn to use it.

They'd assured him they loved him and were proud of him for doing what he felt he had to—for making a choice and sticking to it. They didn't agree with his decision, but they'd have been disappointed if he hadn't made it simply to pacify them.

By the end of his third case, though, their view of him had shifted uneasily. He was changing, they'd said. There was something growing in him, something violent. He was starting to enjoy his role among the criminal element too much, and that made them afraid. Of him.

He stopped and wrapped a hand around a tangle of wild grapevines. He'd stopped going to see his family because he was aware—even though he was unwilling to admit it then—that they were right to be afraid of him. Something hard, inhuman and violent *was* taking root inside him; something intolerant, unforgiving and bitter aimed as much at himself and the bureaucracy he battled almost daily to allow him to make his cases, as at the criminals he risked his life to build cases against. But he figured he'd made his choices; he'd lived by them. No one got through life without a few skeletons lurking in their memories. Some had more than others; many were worse than his. Some dealt with memory by confronting it, letting it rise and fall in a natural day-to-day progression. He'd dealt with his memories by burying them alive and changing his identity with his cases so that when his ghosts came out to haunt him, they wouldn't be able to find him. For the most part it had worked. Until Alice.

He ran a hand through his hair trying to come back to the present, get his bearings, remember which persona to put on. Damn, he might have known he'd been enjoying himself too much with her. And her family. He might have known that if he let himself relax even a little he'd start to question who and what he was again.

He stiffened at the sudden cold flick of her shadow on his back, heard her puff in the clutter of branches behind him. *Don't,* he thought, a warning to himself. Or was it to her?

"Gabriel?" His name was a tentative sound in her throat. "I'm sorry. I didn't mean—"

"Who are you, really, Alice Meyers?" His voice was controlled, intense, almost savage. Even now, when it was the last thing on earth he wanted to feel, he had the powerful urge to turn to her, touch her, ask her to hold him. His fists clenched at his sides. He'd never asked anyone to hold him. "What is it about you that lets you twist me in knots one minute and makes me want you under me the next?" He swung about and advanced on her, backing her into a tree. "What makes me want to tell you things I don't even want to think about?" He ran a finger along her jaw, watched her pupils dilate, her breath quicken, felt desire rise. "Why, when I can't seem to get far enough away from you, can't I get close enough to you, either?" He dragged his finger across her lips, touched the heat and moisture of her mouth. "Why do I know how you'd feel if I—"

"Don't."

She could barely breathe, he was so close. Blatantly sexual, his gaze moved lazily across her face, aroused, rousing. His breath brushed the corners of her mouth. His body didn't quite press hers, but she could feel him, taste him . . .

"—if I touch you—"

"Don't!"

"How long has it been, Alice?" He braced his hands on the tree behind her head. "How long since you've been touched, treated like a woman?"

Long enough. The thought leapt between them, guilty and revealing. Gabriel's mouth lowered toward hers, and Alice knew he'd read the evidence in her eyes before she could blink it away. Her feet clung to the earth, wanting to run, unable to move.

"Please, Gabriel," she whispered. Why did she want to justify her reaction to him? Why was she afraid of what he might think? She shouldn't be ashamed of not sleeping with anyone since Matt, of being cautious with both her body and her emotions. "Whatever you see, whatever I've done, I didn't mean—don't want—I don't *know* you. I *can't*—"

Gabriel's mouth sought hers briefly, impatiently, stilling the words. "But I've known you forever, Alice," he said thickly, "and I need—"

He stopped abruptly, stunned by the truth. Oh, God, what was he saying, what was he *doing?* He *did* need her. Fiercely. Passionately. He *did* know her. Every nook and cranny of her soul. Had forever. Where he'd always thought he ended, she began him again. His hands crushed dead bark from the tree as he withdrew them from behind her head. The idea was madness. It was impossible.

But it was also true.

His eyes found Alice's, read the confusion, the latent desire, the concern. The same mocha-chocolate eyes that had feared for him—been afraid of him—yesterday morning. The expressive wanting eyes that had called him to her last night, then stopped him from kissing her all in the beat of a pulse. Damning eyes. Samaritan eyes. Forgiving eyes. Hungry eyes.

He spun away from her, back onto the trail he'd crushed through the bramble coming in. And stopped. He couldn't run from her this time.

He turned, but she was already there, hand on his arm, speaking his name. His skin quivered at her touch. "Gabriel—"

"Don't touch me, Alice, not now." His voice was strained. "This is something I haven't planned for, I've never felt. If you keep touching me, I don't know what I'll do."

"Gabriel, please." Again she was pleading with him, but differently now, for understanding. "You—I don't understand what I feel. You confuse me. One minute we're so close that the only things I don't know about you—or care if I ever know—are the details. The next minute you're someone else, someone I don't want to know—*couldn't* know. When I remember that it was only yesterday, and how I found you, I'm frightened. *You* frighten me. Everything in my life is changing so all at once, and I don't know if the way I feel around you is part of that or because of it, and I don't know if this is just a game of pretend that got carried away and . . ."

She was dithering, just like Aunt Kate at Cousin Mamie's wedding. She hated that about herself, hated not being able to put her thoughts into words coherently. She plunged recklessly on, anyway. "And I don't like feeling like this—like I keep inviting you to do something, then pushing you away. But I've never—and I don't know how—and if I let go of you—somehow that seems like it'll make it all even worse and—"

Gabriel's hands cupped her face, were in her hair. His mouth was warm on hers, stilling, demanding, gentle. "Alice," he murmured. "Be quiet. You're rattling on."

Her hands were on his arms, holding tight. "Am I?"

"Yes," he assured her between kisses. "On and on and on."

"I'm sorry." Breathlessly, Alice sought the dangers of his mouth, moth to flame.

Gabriel's hands slid down her sides, found her waist, dragged her close. "I'm not," he muttered, and then there was no more room for speech, no breath to spare for anything so mundane. Alice's arms sought the path along his shoulders, around his neck. Fingers slipped easily into his hair, tightened. His tongue touched hers, claimed it, branded it to the deep-seated tone of Alice's encouragement. His hands curved over her hips. She stood on tiptoe straining to get near, called to him by the rumble in his throat, a sound without words, a plea.

And then he lifted his head and let her go, drawing her hands from his hair, pushing her away.

"Gabriel."

His name was out before she could stop herself from saying it, calling him back. He shut his eyes, jammed his hands deep into his pockets.

"I can't, Alice. I want you too badly. If I don't stop now, I won't be able to stop at all. I'd take you down right here, but I don't want you to remember me that way. I don't want you to regret it."

"What about you?"

Gabriel looked at the sky, at his recent past and indefinite future. What had she called their possibilities last night? *Temporary.* "I don't matter a damn past Saturday, Alice."

She was in front of him, insistent. Her eyes were damp. "What if I said you did? You could?"

"You like to be sure of things before you commit to them, Alice, and I am not, by any stretch of anyone's imagination, a sure thing."

"Because of your job?"

"That, and who I am."

"But who—"

"I'm never sure, Alice." He looked at her sadly. "And I do wish I knew."

Chapter Seven

A dithery-looking white-haired woman in a fluttery dress of orange-flowered chiffon stood on Alice's porch wiggling her fingers excitedly at them as they pulled into the driveway after a silent journey home.

She was flanked by a squat gray grizzled-looking man in his late sixties, three dubious-appearing red-haired boys of varying sizes and ages, a forty-five-year-old whiny-looking female in shorts and a halter top who bore a marked resemblance to the chiffon-clad woman, and a tall stalwart-looking gentleman with orange hair and an expression eternally wishing to be somewhere else. Alice stared at them aghast. After what she'd just been through with Gabriel, the last thing in the world she needed was Aunt Kate, Uncle Delbert, Cousin Mamie, her husband, George, and their children dumped, like so many puppies, on her doorstep. She lifted her eyes skyward with a silent *Why me?*, realizing, as she had in the past, that God undoubtedly appreciated this joke very much, since He apparently had the same sense of humor that Helen had.

Beside her, Gabriel roused himself from his black study to view this diversion with interest. It certainly beat self-castigation all to hell. "Is that . . . ?"

"Aunt Kate." Alice nodded blankly. "Uncle Delbert, Cousin Mamie, George and the boys. I forget their names."

"Were we expecting them?"

Alice struggled with a long-suffering sigh. "No. But then, we never are."

The grin that formed his mouth caught Gabriel unprepared. He coughed and cleared his throat to hide it. His "I see" sounded strangled.

"Yoo-hoo!" Aunt Kate wobbled down the three concrete steps on her orange sling-back stilts, took one step off the walk onto the grass, which last night's rain had left soft, wet and muddy, sank deep, recovered and remained on the walk, waving. "Alice dear, *do* come let us in, will you? We've waited simply *hours* and we're all just impossibly *exhausted* and *famished*. We absolutely *must*—"

Aunt Kate, Alice observed to Gabriel with a shudder, always seemed to speak in exclamation points and emphatic italics, laboring under the mistaken impression that this was 1920, and she was Southern, cute and perpetually twenty-three. Which was what, she added, made Aunt Kate fascinating to observe—from afar. She left the car, mentally cringing, and crossed to greet the relative who lifted her cheek to Alice.

"How are you, Aunt Kate? We weren't expecting you until tomorrow."

"Now, don't be upset, Alice dear," Kate urged. "Your uncle and I decided to come down a day early to see if we could help your mother with anything. Mamie and George and their *darlings* drove in with us to do a little shopping and sight-seeing because we knew you'd be the only one not too busy to *take* them. I mean, you know, there's simply *nothing* like Detroit around us." She slapped a dramatic hand over her heart. "And, well, you know, the prices are *simply* atrocious in the stores up there. And then when that hotel *mysteriously* lost our reservations, Helen told us arrangements were made for Delbert and I to sleep here. Mamie and George's reservations aren't even *good* until *Friday,* and well, you *do* have a sofa bed, don't you? And of course, the *darlings* can make do with air mattresses and sleeping bags on the floor, and—"

Aunt Kate stopped abruptly and drew in a soft breath, hand to her throat and eyelashes fluttering as Gabriel's shadow brushed her face. She captured his hand. "Oh, my," she breathed. "So *you're* the gentleman they say has taken up with our Alice. You are the handsome devil, aren't you? My Delbert reminded me of you, once." She linked her arm with Gabriel's, leaning on him as she climbed the porch steps. "That was a long time ago, of course, but to see you now does take me back to *our* courtship. . . ."

She blushed prettily, tugged Gabriel down to breathe in his ear. "I am so sorry about spoiling your sleeping arrangements, you understand, but they *did* say you weren't married and, well, it *may* do for you to share a bed when there's nobody about, but you do see, don't you, how it looks to the relatives that you may just be *using* our Alice. I mean, how *plain* she is and all, not like my Mamie. And really, it may just be best if you'd bow out now and shack up somewhere else while there's someone here to comfort her, if you see what I mean, because the *example* for Mamie's boys and all, well, you know, it's just *not* what we want, and—"

"Aunt Kate." Alice grasped the other woman's free arm, smiling, but her voice was low and dangerous. "You're overstepping again, Aunt Kate, and I don't care what Helen says, there must be some lumpy-mattressed motel around here somewhere with a room and a restaurant where you can go and pay for all your meals, and if you don't behave, I will find it for you."

"Oh, but Alice *dear.*" Aunt Kate looked shocked. "I was only thinking of your best interests. You're all alone in the world and with one disastrous marriage already behind you, why it's obvious you simply *don't* understand a *thing* about men. *Someone* has to protect you."

Alice glanced at Gabriel, whose mouth fought a valiant battle with laughter, but whose eyes warmed her, stirring the still-smoldering coals inside her. Her hand shook as she tried fitting her key into the front door lock. "Thank you, Aunt Kate, but someone does—" her eyes unconsciously slid Gabriel's way once more, and her cheeks pinked slightly "—protect me from myself. Now—" she controlled her trembling with an effort, unlocked the door and pushed it open, letting them all in "—I think we'll pitch a tent in the backyard for the boys, and..."

Her hand ready to snap the bowl off the stem of the wineglass she held, Alice surveyed the six new tiny punctures Aunt Kate's stiletto heels had put in her kitchen floor, the bits of shag carpeting that littered the woman's knife-heeled path through the dining and living rooms. Bits of clothing shed by the travelers lay draped over available chairs; dresses and suits to be worn to the two or three planned family functions hung from the curtain rods and lamps. The boys' sleeping bags, car pillows and suitcases obliterated a corner of the living room; mud flecked the floors and carpet, marking the passage of boys from the side door, through the house and into the bathroom.

Barely two hours had passed, but already, no matter where Alice turned, her formerly tiny-but-adequate house looked the way she felt, ransacked. What was it the nuns used to say about cleanliness being next to Godliness and an orderly desk meaning an orderly soul? Apparently they'd been right, because right now she had neither. She was al-

most as confused by and about . . . everything as her house
was confused about whom it belonged to. And in less than
two hours she had people arriving to gossip, relax and party
before the actual prewedding gossiping, relaxing and par-
tying began tomorrow.

She'd get no help from Aunt Kate or cousin Mamie, that
was clear. The former had breezily suggested everyone help
themselves to lunch from Alice's cupboards, then gently
informed Alice that proper etiquette forbade guests from
actually lifting a finger in the host's house. And Alice, who
realized she herself had thought Gabriel impolite for taking
uninvited liberties with her kitchen—was it only this morning?—had opened her mouth to disagree with Aunt Kate,
then been left with nothing to say.

Instead she'd mutely watched Aunt Kate go off for a long
soak in a refreshing lavender milk bath in Alice's tub, while
Mamie, complaining of a migraine, had retired to Allyn's
bed with her soothing aquatic face mask and a bag of choc-
olate-chip cookies from Alice's freezer. George had gotten
directions and volunteered to go for beer. Uncle Delbert had
corralled Gabriel in an under-the-hood-of-the-car-getting-
to-know-you discussion of "men things" that included,
Alice suspected, having overheard bits of the "men things"
discussions before, the proper set for spark plugs on a
Cadillac, the ungodly state of baseball in the American
League and the current price of tea in China. And, after
setting up Alice's tent and devouring everything that wasn't
nailed down in the kitchen, Mamie's boys were glumly
mucking about on the top deck of the play structure, re-
senting the way family weddings interfered with their lives.

Setting the dirty wineglass carefully on the counter, Alice
glared at the walls around her, heaping curses on the Army
for allowing Helen to leave Washington state before she had
to, on Grace and Phil for not having the consideration to
elope and spare the details, and on Gabriel for having the
bad taste to fall half-dead at the side of a road where she'd

find him and then having the gall to turn her emotions inside out at a time when they were hardly right side in.

She knew what they'd agreed to be to one another, knew the appearance they were supposed to keep, but something was happening beyond "pretend," something was changing—had changed—almost from the moment they'd agreed to *pretend* to be lovers. Because of him something that had lain dormant for years was waking inside her, filling her with an unfamiliar longing. She'd wanted him. Badly. Desperately. He'd touched her senses and her heart. She couldn't concentrate. She was nervous, she was restless, filled with the desire to do something naughty, wild. And it would be easy to take that short step between pretense and reality, except...

She dumped the remains of that morning's coffee over the dishes that lay piled in the sink, turned on the water and began to rinse plates. Relieving this particular fit of restlessness could be expensive. Because she couldn't guarantee that physically becoming lovers would actually make them so. From what she'd read, undercover agents had to be likable con men—consummate character actors who never went out of character during a case, no matter what, because the case and the cause came before anything else. Before family, friends, children, lovers...

She viciously attacked a cheese-crusted plate with a table knife, trying to scrape away unaccustomed desire as she scraped the scorched remains of someone else's lunch. Life had walked right around her without her ever even noticing where it had gone. The knowledge irritated her at first, then made her angry. She'd already spent too much of her life with her face pressed up against possibility's windowpane watching the opportunities pass her by. If she wanted anything to come from her life *now*, post-children, post-bookstore, post-past mistakes, she couldn't afford to let her body—or her emotions—dictate her behavior because of one earthshaking soul-shattering absolutely-to-die-for kiss from an undercover impostor she'd met, for Pete's sake, *yesterday.*

Schoolmarms and desperadoes. The attraction was classic. The knowledge played havoc with her thoughts.

"I want you too badly," he'd said to her. "I'd take you down right here, but . . ."

Oh, God, why hadn't he? Why hadn't he just done it and gotten it over with so she could hate him for taking advantage of the situation, instead of hating herself for still wanting him to? Damn it to hell, for a thirty-five-year-old un-virginal mother of two she was awfully confused.

Furiously she clattered the dishes out of the sink, stacked them, ran the sink full of scalding water and dumped the dishes back into it. Her hands resembled lobsters by the time she'd finished, but she barely noticed, turning from dishes to straightening, vacuuming, dusting and food preparation with a dogged let's-avoid-thought zeal and concentration.

To and fro, past her while she worked, Mamie's boys came and went, leaving a trail of blue Kool-Aid in their wake. Mamie and her aquatic face mask surfaced long enough to crack the seal on tonight's rum, mix it with pink lemonade, sugar, ice and grenadine in the blender and depart toward the bathroom with two large glasses of the mix to have a chat with her mother.

George returned with two cases of beer, six bottles of pop, several bags of pretzels, some crushed ice and a cellophane-wrapped bouquet of carnations that he gruffly handed to Alice as he asked for directions to her ice chest.

Uncle Delbert left greasy fingerprints on her doorknob as he asked for a rag on which to leave greasy fingerprints.

Gabriel laughed and chatted, outgoing and likable, betraying nothing of himself to anyone. Vacuum cleaner in hand, Alice stared at him through the lace curtains on her dining-room windows, watching him move, involuntarily moistening her lips and catching her breath when he removed his shirt to lean further into the engine of Uncle

Delbert's Continental. Sunshine glistened on the sweat staining his back, and before she could help herself, she thoroughly appreciated every lean tan line and angle of his back, the ripple of every muscle in his shoulders and arms.

Mamie came silently out of the bathroom and, following the drift of Alice's gaze, watched Gabriel, too. "Nice," she observed in her sulky sultry voice. Alice jumped guiltily and turned. Mamie's eyes were slightly glazed and the glass in her hand was empty. She giggled and shook her head, putting a dilatory finger to her lips. "I won't tell," she whispered, patting Alice's arm. "Our secret. But you can always recognize the women who live on nothing but fantasies. Mmm-hmm." Mamie eyed Gabriel again, drew a regretful breath and continued on toward the kitchen. She stopped suddenly in the doorway, swinging back to Alice. "If you want to sneak off with him somewhere for a bit, I'll cover for you. 'Course—" she pursed her lips thoughtfully, narrowing her eyes "—first time's better if you let it build—you know, if you're forced to abstain for a while." She lifted a confidential brow and shut her eyes, shivering theatrically. "Anticipation, you know? By the time we all leave..." Her lips curved in a secret smile and her eyelids drooped for a moment, then she confided, "Anyway, it works for George and—"

Alice yanked the vacuum cleaner plug from the wall, stepped on the retractor that brought it whipping back into the machine and fled in horror. She didn't want to hear about Mamie and George, didn't want to dish up girl talk complete with suggested sex. And she didn't want to be spied on by unwelcome relatives with big eyes and mouths who figured they could say anything because blood ties gave them the right—no matter how thin the blood. What she felt about Gabriel was personal, what she wanted or didn't want from him was private; what she'd done—or not done—was nobody's business but her own. She was not on display for the kinfolk's entertainment. What she was, was tired, embarrassed, full of rebellious hormones and . . . and . . .

She felt the moist track of tears down her cheeks and scrubbed at them with an ineffectual wrist. On top of everything else, she was crying in the back hallway. Because she had ninety-five seed pearls left to sew on Grace's veil in the next three days, a houseful of strange family members who would never leave her alone, and a "thing" the size of Cleveland for a man who was pretending—far too effectively for comfort—that he loved her.

With a silent "Grow up, Allie," she shoved the vacuum cleaner into the hall closet and for an instant contemplated climbing into the comforting anonymous darkness. Then she resolutely drew herself erect. This was dumb, she advised herself silently. It was stupid. It was stress. That was it! All she needed was to rest, relax; to spend a month out of touch in the Marquesa Islands with nothing but biting flies and soughing winds to distract her. Alone. As far as she was concerned, heaven would be the place without telephones, weddings, relatives or men named Gabriel.

"Alice, do you have any—" Gabriel asked and stopped, concerned. "Alice?" he said uncertainly.

With a start, Alice jerked the tail of her shirt from her pants and blotted her eyes gently, mindful of the appearance rubbing them would create. She'd been so busy feeling sorry for herself she hadn't heard him come in.

"Do I have any what?" she demanded, trying to keep the sniffle out of her voice.

He ignored the question, ran a finger down the collar of her shirt. "Are you crying?"

"No." The lie was ragged from the clog in her throat. She looked guiltily at the floor, trying to swallow the lump of mortification that wanted to raise more tears. She wanted to run, but there was no place to go. She was boxed in by a closed bathroom door with a full-length mirror reflecting back at her everything that was going on, a closed closet door, a closed bedroom door and a man who smelled of sunshine and salt, whose arms would probably feel just too darn good and secure if she let him put them around her. The tears ran before she could catch them. She was so damn tired of not being in control.

Gabriel took a step nearer, yesterday's knowledge that she would pull herself together better if he left her alone forgotten. He didn't want to leave her alone to handle anything. His fingers closed on her chin, tried to force it up. Alice jerked away, turned away. The mirrored door hid nothing. She averted her face and confronted the closet. Tucking his hands in his back pockets, Gabriel retreated a minute half a step.

"Allie, let me help. Tell me what I can do."

Alice shook her head. "Go away," she mumbled miserably. "Don't touch me. Don't be nice to me. And don't call me Allie. People I like call me Allie, and I don't want to like you."

"You're not making sense."

"I *am.*" She tried not to make the tears worse by being too adamant; they got worse anyway. "You're the one who doesn't make sense." It was hard to whisper through a sob. "You touch me and kiss me and it's all pretend. They all know that, and we know they know, but we pretend, anyway, and I feel like such a *virgin,* which is stupid when you think about it and—" Her forehead bumped the closet door. "Why am I telling you this? I didn't even know you yesterday morning and when you get down to it—"

"Alice."

"—it's really no better now, we just look at each other and know things and, really, doesn't that frighten you just a little bit—"

"Alice."

"—and I know I'm babbling, but you make me nervous because I never know what you're going to do, except that

I suspect things, and then you do them and I don't know if they're real or part of an act—''

"Alice." Her distrust tore at him. More than anything in the world, he wanted her trust, needed it. She had to know. He had to show her—

He caught her wrist and hauled her to him, sliding one hand down her back to anchor her hips to his, twisting the other in her hair. Frightened silent, Alice stared up at him. "I don't do theater for just anyone," he whispered savagely. "Certainly not for you, not this..." He rubbed himself against her, offering the painful hardness in his jeans as a graphic illustration of her effect on him. "If you can't believe anything else, believe this—I want you, I want to be inside you, no one else, and I haven't for a long, long time. I look at you and this is what I feel. I want you hot and wet and melting around me. I want to fill you with me. I want to lose myself with you."

He shut his eyes, stopped to collect himself, the breath shuddering through him. There would be no calmness while he held her; he wouldn't let her go. Something irrevocable had happened to him today, something wisdom dictated he avoid. But he wouldn't. He couldn't.

He didn't want to.

He opened his eyes. "I've never wanted to lose control before, Alice, never thought I might. There's more to it than this, but even this is more than I can afford to offer you right now." He took her unresisting hand, guided it down between them so that she cupped him, held him. His groin tightened, and he pressed himself up into her palm with a stifled curse. "You do this to me whenever I look at you, think of you." He swallowed. "Believe it. And be careful."

Then he let her go. Alice staggered back, shocked by his intensity, her sudden freedom, and reached for his arms to support herself. Gabriel's hands locked beneath her elbows. Breath fluttered in her lungs, knots of expectation formed in her stomach; she couldn't take her eyes from him.

If was no longer the question; *might* no possibility; only *when* maintained the distance between them. This was not Matt in the back seat of his father's Ford fumbling to unfasten her bra and get inside her pants. This was a man, adult and dangerous, issuing her an invitation and at the same time warning her to be wary with her RSVP. And her confusion.

There was a whirring from somewhere in the house—the blender in the kitchen. Outside, boys screamed and hollered, the hood of Uncle Delbert's car thunked shut. Through the bathroom door behind them, they could hear the slippery squeak of Aunt Kate rising from the tub, the sound of water gurgling down the drain. The hallway was dusky and intimate, airless and warm. The skin over Gabriel's biceps was smooth and sweaty, slippery; the muscles beneath it hard. The skin over Alice's elbows was soft, sensitive over the inside of her arms. The texture of Gabriel's fingers was rough by comparison, eliciting skittish leaps from Alice's pulse when his hands stroked up then down her arms. He lifted a hand to brush her mouth with his thumb.

"I won't play make-believe with you, Alice," he promised softly. "I don't think I can." His knuckles caressed her cheek. "I don't think I want to."

"Gabriel, please, I don't think I'm ready to handle—"

The screened front door whined open, banged closed.

"Alice," Meg singsonged from the middle of the living room. "We're he-ere...."

Chatter and laughter assaulted the house at every turn.

"So, what, do you think Jack's going to do it?" Meg blotted the lettuce she'd just shredded between two paper towels, then dumped it into the available salad bowl. "We need the kitchen done, and I've got to tell Tim something so he doesn't go out and hire somebody else—which I don't want because Jack'll get what I want done right the first time."

Sam shrugged and crumbled a lump of Danish blue cheese over the lettuce. "I don't know, you'll have to ask him. If I try to talk to him about it he thinks I've been out digging up charity for him. It drives me up the wall. He's out of work two months and already his pregnant working wife has emasculated him. Never mind he's the best fool carpenter in six states—'fool' being the operative word. I mean really, I knew the guy could be Mr. Sensitive when I married him, but—"

"-no, no, no!" Helen exclaimed into the phone. "I said eight *large* pizzas, one with everything but anchovies, one with everything but hot peppers, one with half black olives and half green peppers with Italian sausage over the whole thing, one—"

"—oh, yes." Aunt Kate nodded violently at Twink as she took another long sip of a tall rum-and-something. "She said it was a dreadful trip. Dysentery, spitting camels, sometimes bombs—horrible! Never go to that country in the summer—"

"—no, Uncle Del," Edith shouted down the basement stairs. "Mom said to *bring* Mamie, George and the boys when you meet her for dinner. She said she *doesn't* want to meet you alone. Oh, no, that's not what I mean—"

Thoughts in an uproar, Alice bent over the dining-room table slicing oranges for a fruit tray, trying to close her ears to the hubbub around her. She rolled her eyes heavenward to beg the ceiling for five minutes peace. That's all, please? Just enough to collect myself—

"Do you have family, Gabriel?" Edith asked.

Guiltily, Alice's eyes detoured toward the sound of her sister's voice, found Gabriel where he hadn't been a second before—slouched against the kitchen doorjamb studying her. The orange she was about to slice spit juice into her face when she jammed the knife into it with more force than intended. Gabriel's lips twitched, and he winked at Alice wickedly. Alice dropped her gaze, embarrassed, then her natural ability to laugh at herself took control and she shrugged and grinned wryly back.

Gabriel lazily picked a paper napkin out of the holder on the table and blotted at the orange juice on Alice's face. "I don't have a family like this," he told Edith.

"Nobody has a family like this." Helen laughed. "It's inflicted on you at birth."

"Or by marriage," George mumbled darkly, passing through.

Alice's sisters sent one another secret grins and giggled.

"Blame that on Grandma," Twink called after him. She turned to Gabriel. "Ma always said Gram couldn't abide children who were unChristian, unprincipled or boring."

"Don't you mean 'or barren'?" Sam asked dryly.

"Sam!" Edith exclaimed in feigned shock.

"Edith!" Sam mimicked back.

"Don't worry, Sam." Helen slipped a theatrically comforting arm about Sam's shoulders, then patted her sister's still-flat belly. "Pregnant ladies are allowed aberrant comments and behavior. You'll understand if we just ignore you for the next year or two, won't you?"

"In a pig's eye," Sam stated flatly.

"Bravo!" Twink cheered and added most of a can of black olives to the salad.

Gabriel's hands were warm on Alice's hips when he tossed the napkin down and eased himself around her. His breath was a moist tickle in her ear. "Hi," he whispered. "Long time no touch. How you doin'?"

"Mmm." Caught off guard, Alice smiled and instinctively arched her neck and sank back into his arms as though they'd never had the conversation in the hall. He made it easy, within the security and presence of all this family, to forget who she was and how scattered she felt—and that when she was alone with him, her involuntary naturalness with him frightened her to death.

Safety came in numbers for Gabriel, too. In front of all these people he was merely a performer doing a role he'd been born to play, opposite the costar he'd been born to play it with. And never mind what this particular costar did to his pulse. His hands grazed lightly up and down Alice's sides. "I stuck the board under the mattress and changed the sheets for Kate and Delbert," he murmured, nuzzling her neck. "Hospital corners and everything. Want to check it out?"

"No." Alice grinned at him. "I think I can trust you to do that on your own."

"Less fun that way."

"Safer, too."

"You could be right." The skin of her neck invited his inspection. His lips teased the column beneath her ear deliberately when he reached around her to swipe a piece of orange. "But I thrive on the danger."

Alice's breath stopped, sighed gently between her lips. Don't think, she urged herself silently. You're safe here, so enjoy it. It's a game, just a play, an act. "You would..."

The buzz went on around them.

"Don't they look cute together?" Aunt Kate gushed.

"He does sort of fit her, doesn't he?" Meg agreed.

"When do you think the wedding will be?" Mamie asked. "I'll need to schedule the time off work."

"Should they be doing that in front of the kids?" Uncle Delbert's arthritic hands knotted worriedly. "Kind of suggestive, isn't it?"

"Oh, Uncle Del, he's only biting her neck—"

"Hickey bait, hickey bait," Mamie's boys hooted....

"Ignore them," Gabriel suggested when Alice stiffened and started to pull away. "Grin and enjoy it."

"I am enjoying it," Alice hissed back, blushing furiously. "Sort of."

"Anything I can do to make it better?"

"No! Stop that!" Alice slapped at the hands that slipped around her waist and held her hostage. "Let me go. I hate being on display." Face flaming, she ducked out of Gabriel's grasp and around the table.

Helen lightly socked his arm. "Leave my sister alone, hey?" she ordered, grinning. "You're makin' her all blotchy."

"I think she looks great blotchy," Gabriel returned lightly, but his eyes on Alice were thoughtful and apologetic.

"So, Gabriel," Twink said, changing the subject abruptly, "how long have you been in town?"

"How much family do you have?" Meg asked.

"And where are you from?" Edith added.

Ignoring the first question, Gabriel answered the second. "Parents, maybe a couple of distant aunts, two or three cousins." It was easier to tell them about himself than it was to tell Alice; he didn't feel quite the same compunction to be as brutally honest with either them or himself. He could shave the finer points, couch them in terms that suited his needs without quite lying. Without quite facing himself the way he was compelled to do with Alice. What was it Churchill had said about war and truth? *In war the truth is so precious she should always be attended by a bodyguard of lies.* He swiveled to Edith. "New York by way of Iowa and the South Pacific."

"Oooh! Really?" The interest hummed from Alice's sisters in unison. "Tell us..."

Still red, Alice whisked the fruit tray into the kitchen to finish filling it, thankful for, and jealous of, her sisters' innate curiosity. God, they hadn't had him cornered for ten minutes and already they knew as much about him as she'd learned in two intense days. Envy struck her an unexpected blow. How did they do it? And why couldn't she?

She settled sliced orange on a plate and peeled a banana, studying her sisters. It was easier for them to ask Gabriel for information about himself than it was for her to do it—despite what she'd shared with him. It had always been like that where boys were concerned. Where they were loquacious, vivacious, flirtatious, Alice was ever tongue-tied, ever fourteen. How she and Matthew had ever managed to get together...

She swallowed and dropped her gaze from the sudden all-seeing glance Gabriel sent her that took her breath and made her senses buzz. She wasn't in eighth grade anymore, dammit!, and didn't want to be. It was okay, even nice, to feel gawky and awkward, inexperienced and undeniably feminine, uncomfortably and completely adult. Electrified. To *feel,* period. Why couldn't she seem to grasp that? And deal with it?

But then she supposed men were very much like pregnancy that way. There was never really a perfect time to experience either, but only, if you were lucky, a better time. And sweet St. Christopher, wasn't *that* cynical!

"Got it figured out yet?" Gabriel asked.

"Not quite." Alice shook her head, then glanced up at him, startled. How did he always seem to know what she was thinking? And why did she always seem to answer him as if he did? "Do I have what figured out yet?"

Gabriel motioned at the kiwi fruit she'd been staring at. His eyes swept the line of her jaw, the tilt of her head in profile. He'd felt a gut recognition and attachment to her, felt protective, possessive. He had wanted to bed her for the past two days, without even *seeing* her...the sweeping length of her eyelashes, the small vulnerable stubborn chin, the perfect line of her nose, the at-once tentative and decided set of her mouth. The eyes that could simultaneously make his chest ache with some unnamed emotion, make it swell with invincibility, laughter or pride. He leaned into the cupboards watching her, losing his train of thought.

Alice studied the gold flecks in the countertop, uncomfortable and exhilarated under his scrutiny. "Gabriel?"

Gabriel roused himself with difficulty, trying to remember what he'd meant to say. Again he gestured inanely at the fruit in her hand. "The kiwi looks good. Do you know what you want to do with it?"

Alice self-consciously looked at the knife, the ripe fruit she'd forgotten she was holding. "Um, slice it?" She suited action to words and cut a chunk. The juice ran down her fingers when she offered the piece to Gabriel. "Want some?"

His eyes warmed, fingers closed around her wrist, held her hand still halfway to his mouth. "You trying to seduce me?"

"I'm not sure what I'm doing," Alice breathed. "You look at me and I do things I never imagined I'd do. You know how it is for repressed schoolmarms when they get around handsome wounded desperadoes. They lose all sense of propriety."

Jolted by her honesty, Gabriel relinquished her wrist. She had her own way of making him do things he'd never imagined he'd do. Or think of doing. Her assessment of their...relationship hurt. "Is that the way you think of us? Desperation and misplaced virtue? No matter what I tell you?"

"I guess I—don't know—I can't think—I..." Alice's voice trailed off and she dropped her chin, concentrating on cutting kiwi and arranging it on the plate, then edging around Gabriel in the crowded kitchen to rinse the knife and her hands. Her chest was tight; she felt culpable; she hadn't meant to hurt him. Hadn't thought she would. She flicked the water from her fingers, turned to lay a hand on his arm. "I'm sorry, Gabriel. I guess I'm not sure what else to think. This—I've never—" She hesitated. "I'm such a plain old insecure fuddy-duddy," she said softly, "but you're so— and you react to me. You make me forget myself, that I'm suddenly old enough to be somebody's grandmother. You make me feel out of control, and I kind of like that, but it also makes me not—quite trust—you or me. Do you see?"

Too clearly. Because he felt much the same way himself. Her description fit. They *were* a schoolmarm and a wounded desperado stealing an unpredictable moment that couldn't last.

He brushed her cheek with an open palm. "Alice—"

"Hey, you guys," Sam interrupted impatiently, "get romantic someplace else and quit hogging the sink. I need to wash my hands."

"So use the bathroom," Alice snapped, rousing too suddenly from a place she didn't want to be roused from. "We're in the middle of some serious bonding here, if you don't mind, and we'd rather not be interrupted."

"Oooh, Alice, touchy, touchy," Twink teased, coming in to collect the plate of fruit. "Serious bonding? What have you been reading lately? One of those magazines I gave you?"

"No, I'm merely parroting back at you the last conversation you had with Grace about Phil."

Meg stuck her head into the group, eyes alight with interest—or a wicked facsimile thereof. "Would that be the conversation where Twink advised Grace that the best coupling—er, bonding—"

"Shut up," Twink warned.

"—begins with—"

"Meg," Twink said carefully, "we're in mixed company. If you don't shut up right now I'll—"

"You mean to tell me," Aunt Kate exclaimed shrilly from the living room, "that there was a murder just around the corner from here the night before last and nobody told us before they invited us to stay here?"

"No, really, Aunt Kate," Edith soothed. "I'm sure the paper is wrong, it must be perfectly safe by now. *Aunt Kate!*"

"Alice Marie Brannigan!" Aunt Kate clicked agitatedly into the kitchen, evening newspaper flapping. "You didn't tell us about any loose psychopath who could come in and murder us all in our beds when you invited us here! I really think that's something we should have known about before we agreed to stay with you."

"What are you talking about?" Arms akimbo, Alice faced her aunt squarely. "I don't have enough room to have willingly invited you to stay here and I don't know anything about a loose psychopath."

"This, this is what I'm talking about!" Indignantly Aunt Kate thrust the paper at her and Gabriel, pointing to the fuzzy news photo of police bending over a blanketed victim at a wooded crime scene. Gabriel took a good look. The picture was of the once-smiling-but-now-dead special agent who'd been his partner. "Why didn't you," Aunt Kate repeated shrilly to Alice, "tell us they were killing policemen practically in your own backyard?"

Chapter Eight

Gabriel viewed the newspaper blankly, feeling the violence rise in him.

Memory returned like a physical jolt, a freeze-frame waking nightmare of the moments that had led to Sunday night, Nicky's shooting, the face he'd almost glimpsed behind the gun when it was aimed at him. Damn, he'd been so absorbed in Alice that he'd actually forgotten what had brought him here.

His hands dropped to Alice's waist, tightening painfully to support her when she took an involuntary step back and trod on his toe. Her hands closed instinctively, protectively, over his, refusing to let him go when he would have set her away from him. Trapped against the sink, he strained to control the bile rising in his throat, fought the claustrophobic urge to shove Alice aside and give in to the impotence of rage. God, she had to let him go. He didn't want her warmth or her protection, didn't want to touch her until he got control of this desire to destroy.

Hang on, Book, stay cool, he urged himself mutely. *You won't gain anything if you lose it now. Keep it together, babe, keep it together.* He could feel himself twisting inside, losing touch with sanity. This was the hard part about undercover, the lying to himself, the duplicity between what he had to do, how he had to appear, and what he had to feel in order to remain honest on the job. Nothing must show. Everything had to stay tucked inside deep out of sight, unexpressed, unacknowledged, where even he himself couldn't be sure it existed.

He smiled blankly, blindly at the gathering family, pretending. Alice stiffened imperceptibly, and her hands, her arms, tightened on his when his hands on her contracted more harshly. Gabriel swallowed painfully. How did she always seem to know what he was feeling? Why wouldn't she let him go? *Damn it, Alice, let me go,* he screamed silently. *You'll give me away and I'll hurt you. I don't want to hurt you. Damn you for dying, Nicky. Damn Markum for setting us up. Damn Scully for sending us in. Damn you all to hell. I'll be damned if I don't send you there....*

In front of him the paper rattled when Alice released his hands to take it from Aunt Kate and fold it up. "Look, Aunt Kate, calm down," she said. "This did not happen in my backyard. I live in the city, remember? No woods. And that's—" she snapped the picture in the paper "—at least three miles north of here, and it happened two nights ago. Whoever did it's long gone by now."

"Just the same, you never know." Aunt Kate's fresh purple voile caftan billowed with the anxious flounce of her arms. "I'm sleeping with the butcher knife under my pillow tonight."

"Not in my house you're not," Alice assured her firmly. She rolled her eyes to find Helen standing on the fringes of the discussion and gave her sister a you're-dead-for-doing-this-to-me look. Helen cleared her throat to rid it of a laugh. "There are too many people here, Aunt Kate," Alice went on, frowning at Meg, Twink, Sam and Edith to step in any time and help her out. They ignored her. Alice glared profoundly at them. "I don't want any of them hurt if you sleepwalk or have nightmares."

"But who will protect us?" Aunt Kate moaned, wringing her hands. "We have children here. Someone has to protect them." She grabbed Gabriel's arm, her face turned up to him beseechingly. "Don't you think we should get a gun? You'll handle that for us, won't you? You'll get one and take care of us...."

Gabriel stared down at her wishing he could laugh at her just to take the edge off. He'd been an undercover cop too long to let his true feelings show, but they were reaching for him now. And this wasn't funny. He fumbled for his voice, trying to sound normal. His throat was tight; his eyes sought Alice's. *Get rid of them,* they told her. "I don't think . . ."

Eyes narrowed on Aunt Kate, Alice laid a hand on his arm. "Don't let her put you on the spot, love," she told him. "This is my house, I'll handle it." She aimed a stiff finger at Aunt Kate. "No guns," she warned her. "No knives, no weapons of any kind. None. Now." She took Aunt Kate's arm and turned her around, maneuvering her into the dining room where evening had begun to lay in shadows. "My mother is waiting for you. You should go, have dinner, a couple of drinks, relax, forget about the news. In the morning, Helen will find you a nice secure hotel far away from here." She glanced back at the kitchen and gave Helen a dirty grin. "Won't you, Helen?"

"I live to serve," Helen returned mildly, but her eyebrows waggled dire and unspeakable messages at Alice.

"Don't worry, Mother Kate." George took her arm from Alice, tucked it through his and guided her out the front door, motioning his wife, his father-in-law and his boys after him. "Julia will take good care of us, you'll see. We'll have some of those tropical drinks with the little umbrellas you like, then maybe some shrimp cocktail, and for dinner..."

His voice trailed off into the slam of car doors and the roar of its engine. The car scraped over the bump at the bottom of the driveway, paused momentarily and was powered away. Alice's sisters maintained their decorum for a five full seconds, then exploded.

"God, did you see the look on Allie's face when Aunt Kate asked for a knife?"

"I thought I'd die when she said she wanted a gun!"

"Who's the disaster-monger who told her that happened near here, anyway?"

"Edith!" they chorused, laughing, moving toward the kitchen door.

"What did I do?" Edith asked indignantly and followed them into the living room.

Alice turned to Gabriel. "Are you—"

"No," he said shortly, voice low. "I'm screwed to hell. Damn." He ran a savage hand through his hair, flipped open the paper where it sat on the counter, slapped it closed. "Uniformed officer killed in the line of duty by an unknown assailant or assailants. *Uniformed!* God." He laughed harshly. "They *dressed* him. He was undercover and they stopped after they killed him and took the time to dress him. Why? What was the point? Sympathy? Misdirection? It doesn't make sense. Oh, man." He threw up his hands; his laughter wore an edge. "I am flippin' out here, Alice. My partner's lying in the leaves waiting for someone to find his body and all I can think about is making love with you. Man, somehow that doesn't balance, does it?"

"No," Alice answered, "I guess it doesn't. Not so you can tell, anyway."

"What's that supposed to mean? Everything happens for a reason, but sometimes it takes you a while to see it?"

"Yes."

"Bull." The violence was creeping up in him again. He could feel it in his fingers, in his hands, clenched into fists that wanted to strike out at whatever they could reach. He dug his palms around the edge of the counter, trying to contain himself. He wanted to move, had to move to relieve the fury, but her kitchen was too small, her sisters too near. "Not everything happens for a reason, Alice." The strain told in his voice. "Some things are just done for the hell of it. This—" he picked up the paper, threw it down "—this was done for thirty pieces of silver and a kiss on the cheek by some greedy bastard who thinks murder and shortcuts are the only path to a richer life."

"What do you want me to say?" Alice asked. "That I'm sorry it happened? That I wish to God it hadn't? Well, I *am* sorry it happened and I *do* wish to God it hadn't. But, damn you, I'm glad you weren't killed, too. I'm glad you're still alive to do something about it, even if everything does take longer than you want it to."

"Well, ain't that the cliché of the month," Gabriel sneered. He rocked himself away from the counter, swung to face the kitchen window. He struggled to locate the cool calculating part of himself that had always protected him, distanced him from a situation, allowing him to observe and document everything as though he wasn't part of it. Two, three more days, and the man he'd contacted last night would have the missing pieces of this case together. All Gabriel had to do was hold on to his sanity—sometimes not an easy task.

Spend only what you have to, to survive, he reminded himself. *Save what you can.* He reached down inside himself, digging deep to find the single piece of calmness and humanity left in him, and drew a long breath of it. "Look," he said more quietly, "I don't really want you to say anything, Alice, nothing. There's nothing to say except I'm sorry. You don't need this from me. It's not your battle."

"But it is, Gabriel." Alice stood beside him, earnest and determined. "You may be the law, but I'm a taxpayer, that makes it my battle, too." She touched his chest, made him look at her. "Even if I wasn't a taxpayer, it'd still be my battle because you're my friend."

Gabriel made a gesture of disbelief and laughed without humor. "Friend. Is that what you call it?"

"'Friend' was your term this morning," she prodded gently, "not mine."

He huffed an impatient breath. "I was wrong then—or I lied, Alice," he said. "Things with you move so fast I can't be sure of where I stand or what I feel from minute to minute. But we're not friends. What I feel for you is not friendship—not by itself. I can't." He studied her face for an instant, let his fingers touch her cheek, drop again to his side. "I wish…" he began softly, then stopped himself, shook his head. Wishing was for the innocent. "Thanks for the offer, but I've got to take care of this on my own."

He paused, looking down at her, half-poised to touch her again, to memorize her face with his fingers. The sound of voices reached them from the front porch. "Grace is here," Sam called. "She brought the pizzas and Phil. How are you—"

"Gabriel?" Alice whispered.

She hadn't brushed her hair since they'd come in from the car; it was still textured from the wind coming through the open windows. He stroked her hair, smoothed it, aware of every strand that passed beneath his palm. "I just need some time to sort it out, Allie. I'll be all right."

Her hands fit his waist naturally. Anxiously. "You won't go off half-cocked?" she asked.

Gabriel grinned in spite of himself. "No, I promise," he assured her. "When I go off I'll be fully cocked."

"That's fine then." Alice nodded and patted his chest, then took two steps toward the door, eyeing him over her shoulder as she went. "You understand," she said slyly, "that when you do go off, I'll at least want to watch?"

Laughter caught him by surprise. "That's bad." He made a grab for her that she eluded. "What was that supposed to be? Sexual innuendo?"

"No." Alice shook her head and rounded the dining-room doorway. "It was merely a suggestion. Like, um, take a witness and, um, cover your assets."

Shoulders shaking, Gabriel stared after her, laughing until his chest ached and his eyes teared. Ah, hell, what a roller-coaster ride, huh? he thought. One second around her he felt gutted, the next full, the one after that slammed back against his seat taking the full force of the wind in his face. She was only mixed up about her own emotions, her own needs, desires. *His* she handled like a pro. Whatever he needed, there she was, pulling him back from the brink of... Of what? he wondered, damnation? Whatever brink she drew him back from, it was incredible how easily she did it, extraordinary how badly he wanted her to. But maybe where emotions were concerned she understood what he didn't. Maybe the true trick to balance and survival was not resolution, but compensation, offsetting bad with good, sin with penance. An old friend's betrayal with someone new to trust.

Laughter sighed away on the thought. For an instant he simply stood, drained, contemplating the possibilities. Then he rolled his shoulders and flexed his legs, trying to alleviate the angry tension left in the muscles Alice's laughter hadn't touched. What he needed was a workout, an exhausting physical release of energy that would allow him the latitude he required to put the past few days in perspective for himself; to build a case that would pull everything together so it made sense: Markum-Alice-Scully-Alice, the story in the paper, the lies...

Alice.

He shut his eyes against the instant buildup of tension thinking about her inspired and headed for the side door, the approaching twilight, the only place around here he could think of where he could get a workout on short notice—the kids' jungle gym and swings.

Exercise numbed, sweat cleansed.

Again and again Gabriel pulled himself up to the bar that held the swings, doing chin-ups the hard way, like the marines. He felt nothing but the flex and strain of muscle on muscle, the drag and weight of his body pulling against him. He couldn't get away from his thoughts; they intruded no matter what he did. Markum-Scully-Alice-Nicky-Markum-Scully-Alice . . .

Don't think, he ordered himself. Concentrate: Up, down, tug, release, breathe. Markum, he thought. Not Scully. It had to be Markum. Scully was too far removed from all this, and putting the uniform on the dead Nicky was too subtle a message; Scully was more direct than that. If he'd thought Gabriel and Nicky were getting too close to him, he'd simply have met them someplace and pulled the trigger himself. One thing about Scully was you always knew where you stood.

Markum was something else. Markum could lie with his heart in his eyes; Gabriel had watched him do that more than once. Markum also liked games. He played them well, he played to win, and he wrote the rules as he went along. Dressing Nicky in uniform was Markum's means of sending a message to Gabriel that *this* was the way it would go down. He and Nicky had been assigned the kind of deep cover that forced them to abandon the protection of their official identities and adopt new ones as criminals—in this instance to become corrupt cops, instead of remaining special agents. Markum had set them up to take the fall for him. He'd leak their adopted identities little by little to the press: *Cop* on the take killed by *cop* on the take. He'd destroy Nicky's credibility and his family, then do the same to Gabriel's. Without credibility in the press, even if Gabriel stayed alive it would be hard to get a jury to believe him about Markum.

Gabriel shut his eyes and forced himself to do ten fast pull-ups in succession, making his arms shake.

Scully must have suspected Markum's duplicity from the start, must have seen what Gabriel had been blinded to by friendship. And trust. Scully should have leveled with him before tossing him face first into the frying pan, Gabriel thought bitterly, given his undercover a sporting chance.

But even as he thought it, Gabriel knew why Jack had remained silent. Because he would have defended Markum, then confronted him with Scully's suspicions—and Si would have had time to deny everything and cover his tracks.

Gabriel squeezed the swing bar in his fists until his knuckles ached from the strain. What a jerk he'd been.

Sometimes, he knew, you trusted the wrong people; it was that simple. Sometimes it just got away from you. Sometimes, in attempting to defend what was right, you became what was wrong. Intellectually he could see how that happened: you spent so much time portraying sleaze in this work that sometimes you forgot who you were and became sleaze. When had that happened to Markum?

Exhausted physically and emotionally, Gabriel went up and down on the bar, hearing and feeling nothing.

The tail end of the sunset hanging in the sky bronzed him, glowing in the perspiration that coated his bare torso. Coming around the side of the house a short time later to find him, Alice paused and drew a shallow breath, startled by the picture of raw power and vulnerability he presented, the sudden realization of the emotional investment she was making in him by coming out here after him. Had already made when Aunt Kate had thrown the paper in his face. She was no longer out to help him because she was inherently a Samaritan. She was out here to be with *him* because he was

Gabriel and she felt for him. And because she wanted to offer him something to hold on to, wanted to hold him.

She set the closed pizza box she'd used as a tray to carry out a variety of cold drinks on the bottom floor of the play structure and watched him for a moment. He was not a tame man, she realized not for the first time, but one who could be infinitely dangerous to both her body and her heart. If he chose to be, that is. And if she let him. Ian, the rebel-without-a-cause she'd fallen for in high school before she'd wound up with Matt had been like that. Sort of. He'd been her first true crush. Without touching her he'd made her sheltered Catholic inexperienced body and heart feel everything she'd never felt before. She'd really been one of his groupies rather than anything else. But she'd have done anything for him, literally anything, and that's what had scared her about him: the way she'd wanted to let him swallow her up, think for her, tell her what to do.

The memory made her shudder. She supposed everyone had a past that was blemished to one degree or another, but that didn't make hers any easier to look at sometimes. Ian had also had a reputation for violent antisocial behavior that she'd believed was merely rebel-biker hype. Except, as she'd discovered almost too late, it wasn't.

But where teenage Ian had been controllingly manipulatively dangerous, Gabriel was different. Older, more mature—in charge of himself, angry for a reason. Concerned for her, instead of immersed solely in himself. And, as one human being to another, she cared very much about him. Or maybe more than that. *No sense in doing anything halfway,* she reminded herself dryly, and swallowed. For all her other flaws, committing herself less than wholeheartedly to anything was not something she had to worry about—not even when she should. A sense of impending decision lodged her heart in her throat; she gathered her emotions about her and crossed to him.

"Gabriel."

She touched his back where he hung from the bar of the swing, and he recoiled, startled, then dropped to the ground and swung on her defensively. Prepared for this response, she slipped past his fists and framed his face between her hands, drawing his mouth to hers, pressing herself into his arms. "It's me, Gabriel," she murmured. "Don't worry, it's only me."

"Alice?"

His face was half in shadow, half in fading sun, reminding her again of the two sides of him, one the professional liar, the other very, very real. She stroked his face with her fingers, brushed her lips over his again. "Yes, Gabriel, I'm here."

He pulled his face up but not away, holding himself rigid, reaching for the frame of the swing, not sure whether he should trust his numbed senses or not. Not sure if she was real. "Why?"

She stood her ground, not afraid of his distrust, his apparent rejection, only dipping her chin slightly to kiss his chest below the hollow of his throat. Then she looked up at him again, eyes steady, lips bowed. "I didn't think you should be alone. I didn't want to leave you alone. I wanted to be with you." Again she pressed toward him, slid her hands down the sides of his neck. "Hold me, Gabriel," she whispered. "Hold on to me."

"Do you know what you're doing?" His voice was strained, his arms were folding around her. "Do you know what you're asking?"

"Yes." She fitted herself to him, feeling the possessive rightness, naturalness, between two bodies that somehow belonged to one another. "I'm asking you to let me be with you. I'm asking you to share what hurts you and what makes you feel good with me. I'm asking you to touch me, Gabriel, and let me touch you."

His arms tightened around her. "I don't want you to think you're rescuing me from anything, Alice. I don't want this kind of charity from you."

"So help me, Gabriel," she whispered fiercely, "I'm not capable of this kind of charity. Believe me."

"I want to, Alice." His arms were beneath her shoulders. His hands pressed around them, then up, into her hair. "God, I want to."

"Then do," she urged. She struggled to get closer to him; he held her away.

"Be sure." The warning was filled with passion. "God, Alice, please, be sure."

"I am, Gabriel. Trust me. I feel like you belong here. I belong here. I don't know what else there is, but for now…" Her hands moved restlessly through his hair. "Come to me, damn you, Gabriel. Please."

"Alice." Her name was a hoarse sound in his throat. "Allie…" He held her away an instant longer, searching her face for any hesitation, then crushed her to him.

There was no gentleness in his kiss. His mouth bruised, plundered, demanded, and then quite suddenly gave, gentling, caressing—worshiping—moving from her mouth over her face and throat, along her neck, into her hair, then came to rest at her ear. His heart pounded; his breathing was ragged. She felt the rhythm of both against her breast, felt the staccato tremble of her own heart and lungs matching his. He dragged his lips, parted, warm, moist, over her ear. Around them the twilight deepened, closed them in the dark and intimate shadows cast by the maple trees and the play structure. Gabriel slid his hands down Alice's back, up her sides. He stroked the curve of her breasts with his thumbs.

"We can't do this here," he muttered. "I want to make love with you, but not in front of the whole neighborhood."

"What about the top of the play structure," Alice whispered. "It's enclosed, private—"

"Cramped," Gabriel murmured. "Hard."

Alice pressed her forehead to his chest and slid her hands boldly down his back, settling her hips against his. "That's not the only thing that's—"

Gabriel made a sound low in his throat and sought her mouth, silencing her. "Quiet, woman," he mumbled. "Didn't your mother ever teach you it's impolite to speak to people about afflictions they can't do anything about."

"Afflictions they can't do anything about, yes." Alice nodded and leaned back into a play-structure upright, wantonly dragging him to her. "But not about things we could find a solution for."

She rubbed her chest provocatively against his, dropped her head back, eyes open, lips parted—full—promising. He couldn't resist her. He bent to her again, immersed himself in her. As though they had a will of their own, his hands moved deeper between them, across Alice's breasts. She released a soft sigh of pleasure and frustration when they peaked at his touch. Her hands moved restively up and down his back. His fingers opened a button on her blouse, knuckles grazed her skin. In some distant part of his brain, he knew he shouldn't do this, knew it would only make things worse when he had to call another halt. But she touched him where reason did not, filled his heart, took away the pain, the loneliness, the internal affairs and undercover cop's constant sense of not really belonging. He undid another button, let himself be dragged deeper into the moment by her inarticulate murmur of encouragement. He'd stop soon, he promised himself, but not yet. He couldn't let her go yet—

From somewhere out of the lengthening dusk, car doors slammed, then sneakered feet slapped on concrete.

"Could not."

"Could so!"

"Bet ya!"

"You're on."

The sound of boys' arguing voices carried over the clang of the backyard gate opening then closing. On reflex Gabriel shoved Alice's buttons back through their buttonholes and thrust her behind him, grabbing his own shirt off one of the swings in the same move and sliding it on. Mamie's sons rounded the corner of the house, crossed the yard and burst into the tent they'd set up earlier. Gabriel seized Alice's hand, kept his voice low.

"Come on," he urged.

"Wait," Alice protested. "I've got to get—"

"Leave it. Let's get out of here while we've got the chance."

Alice tugged her hand free. "Gabriel, what's with you?" she asked, matching the pitch of her voice to his. "This is *my* backyard. I'm allowed to be—" She stopped suddenly as a thought struck her, and she reached out to feel his cheek. It was warm and, she imagined, red. The idea delighted her. "You're embarrassed."

Gabriel stuffed his hands in his back pockets, swung away from her. "Ah, hell."

Alice laughed soundlessly. "You are!"

He looked over his shoulder at her. "Aren't you?"

"No." Alice tilted her head, surprised. "It's weird, but I'm not. Oh, if we'd been caught, I might be. But we weren't. I don't know, maybe I'm finally starting to mature, after all."

"You're maturing and I'm regressing then," Gabriel said dryly. "It's been twenty years since the last time I was caught doing any heavy necking on the swings, but I can still feel Aunt Sarah's broom on the back of my head." His quiet laughter was full of self-mockery. "You make me feel about as in control as a teenager on his first car date, Alice," he said. "I'm not sure I like that. I know I can't afford it. At least not until this case is over."

Alice cupped his cheek in a palm, stood on tiptoe to brush a light kiss across his lips. "You make me feel incredible," she told him softly. "Alive, sexy, special, beautiful, adolescent, more than myself, confused... I don't think there's anything you don't make me feel. Even though it's only temporary—"

Temporary, Gabriel thought, *not permanent, transient.* The damned words that spelled out what he was. Had always been. He didn't think he'd ever hated them more.

"—just learning that there can be more to life than... Learning that maybe there's more to *me* than I thought. That makes it worth it."

She hesitated, and for a moment the night held only darkness and possibility, the murmur of boys squabbling in the tent near the house. Then Alice dropped her hand from Gabriel's face and drew a settling breath, turning to collect the pizza box and drinks from the play structure, becoming herself again. "I thought you might be hungry so I brought out a few different kinds of pizza and some beer, only I didn't know if you drank beer, or what type—light, regular, dark, dry—so I brought out some pop and some diet pop and some juice boxes, and—"

"Alice."

She looked back at him, waiting. Gabriel studied the darkness around his feet. It was crazy, but what he wanted to say was, "When we make love it won't be temporary. When we make love, it'll be for keeps." Instead he took the pizza box from her. "When I'm not driving I drink beer with pizza," he said. "Let's take this back inside and have some."

Chapter Nine

The party was breaking up by the time they got inside. Aunt Kate's stockings were rolled around her knees and she was carrying her teeth in a glass. Uncle Delbert had stripped to his undershirt and loosened his pants. Mamie and George were nowhere in sight. Alice's sisters, Grace's Phil, and Skip, who had arrived late, milled about near the front door sealing two black plastic garbage bags filled with the evening's litter.

"Oh, Alice, there you are," Helen exclaimed, sliding neatly away from the possessive hand Skip had settled on the middle of her back. "We've been wondering where you'd gone. We've got to go, but you should know Skip has a proposition for you."

"Helen, I don't think now's the time." Skip squirmed uncomfortably. "I really think it would be better if I wait until after I've talked to my partners to ask—"

"Nonsense," Helen said firmly. "No time like the present." She turned to Alice. "Skip thinks maybe he and a couple of friends of his would like to invest in a book-store—or something retail like that. They thought maybe in an office building—you know, captive audience—and that maybe you could scout locations, put the plan together, oversee the design, hire and fire—you know, run it.''

Alice turned from Skip, to Helen, to Gabriel and back again. "What?"

Skip shrugged uneasily, nodded. "I know your store is shutting down and I mentioned the possibility—there's nothing firm yet, you understand, but the idea makes sense, and I could use the investment—''

"Ahh." Alice ran a hand through her hair on a puff of disbelieving laughter. Was the man really desperate enough to try buying Helen's affections by attempting to solve her sister's unemployment problem? If so, then for all the years her mother had said he'd been coming around, Skip had a lot to learn about Brannigans in general, and Helen in par-ticular. Where matters of the heart were concerned Bran-nigans dealt strictly from the gut, never from the size of the pocketbook. She gave Gabriel a didn't-I-tell-you-about-her and damned-if-you-didn't-hit-the-nail-on-the-head-about-him look. "Ahh." She laughed uncomfortably again, shook her head. "Skip, I appreciate the offer, but you look like she's railroaded you into this, so I really don't know what to say."

"Don't say anything," Helen urged. "Just think about it. Keep your mind open to the options. Skip's going to talk to his partners tomorrow. He'll be at the picnic tomorrow night—you'll discuss it then. Now, Gabriel—" Helen grabbed Phil's arm and pulled him forward "—this is Phil, the bridegroom. Phil, Gabriel. We got him a tux this morn-ing. He's your new usher. That means we'll put Skip with me and let Gabriel escort Alice. Now you don't have to worry if your brother's wife goes into labor. We're still two by two. Right. Well!" She kissed each of her sisters quickly. "Gotta run, got people arriving at the airport and train stations simultaneously in the morning, got car pools to figure out. Meg, will you—"

"No."

"Edith?"

"Uh-uh."

"Sam—"

The screen door slammed behind them. Gabriel looked at Alice. "Did you ever feel like you were living with a tornado instead of a sister when you were growing up?"

"Frequently. It got worse after she went to the Point."

"Who went to the Point, Alice dear?" Aunt Kate asked fuzzily from behind her.

Alice turned. "Helen."

"Oh, Helen!" Aunt Kate rolled her eyes as though the subject was a lost cause. "I don't understand why they want to let women play army, anyway, but I guess that's none of my never-mind, is it? I tried, but when your father let her go off—humph, well! Let me tell you—"

"Aunt Kate," Alice interrupted, "did you need something?"

"Hmm? Oh, no, dear, everything's just fine. I just came out to say good-night."

Alice brushed her aunt's cheek with a kiss. "Good night, Aunt Kate. Sleep well."

"Thank you, Alice dear. You, too." Aunt Kate sighed, patting Gabriel's hand. "You sleep well, too, young man, and since we couldn't get you to sleep somewhere else tonight, I *do* hope you'll at least *think* clean thoughts while we're here."

"Aunt Kate," Alice warned.

Gabriel's lips twitched.

Aunt Kate waggled a placating hand in the air and headed for the bathroom. "I know, I know, it's none of *my* affair, and it really shouldn't be yours, either. But that's all right, don't listen to me, go ahead and fornicate right here in the living room. I promise I won't listen . . ." Her voice trailed off behind the click of the bathroom door.

"Fornicate?" Outraged, Alice pulled the cushions off the couch. "Listen?" She dumped the couch cushions on the floor and made a gagging shuddery noise. "What does she think I'd do? Bellow for her benefit? Oh, no." She slapped a hand over her mouth and blushed crimson, mortified. "Did I say that? I can't believe I said that. Strike that. Oh, God, that's so tacky!"

She heaved on the strap that opened the sofa into a queen-size bed. It resisted. "It's this family," she ranted, tugging at the bed. "These women! Grandma Brannigan says they're all shatter-pated. Of course, she would say that—they're my mother's relatives. But they make me so crazy I don't know what I'm saying—" she sneaked a glance at Gabriel over her shoulder and her flush deepened "—*doing*. When they're around I do the most unbelievable things—things I'd never do." Still struggling with the bed, she shook her head vigorously at Gabriel. "If you're around at all after the wedding you'll see right now I'm not myself, I'm somebody else. I'm living in the *Twilight Zone*. In a second we'll hear the doo-doo-doo-doos, and Rod Serling will show up to tell us the story of Alice in Nuttyland, about a woman haunted and hunted by her relatives and their raving idiosyncrasies."

Trying not to laugh, Gabriel took the bed strap from her and pulled straight up. The sofa opened without a squeak. "They care about you, Alice. All of them."

"Phooey." Alice glared from him to the bed, then spun about and headed for the hall linen closet. She returned with pillows, blanket and sheets, and started to make the bed. "Honest to John," she muttered. " 'Fornicate in the living room.' As if I'd really consider—" She stopped abruptly, gazing down at the bed and blushed again. "Well I suppose I did actually consider that, didn't I? Oh, jeez, am I that depraved that I'd—when they're—" Her blush deepened.

"Oh, no, I don't believe it. I might have if she hadn't— Oh, Gabriel." Embarrassed, she sat down on the edge of the bed and covered her face with her hands. "I'm sorry. Oh, God, you must think I'm a sex-starved lunatic coming on to you like that when they're—and I've only known you—"

"No." Gabriel sank to his knees in front of her and caught her hands in his, forcing her to look at him. "I think you're beautiful and generous and loving and so damned sexy—" He buried his face in her hands, kissed each of them with gentle passion. "If we had doors to close behind us, Alice," he promised softly, "if we had time, I'd show you what I think of you. I'd make love to you—" His mouth curved, eyes lit. He leaned his elbows on the bed on either side of her, placed a lingering kiss on her mouth. "I'd *love* you," he repeated for emphasis, "until the cows come home and beyond. If I could."

As though wrapped in a spell, Alice swayed toward him. "Oh, my," she breathed inadequately. "Oh, my golly jeepers gee. You sure can talk. Is that what makes you good undercover?"

"Hmm." His smile brushed her cheek when he lifted himself on his arms and pressed her back onto the bed; his tongue outlined her mouth, made a brief enticing foray into its interior. "That and knowing when to press an advantage."

"Oh, my." Alice gulped, staring up at the face so close to her own. Feeling the press of his weight on her chest, the smoothness of denim against her skin where his leg had hiked her skirt up her thigh. Feeling the flutter of tension and anticipation inside her when he shifted forward slightly. Wondering how mature she really was the second after she wondered how far she'd let him go. *All the way,* she assured herself honestly, distrustfully. *I'd let him go—no, I'd take him all the way.*

"No," she moaned, and rolled away from Gabriel. "Not again. Not now. I'm a grown-up, not sixteen. I'm supposed to have some self-control. Oh, damn." She scooted off the bed and stood in the pool of yellow light cast by the floor lamp, gazing at Gabriel, hand to her mouth. "Oh, what is it about you, me—us—that I keep doing this, acting like this? Yesterday morning you had a gun in my face, tonight I'm trying like hell to climb into bed with you. I can't trust myself around you. You look at me and I feel like I'm going to burst. My chest gets tight and my heart pounds and I can't breathe."

She rubbed her forehead, dropped her hand to her side with a short unamused laugh. "If I were one of my daughters I'd tell myself this was a crush—something to be enjoyed, maybe daydreamed about, but not acted upon. But I'm not one of my daughters, and this isn't a crush and I don't want to feel like this about you or anyone. Not now. Not when I'm finally going to get the time I've always wanted to figure out who I am."

"How do you feel, Alice?" Gabriel came intently around the end of the bed wanting her answer, afraid to hear it. "How do I make you feel?"

Jaw working, Alice looked at him, then away. "Like I'm not safe. Like I'm about to fall in love, lose my mind and go to hell on good intentions." She swallowed and looked at him again. "Is that what you were trying to tell me this afternoon, Gabriel?" she asked. "Is that how I make you feel?"

Gabriel studied her for a moment before replying. He considered lying to make things cleaner, easier for both of them, but he'd promised her he wouldn't. "Yeah." He nodded. "That's close. Given time and opportunity, I don't think I'd find it difficult to love you, Alice Meyers."

"Oh, God, do you want to?"

"Do I *want* to?" Gabriel's shoulders shook with wry laughter. "I've never been under the impression it's a matter of choice, Alice. It's what we do about the situation that counts.''

"What are we going to do about it?" Alice whispered.

"Enjoy the moment. Make a memory." Gabriel closed his hands in a gesture of defeat. "Nothing. You deserve someone who's got time to love you right, Alice, to love you completely. You're worth time. A lot more than I have to give you.''

"Oh, Gabriel." Hands outstretched, Alice took two steps toward him before catching herself, stopping. "Damn." She flung herself into the dining room and wrapped her hands around the back of a chair. "My grandmother always said idle hands were the devil's workshop," she muttered. "Now I know what she meant.''

"Alice."

Gabriel crossed the room, gripped her arms. Alice slipped away from him, dodging around the table to pick up Grace's veil, her pincushion and the bag of seed pearls from the shelves indented in the dining room wall. "I—I can't...talk about this anymore, Gabriel. I don't know what to say. I don't know what to do. Y-you go to bed. I—I'll sit up, work on this veil—keep my hands busy so I don't tempt the devil anymore. Besides, I do have to get this thing done.''

"Alice." Half-serious, half-laughing, Gabriel caught hold of the chair she'd vacated, rocking it. "Alice, listen to me. You don't need to worry about the devil tonight. We're between the backyard and the bathroom and between the bedrooms and the kitchen. We're sleeping in the middle of the main drag. Now—" his mouth worked around a grin "—I know I'm many things, but I'm not an exhibitionist.''

Alice ducked her head in consternation. "I wasn't worried about you attacking me, Gabriel," she mumbled. "I was thinking more along the lines of me attacking you. 'Cause like the song says, you rattle my brain. When I kiss you I forget to think.''

Gabriel's grin broadened. "I can sleep in the yard with the rest of the boys," he offered.

"Well—" Alice set the pincushion and pearl bag on the table and toyed with the dimmer switch for the dining-room light. "—it's not a bad idea, but it also kind of brings us to another problem."

Gabriel coughed to hide a laugh. "I hoped it might."

Alice sent him a severe look. He made an expansive gesture, motioning her to continue; he wouldn't interrupt. Alice nodded, grimaced and took a breath.

"Y'see," she said tentatively, "what I was saying, we'd probably be ever so much more comfortable if you slept outside, except, well, the extra sleeping bags are in the girls' room with Mamie and George, and there's only enough room in the tent for the boys, and the ground is kind of hard, and you said yourself that you're not as young as you used to be and, well—" she made a face "—it's a big bed. I mean, it'd be silly to waste the space, you know and—" she hesitated, then plunged on "—I kind of like the idea of you being in it where I can see you. Very strange, I know, except that if you do go to sleep, then maybe I could calm down and come to bed, too, and you know—" she sighed in half-sincere despair "—just sort of be near you."

"Sounds frustrating," Gabriel commented dryly.

"Yeah—" Alice nodded "—it does, doesn't it." She gazed at him apologetically. "I told you it was a problem."

Gabriel pulled off his shirt and came around the table to her while unbuttoning his jeans. "If I do fall asleep and you do come to bed," he said slowly, and Alice swallowed, then nodded that she was following his drift. "If that happens," he went on, "and I reach out to hold you—in my sleep, of course—will that be a problem?"

"Definitely," she murmured, eyes on his mouth. "But feel free to do it, anyway."

"I will." He stepped out of his pants, leaned toward her. Alice met him halfway. His kiss was rough, thorough, sweet.

"Good night, Alice," he said and touched his mouth to hers again. "Don't stay up all night."

"No," Alice said shyly, "I won't."

The dream went something like this:

She was standing in the middle of her bedroom with Gabriel. The door was closed and they were undressed, in one another's arms, about to make use of the bed. There was a knock on the door. Without waiting for a response, Julia Block Brannigan opened the door and entered her daughter Alice's room.

"Well," she said, circling Alice and Gabriel thoughtfully, "what have we here? Sneaking boys into your room now, Allie? What would your father say?"

Gasping, Alice lifted her face from Gabriel's shoulder and gazed at her mother, glassy-eyed and irritated. "Ma," she snapped defensively, "could you get out of here? I'm in the middle of something."

"So I see," Julia reproved. She shook her head sadly. "Allie, Allie," she said, "when will you learn? Didn't Matthew teach you anything? Didn't Ian use you enough?"

"Ma-a," Alice singsonged, "what do you mean, didn't I learn anything? I waited eighteen years, didn't I? I mean, you have a lot of nerve disapproving of what I'm doing, what with all the men this family has thrown at me over the years."

"Fodder," her mother said, dismissing the men with a shrug. "Company. Family prerogative. Nobody you'd go to bed with. We've always been very careful to select only men who'd irritate or distract you, instead of someone who might be *right* for you."

Nonplussed, Alice stared at her mother. "Then what was the point, Ma? If you weren't looking to find someone who'd take care of me and the girls, what the hell was the point?"

"We love you," Julia said. "You've been so wound up in Allyn and Rebecca all these years that you've never taken any time for yourself. You're getting old and crabby. We just wanted to take your mind off. We want you to be happy."

"But, Ma, Gabriel makes me happy."

"Ffftt!" Snorting, Julia tossed up a hand. "How would you know? You know him five seconds and you're off to bed. You know what I think? Proximity, that's what I think. A man and a woman living closed up in the same house with a bed and active imaginations—that's a lot of temptation. Things happen. 'Happy' is just a word you use to justify the choice."

"Mom..." Locked in Gabriel's arms in her dream, naked emotionally as well as physically, Alice stared at her mother, remembering. Hadn't she had almost this same conversation with Allyn five minutes before her daughter—Julia's *grand*daughter—had driven off in the van with two girlfriends, three boys and a bed? And she'd had it almost as successfully, too. "Ma," she complained almost as Allyn had, "I'm thirty-five years old, and I've been making my own decisions for years. Don't you think it's about time I go back to making my own mistakes, too?"

Julia touched Alice's shoulder with a daughter-irritating mixture of compassion and love. "A lot of things have happened in your life lately, Allie. Don't fall into bed with him just because everything around you is changing and you figure one more change thrown on top of the others won't make any difference. Your confusion may make him seem right to you when he might not be."

"I'll be careful, Ma." Alice nodded and turned her attention back to Gabriel.

Her mother shook her head—down, but not defeated. She got in the parting shot even as her image began to fade from the dream. "He looks at you the way a man looks at a woman, Alice Marie. He expects more from you than flirting and waffling. More than sex. Are you sure you're ready for that? *Are you sure . . .*"

"Are you *sure?*"

Alice awoke with a start, jerking her face off the dining-room table, hearing the voice in her head. Only it wasn't her mother's voice she was hearing now. This voice was masculine. Deeply, richly, despairingly male.

Without comprehension Alice looked around. She was sitting at the dining-room table, Grace's veil in her fist, seed pearls scattered in front of her. Her back ached and she had a crick in her neck. The dining-room light was off.

"You're sure," the voice said again, violently. "That's an absolute? No mistake?" The voice paused, listening.

Gabriel, Alice thought and blinked. Talking to someone in the kitchen. No, she shook her head. That wasn't right; there was only one voice. He was in the kitchen talking to someone on the phone. No, she tensed and straightened apprehensively. He wasn't talking; he was hurling obscenities at someone on the phone as though what he'd really like to hurl was something shiny, sharp and deadly.

"No, don't wait," she heard him snap. "Go to Scully, get clearance and get the damn warrants. This has gone on long enough. I'll call you in a couple of days." He paused again, then loosed another ugly obscenity. "Screw Markum. I'm going to take the bastard down."

Frightened by the sound of his barely contained rage, Alice pillowed her face on her arms on the table again, pretending to be asleep, and watched the kitchen doorway. He appeared there, backlit by the shadows filtering through the unshaded kitchen window. Even in silhouette his anger was tangible, dangerous; it engulfed her. This was not the brown-eyed man she'd shared her confusion with, had wanted to hold her. This was the man with the vivid blue eyes who'd stopped her from taking his gun in the pawnshop. This was the man who knew how to make nice with killers, who was capable of anything.

She watched him twist the phone receiver in his hands, felt the control he exerted not to smash it through the wall. Saw him look at her without realizing she was awake. Watched him drag air into his lungs as though that was hard work; saw him gently depress the phone's plunger and dial.

"How did it happen, Markum?" he said evenly into the phone. "Who turned you? No, don't tell me, I don't give a rat's ass for your excuses. But what you did to Nicky, I'm gonna damn well do that to you, too. You got that, Si? Personally, I'm gonna do it to you."

"Gabriel, what's going on?"

Afraid for him, Alice forgot the cautions of her dream, was out of her chair and at his back. She reached around him, wanting to hold him, to pull him back from the brink of whatever ledge he was standing on. To stop him from letting his anger consume and endanger him, by getting him off the phone and making him think. He twisted under her touch, crooked an arm about her neck and covered her mouth with his hand. Then he cradled the phone and grabbed her arms, shaking her.

"What the hell do you think you're doing, Allie?" he demanded harshly. "Don't ever do that again. If he finds out who you are, where I am, I don't know if I can protect you." He hauled her roughly against him, buried his face in her hair. "God, Alice, I don't want anything to happen to you."

"Gabriel, you were threatening someone on my phone."

"I know." He stroked her hair restlessly, ran his hands the length of her back. "I'm sorry. I let it get away from me." He released her suddenly, strode back into the kitchen and began shoving things around on the counter, unsuccessfully trying to confine too much emotion in too small a space. "I hate this, Alice," he said hoarsely. "I hate this stinking job, I hate the lies and the subterfuge, the damned personal agendas. I hate manipulating people, I hate using them, I hate spying on them. But the biggest crime I've ever committed is trusting someone else's judgment over my own instincts. Letting them use me, manipulate me.''

"Gabriel…'' Alice crossed the kitchen, reaching for him. He eluded her, blindly wedging himself into the corner join of the counter, holding himself still by hanging on to its edge.

"He did it, Alice. Markum. Silas Markum. Not Scully. I've known him fifteen years. He got me into this business, he recommended me for promotions, he taught me what I needed to know to stay alive out there. His thirteen-year-old's my godchild, dammit! The sonovabitch killed three cops and a special agent, embezzled crime-unit funds, stole drugs and drug money after busts. And I as good as let him do it.''

"You can't blame yourself for what he did, Gabriel.'' The words meant nothing to him right now, and Alice knew it. She made the effort to say them, anyway, hoping he'd find at least a glimmer of truth. "He made the choices, not you.''

"Yeah? Well, I do blame myself, Alice. I live in a world of deception. I oughtta know when someone's lying to me. I can't wear blinders out of loyalty because he's a friend.''

"Don't—''

"You know what the worst part of it is, Alice?'' Haunted, Gabriel stared into the darkness, continuing as though he hadn't heard her. "You know the worst of it? At this moment, I don't think I'm as angry over him stealing the public trust or killing Nicky and the others as I am over his betraying *me,* lying to *me,* using *me.* God, it makes me sick. I can't believe how stupid I've been.'' He shoved a hand through his hair in disbelief. "He killed them, Allie. Whether he pulled the trigger himself or just sent them out to die, the bastard murdered them.''

She didn't know what to say. She knew how he felt; she'd felt the same way on a different scale with Ian and then with Matthew. It was hard to forgive yourself for being naive and stupid in a world full of cynics. She opened her mouth to say something, anything, to alleviate the clustered silence. But there were no words, only feeling; a fullness and sadness and understanding that could only be conveyed by touch.

She went to him, outlined his jaw, stroked his chest, put her arms around him. He tried to disentangle himself from her embrace, to push her away, but she held on, anchoring him. He ceased struggling and wrapped himself around her, burying his face in her neck. His sobs were dry, silent shudders through him.

In that instant, the world and her self-designated part in it seemed to shift under Alice's feet. After nearly twenty years of resolute denial, it took her heart barely a split second to acknowledge the irrevocable commitment her head would rather have ignored. She knew now what she'd been looking for in Matthew, what had made her feel like such easy prey for Ian. Gabriel was everything they hadn't been and much, much more. Danger and safety, arrogance and vulnerability, unadulterated passion and generosity. He was adventure, larger than life. He was part of her blood. Not just in it, not simply a burst of adrenaline through her veins, but an essential ingredient of it, like white blood cells and iron.

Given time and opportunity, I don't think I'd find it difficult to love you, Alice Meyers, he'd said.

Alice shut her eyes and clenched her fists on Gabriel's back. She didn't need time to know that she already felt what she'd promised herself not to feel for him, *with* him. She didn't want to live a safe uneventful underdeveloped life anymore. She wanted to be foolhardy. She wanted to be reckless. She wanted to risk her heart on the basis of the last forty hours, to be part of Gabriel body and soul. No matter what kind of future, pleasure or pain that meant.

It won't happen, Alice, he'd said. *We're in the middle of the main drag and I'm not an exhibitionist.*

She opened her hands and hugged him harder, reaching up his bare back to the long hair curling over the base of his neck, tangling her fingers in it and the rough chain that held his St. Jude medal. There was, she thought, nothing quite as impossible as this felt right now. She pressed her face tightly into his neck. Gabriel stilled.

"Alice?"

He shifted in her arms, whispering her name first as a question of concern, then as a knowing caress, soft and erotic. "Alice."

"Gabriel." His name was drawn out of her like a sigh of despair, like an anguished plea.

He rubbed his hands down her back, roughly up, twisting them in her hair, tilting her head back. "I'll take care of you, Alice, I promise," he whispered raggedly. "You won't be hurt. I won't hurt you." His lips, teeth, tongue tasted the taut curve of her throat, left heated imprints along the open V of her blouse.

"Gabriel, please." Alice's breath sobbed in her throat. She raked her fingers down his back, into the rough denim at his hips and tugged, arching to fit him. "Please, Gabriel, I need you. Please."

Her hunger entranced him, spurred him on. Where his heart ached, she soothed it. Where his mind cried out, she answered the call. Where his muscles knotted with anger, she eased them, then built in them a new kind of tension. Where his gut twisted with self-loathing and disgust, she filled him with surety and heat.

He lifted his head to look down at her, letting the beauty his eyes saw quench the thirst in his soul. Her lips parted. "Please, Gabriel," she whispered again, and unable to stop himself, he bent his head and buried his tongue deep in her mouth. He would give her what he could in this shadowed room at the heart of her house where he couldn't give her all of himself, where he couldn't protect her from the consequences of their loving, couldn't trust himself to let her touch him, comfort him, the way she wanted to. The way he needed her to. Not when he couldn't offer her a forever-and-always guarantee. Even though he wanted to.

Her body twisted in his arms, reaching for the union his tongue mimicked. Gabriel dragged his mouth from hers and bent his knees, keeping them from that most intimate contact even as he pulled her blouse from her skirt, freed its buttons from their buttonholes. "No, Alice, not like that, not here. Not now. Like this, love. Let me..."

He parted her blouse and slipped a hand up her back to release her bra, pushing the hindrance aside to expose the fullness of her breasts, to shape, tease, mold. Alice gasped and arched toward him again, moaning softly. He eased her back against the kitchen wall and dipped his head, brushing his tongue across her belly and up between her breasts as he hiked her skirt up her thighs, over her hips. Then, while his mouth outlined her breasts and his hands shaped her bottom, he sandwiched one jean-clad thigh between hers.

Alice's eyes widened and she inhaled sharply, tightening instinctively on him. Gabriel kissed her again, rocking her hips gently. "It's all right, love," he murmured against her lips. "It's all right, Allie, trust me. Let me love you."

Wordlessly, thoughtlessly, Alice tangled her fingers once more in his hair, brought her mouth to his. He tasted hot and sweet; his teeth were sharp and smooth, his tongue rough-textured, rough-playing, sliding against her own. She felt one of his hands massage the small of her back in tiny nerve-tingling circles. The other lightly claimed her breast, stroking it so it swelled to his touch, tracing her nipple without quite touching it until she strained upward in frustration.

Tension coiled inside her like a spring about to burst. Whatever he was doing, she needed more of it now. When he tucked an arm about her waist and slipped his fingers down her stomach and along the elastic waistband of her panties, she surged toward him with relief. When his teeth nipped an enticing passage down her throat and breast, then paused, Alice pressed forward eagerly, begging him to continue. As though of their own volition, her hands roved down his chest to find that he'd left the buttons of his fly undone when he'd pulled his pants on. She parted the denim fabric and reached for him, bent on releasing him, touching him, involving him. Loving him.

With a groan, Gabriel caught her hands, pushed them away. He was already too close to the edge of taking her; if she touched him, he was lost. He wanted this moment to be for her; his pleasure would come from hers.

He flexed his knees and drew her nipple into his mouth at the same time as his fingers found and invaded the damp secret part of her body. Alice gasped and folded mindlessly around him, burying her face in his shoulder as she parted her thighs to his hand. His touch was exquisite. Each intimate stroke made her burn, melt, tighten. Her hips moved to quicken the rhythm, and he turned her slightly, deepening the caress as he turned his attention to her other breast, flicking his tongue across its excited tip until he felt the tremors begin inside her.

Alice bit her lip to keep from crying out her satisfaction when he drew in her nipple deep and hard. The tension inside her built to a peak. She felt herself trying to hang on to it, to keep herself from falling, but she couldn't. Gabriel wouldn't let her. He touched her, and she felt herself let go for him, splinter and float. He captured her mouth, catching the cry she couldn't hold back, holding her while the earth trembled around her. Trembled with her.

"Gabriel," she whispered brokenly, "Gabriel."

"I'm here, Alice. Hold on to me. I won't let you go."

"But you—we didn't—I want to—"

"It's all right, Alice, it's fine. You're wonderful, beautiful. Hold on to me. Don't let me go."

"But you—right now—it's not right—it doesn't seem fair. I didn't mean to use you, Gabriel."

"Use me?" Unnerved by her choice of words, Gabriel rocked back on his heels to stare at her incredulously. "Use me?" he repeated angrily. "Is that what you think just happened?"

Guiltily Alice nodded and turned her face to the window. "I'm sorry. I didn't think, I just—"

"Felt." Gabriel's voice softened. "Enjoyed." He caught her chin, drew her face gently his way. "Trusted me. Gave me the most precious and irreplaceable piece of yourself because I needed you to. Because I asked you to. But, God, Alice, use me?" He shook his head. "No."

"But you're still—" Alice began and stopped uncomfortably.

"Aroused?" Gabriel smoothed her hair behind her ear. "Physically encumbered?" He smiled when she gave him a hesitant nod, and kissed her reverently. "Do you know how beautiful you are when I touch you?" he asked. "What you do to me? How you make me feel inside? Now, I won't deny it'd be a helluva relief to jump your bones right now, Alice Meyers," he said softly, "and sometime when the time's right, I hope to do just that. But until then, know this—" he took a breath "—what you just gave me is worth a damn sight more to me than some temporary physical relief and I wouldn't trade it for anything in the world."

"But—"

"No, Alice." He touched an open palm to her face, inhaling some unnamed emotion when she lifted her cheek into his hand. "I want you, Alice Meyers," he said huskily, "make no mistake about that. But right now what I need more than anything is to hold you, be with you, know you're there. Please," he implored, and Alice thought she felt her heart burst. "Let me hold you."

She smoothed his face, took his hand. "Come to bed," she told him. "Gabriel, come to bed."

She awoke at sunrise to an unfamiliar sense of complete peace and a too familiar sense of impending interruption. Gabriel had pulled the sheet over them when they'd gotten into bed and now slept spooned along her back with one leg thrown over her thigh and one arm tucked around her middle, hand possessively encompassing her bare breast. The feel of him made her ache with anticipation and the need for privacy so that she could wake him the way she wanted to.

She shifted carefully in his embrace, trying to distract herself by straightening the twisted clothing she'd slept in. Instead she succeeded in making Gabriel stir. His hand contracted, thumb stroked across her nipple, making it harden. Alice sighed with pleasure. Gabriel murmured something soft and wordless and repositioned himself more firmly against her back, tucking his leg around her this time, as well as his arm. She thought she felt him smile in his sleep against her neck. She shut her eyes and loved the feel of his smile.

Her sense of impending interruption and disaster increased with her sense of contentment and desire. All she wanted to do was bask in Gabriel's warmth, to at least replay last night to an even more satisfying conclusion in her dreams, but something niggled at her awareness, something that wasn't quite *so*. She glanced uneasily around as much of the living room as she could see. The house was too quiet, she decided, and her everymother's instinct warned her it had been too quiet for far too long. Something, she realized, was about to explode.

Unfortunately, she understood her instincts well.

There was a springy whine, a hesitant click and the front door was eased open into the living room. Before he even woke up, Gabriel flung himself away from Alice and across the four feet to the doorway, surprising the intruder as she came in. He crooked his arm about her neck, bent her arm behind her back and forced her face first against the wall. Then he stood there blinking and shaking his head groggily. The intruder struggled with him, alternately sobbing and emitting tiny shrieks that came out sounding a lot like "Mom."

"Becky?" Alice took one look at her youngest daughter, used another one of the words she'd been saving up for eighteen years and scrambled off the bed, buttoning her blouse as she came. "Gabriel, let her go. It's my daughter."

Chapter Ten

"Huh? Oh." Embarrassed and still yawning, Gabriel released the struggling teen. "I'm sorry. I didn't mean—"

Becky shushed him with a look of teary loathing and threw herself into Alice's arms. "Mom," she sobbed. "Oh, Mom!"

"Shh, baby, shh." Alice sat down on the bed, holding Becky, smoothing her daughter's hair, comforting her child. "He didn't know it was you, darlin'. He didn't know."

"It's not him." Becky gulped and sniffled back a sob. "I don't care about *him*—were you sleeping with him? Your clothes are kind of rumply. It's Michael. He—" She gulped again and threw herself face down on the bed, sobbing. "Oh, Ma! It's such a mess—I've made such a mess. I'm not—and Mike—"

"What's going on?" Mamie whispered from the twins' bedroom doorway. "Is somebody crying? Is it my boys?"

"No, it's—"

"What's going on out there?" Aunt Kate staggered blindly into the hallway, pulling the black sleep mask she'd worn to bed up from over one eye and blinking. "Whoever it is better not try anything funny," she said querulously, patting the pockets of her robe. "I've got a knife here somewhere and I'm not afraid to use it. Alice Marie, where is your bra, and is that your blouse I see unbuttoned? Young man—" she waved a threatening finger at Gabriel and made a move toward him "—I thought I warned you—"

"Mother!" Mamie eased herself into the hall, squinting at Alice's clothing as she took her mother's arm. "Leave them alone. It's nothing. If you've really got a knife, give it to me and go back to bed. Honest to God, I don't understand why I do this..." She maneuvered Kate back into Alice's bedroom and shut the door behind them.

Alice gaped after them for a moment, then crossed her eyes and flared her nostrils, making a they're-driving-me-nuts face at Gabriel before turning once more to Rebecca, who was leaning on her elbows sniffly and watery-eyed, but interested. "Wow, Mom," she said. "Aunt Kate, Cousin Mamie..." She narrowed her eyes and glanced speculatively at Gabriel. "*Him.* What'd you do last night? It must have been a hell of a party."

"Don't swear," Alice admonished automatically.

"God, Ma!" Rebecca shoved herself off the sofa bed in disgust. "I'm eighteen. I don't even live here anymore. I come home to get your advice on this problem and all you can do is tell me not to swear. I'm old enough to swear in front of you if I want to. God, I mean, I don't want to get to be *your* age and find out I'm still curbing my natural speech patterns in front of you like you do in front of Grandma because you're afraid of offending her. I mean, really, is that what you want, Ma?"

"Ah—" Alice began, but the side door slammed open, saving her from replying.

"Cousin Alice," Mamie's oldest son shouted. "Cousin Alice, you up? We can't sleep out there anymore with the sun comin' up, so we thought we'd get up and make breakfast and get Dad and go fishing. We caught some really freaky night crawlers last night. You got a camp stove and some eggs and bacon and potatoes and sourdough? If you don't have the sourdough, we'll take some Jiffy Mix or Bisquick and frozen blueberries. Oh, and a frying pan. Gotta have something to cook in."

Alice rose stiffly and advanced toward the kitchen, gritting her teeth. "Do I have what?" she asked carefully.

Gabriel put a hand on her arm and pointed her at Becky. "You handle this," he suggested. "I'll take care of that."

"Wise choice," Alice muttered and eyed her daughter. "Front porch?" she asked.

"It might be more private," Rebecca agreed and went out the door she'd just come in.

Alice took a quick look down at her clothing. Who the hell had told her life to start imitating her dreams? Her bra was practically around her throat, the front of her blouse was buttoned at an angle, and her skirt was full of static cling and riding up her back. She spread a hand over her face and heaved an oh-God-wouldn't-you-know-it sigh of humiliation, wondering exactly how Aunt Kate would embellish this story. She might as well resign herself to her fate, Alice thought. Because no matter how Aunt Kate told the story, Alice's sisters would have a field day with it when she was through. It would be handed down in the Brannigan annals as The Day—or rather The Night—Aunt Alice Went Mad. It would be like playing telephone; each telling would get more and more ridiculous, until finally the story would have Aunt Alice dressed in a toga wearing grape leaves on her head being fed the grapes by some bronzed young god— who might or might not resemble Gabriel—with oiled skin and wearing very few clothes. Alice yanked her clothes into place with a sound of irritation. Some nights, she thought, it simply didn't pay to go to bed.

But the up side was, she also no longer felt quite so *old*....

Outside, the late-June morning was still cool and soft around the edges, but the stark yellow of the rising sun promised heat when the dew burned off. Alice stretched and for a moment simply stood to take in the morning's beauty, looking up and down the street at the facing rows of matching houses. Sunlight glinted off windows, barely filtered through the cover of maple and locust leaves where the trees farther down lined the street. Lawns, both the ragged and the well-kept, glistened with dew; roses, petunias and pansies were alive with it. Serenity touched the neighborhood while there was no one about to see it.

Except here. Alice looked down at the porch steps where Becky awaited her, head bowed, face peeking out at her mother between long strands of dark brown hair. The big deep-lidded hazel eyes that had first attracted Alice to Matthew and were his unsung legacy to both of Alice's daughters, blinked guiltily when Alice sat down on the chilly concrete.

She's been lying to somebody, Alice thought, recognizing the look. But who to? Me? Michael?

She lifted a lock of Becky's hair and tucked it behind her daughter's ear. Again the red-rimmed dark-shadowed eyes blinked unhappily at her. Some deep-rooted sense of mother intuition told Alice that Becky had lied to her husband and not been quite straight with her mother. Wonderful, Alice thought, this was going to be one of *those*.

"So," she said neutrally, smoothing the rest of the tangled hair off Becky's face. "Tell me about it. Start with how you got here."

Becky hid her face in her knees. "I got a ride from a couple of guys who needed directions to the Detroit waterfront so they could get to Eastern Market or the Ethnic Festival,

I forget which. They dropped me off up on Baldwin. I walked from there.''

"I see," Alice commented carefully. "It's not quite five-thirty now, so that means you must have left East Lansing, what, about four?''

"Three-thirty."

"What did Mike say when you left?''

Becky buried her face deeper between her knees and plucked an impatiens from the bunch Alice had planted beside the porch. "Mike's working the third shift over at the hospital for the summer. He doesn't know I'm gone yet.''

"Ah, Becky—"

"I left him a note," her daughter said defensively. "He'll see it when he gets home."

"Did you fight? Will he know why you left?''

Becky dipped her head deeper toward the steps. Her voice was small. "No."

"Rebecca Sue—"

"Ah, Mom." Becky lifted miserable features to her mother. "When I told him I thought I was pregnant he didn't even get upset. He got this look on his face like I was the most wonderful thing he'd ever seen. Then he started to laugh and hug me and he said, 'Good, now you'll have to marry me.' He went right out and bought an engagement ring and roses and he knelt down and it was so romantic, Ma. We went down to the courthouse the day after graduation, and they told us if we had an hour's worth of counseling, we wouldn't even need blood tests, so that's what we did. And Grace and Phil were there, and we witnessed for them, and they witnessed for us and—"

"Wait a minute, back up," Alice said. "You stood up for Grace and Phil?''

"Yeah." Becky nodded. "Didn't she tell you? She said she would, I mean they helped *us* out, it was only fair. She was so upset about the way everybody was making plans for her wedding and not listening to her, and you know how she is about ceremonies and crowds and everybody just wanting to add 'two more guests.' And you know Grandma. She'd give anyone who asked the shirt off her back, then turn and offer 'em yours, too. She can't say no to anyone. Grace said she and Phil eloped so Grandma wouldn't have to say anything to anybody anymore. They figured all they had to do was hand Aunt Helen the guest list and let her organize calling off the wedding. Didn't they?'

Alice shut her eyes and rubbed her nose. And this was only Wednesday, she thought. What more could happen before Saturday morning? Don't tell me, she admonished the fates hastily, silently, I don't want to know. "No," she said aloud, "Grace hasn't said anything about her wedding yet. But never mind, let's get back to you. What happened to all that romance? Did Mike," she said slowly, hating what she had to ask, "do...anything? Did he...hurt you?"

"No!" Becky was off the step in a flash to face her mother, face flaming with indignation. "How can you even ask? I'm only in love, I'm not stupid! Mike's the kindest, sweetest, most generous, loving—"

"You didn't tell me you wanted to get married," Alice interrupted her, ticking the points off on her fingers. "You didn't tell me you were pregnant, but a week later you catch a ride home to me in the middle of the night with a couple of strangers and Mike doesn't know you've left?" She shook her head, bewildered. "What else should I ask you, Becky? If everything's so wonderful and he hasn't hurt you and you didn't have a fight, *why* did you run away from him? I mean, you wanted him so badly you ran away with him in the first place. Cut me some slack here, kid! If you want me to treat you like a responsible adult, then *be* one. Quit pussyfooting around whatever it was you think you did and *tell* me."

Becky drew herself up to her full height at the challenge and looked Alice in the eye. "I'm..." Her shoulders drooped and she wilted. "Can we go up to Big Boy and get some coffee first?" she asked.

"Is it serious?" Gabriel asked a minute or so later when Alice followed the scent of eggs burning over a charcoal grill around the back of the house to tell him she and Becky were leaving for a while. "Do you need me to beat anybody up?"

Alice tried to smile, failed. "I don't know yet." She looked up at him, troubled, when he cupped her face. "She says Grace and Phil got married the same day she and Mike did and that Grace is going to call off the church wedding. I suppose that's going to tick off a few of the relatives, but why Becky came home..." She shrugged helplessly. "She's having such a hard time telling me, it must be bad. But if Mike hasn't done anything, and they didn't fight, I can't imagine..." She lifted her shoulders, let them drop. "I don't know, maybe it'll be easier for her to say with a table between us. Sometimes being a parent is such a bitch."

Gabriel turned his head to hide a grin. "I wouldn't know," he said. "Would you trade it?"

Alice heaved a long-suffering are-you-kidding sigh. "Not a chance."

"I didn't think so." Gabriel chuckled. "Hey." He caught her hand when she turned to go and drew her back. "Whether it's serious or not, if you need a place to dump it, I'm here."

"I know." Alice looked at him, surprised by a knowledge she hadn't known she possessed. She touched his jaw in wonder, stood on her toes and kissed him hard. "I know you are," she repeated with evident satisfaction, then went.

"My period started last night," Becky announced suddenly after toying with a glass of soda and a plate of scrambled eggs for fifteen silent minutes. "Mom, I'm not pregnant."

Caught off guard, Alice opened her mouth, and coffee dribbled down her chin. She snatched up her napkin to catch the liquid before it dripped onto her blouse. "What?"

"Oh, there, see?" Becky moaned. "I knew you'd be upset. Just think how Mike'll feel when I tell him. It'll be like I betrayed him or something."

Alice cleared her throat around a soundless involuntary *Thank you God!* and remained carefully joyless and noncommittal. "He doesn't know?"

"Mom, how could I tell him? We got married because we thought I was pregnant. Now that I'm not, what's he gonna say? He says he wants kids right away, Ma, but he thought— when he said it—and his parents already think I tried to trap him. He told 'em to go blow, that his wife didn't have to take that kind of crap from his parents and that he wasn't going to let any kid of his grow up without a father. But now that we're not having a baby things might change. You know?"

Alice nodded. "I see," she said, then shook her head. "No, I don't. Help me out here, Beck. Marriage is a tough proposition for anyone at any age, let alone for a couple of kids who are pregnant. I'd think maybe it'd be . . . easier for you and Mike if you're not. To begin with."

"No, Ma, don't you see?" Becky said passionately. "A baby made everything different. Possible, you know? When we went down to the courthouse, I didn't have any doubts about what we were doing. I don't think Mike did, either. We'd have had the baby and struggled to make ends meet and it would have been great." She looked down at her hands. "But now . . . I feel like a fraud—like I married him under false pretenses. I love Mike, Mom. I want to be with him for the rest of my life, but now I sort of wonder if we didn't do this too soon, if I messed up and he's going to feel trapped like his parents said. I mean, maybe we should just call the whole thing off, you know? Maybe . . ."

Alice spread her hands in front of her on the table. I can't think of her as me, she told herself for the thirtieth time. She's not me. And Mike is not Matt. "What do you need from me, Becky?" she asked. "Permission to come home and be my little girl again? It doesn't work that way, babe. You've got a husband, a whole life in front of you. I can't get between you and Mike. Not now. That's not the mother-in-law's job. My house is always yours, but—"

"Tell me what to do, Ma," Becky pleaded. "Tell me how to handle this."

"Oh, Becky, I can't." Alice gestured inadequately. "You made your choices. I can't unmake them for you. Only you can do that. Even if I wanted to, you'd only resent me for it later. I love you, darlin', but I'd rather have you hate me now and get it over with than wait until you're thirty and have you dump my interference back on me in spades." Alice touched her daughter's hand, praying she was saying the right things. "Whatever you decide, I'll back you up, you know that. But it's your choice, Becky. You decide."

Mother and daughter stared at one another across the table, across the span of years and experiences that separated them. They weren't so different from one another right now, Alice realized. They were closer in age than they'd ever been. They'd each spent the past chaotic week vainly trying to get a fit in their new lives, trying to figure out men, and how much a couple of men in particular meant to them—and to their lives, their homes, their beds and their independence.

And to their futures.

Alice took a sip of coffee to wash down her own confusion over that one. Her daughter had been too wrapped up in her own problems to ask Alice anything about Gabriel yet. Alice had no idea what she'd say about him when Becky did. Except that he was . . . special. She watched her daughter take a deep swallow of decision with a mouthful of soda.

"Okay, Mom," Becky sighed. "You got it. I'll talk to Mike. But . . ." Her lips twitched and her eyes sparkled suddenly. "I don't suppose—" She tipped her head and viewed her mother with mock calculation. "I don't suppose," she repeated, "that since you won't tell me what you *want* me to do, maybe you could at least tell me what you *hope* I'll do?"

Alice smiled broadly and shook her head. How could she tell her daughter what she couldn't tell herself? "Not on your life," she said.

Meanwhile, back on the home front, Gabriel was having an equally revealing morning. He learned, for instance, that Aunt Kate liked steak with her scrambled-egg substitute for breakfast and that Alice kept neither in the house. He learned that Uncle Delbert liked his toast burned to a crisp and covered with Alice's homemade mint jelly. He learned that Mamie enjoyed "playfully" swatting men's buns at the end of a joke, and that George was not nearly as henpecked as he appeared. And he learned that the best way to cook breakfast outside with the boys was to put the toaster on the picnic table and hook it up to the extension cord, hand them a jug of milk, a bottle of imitation maple syrup and two or three boxes of frozen waffles and yell, "Have at it, guys," and with that they were perfectly content.

He also discovered with a great deal of surprise that, aside from the odd intrusive thought about Markum, he was thoroughly enjoying himself.

"No," he said into the phone to Edith, who was calling for Helen, who had already called twice in the past half hour. "She cannot bake cookies today. No, when she gets back, I will not ask her to call you so you can make her feel guilty about not doing it. Doesn't anyone else in this family know how to do anything? Yes, I'm sure if she said she'd do blueberry cheesecakes that she did them. I don't care if she's forgotten to do things sometimes in the past. I'm sure it's

because of all the things you all line up for her to do. No,
I'm not sorry for saying that even if I don't know you very
well. There's just something about this family that invites
that sort of comment—uh-huh, yes, I feel . . . right at home
around you, too." He waggled his fingers goodbye at Aunt
Kate and company as they went out the door to spend the
day in Detroit. "No, Edith, I'm sure. You tell Helen, Alice
is tied up, busy, not available all day. No, I'll get her there
tonight, I promise. She'll be there by six o'clock but not before. No, goodbye, I'm hanging up now, Edith. Goodbye."

Gabriel cradled the phone firmly, found the phone's
ringer volume control and turned it off. Then he ran a hand
through his hair, trying to remember where he'd been before Edith called. Now he understood why the few men with
large families he'd met in the past seemed to regard child-
rearing like a course in military maneuvers: you had to treat
a passel of kids like rookie marines in self-defense. Fathers
would never know where they were if they ran their families otherwise—and the truth of the matter was, they probably rarely knew where they were, anyway, and the military-
maneuvers ploy was all for show. It wasn't like him to
forget his place this way, Gabriel thought. In fact, up until
Monday, he didn't think he'd ever before had a problem remembering where he was or what he was doing. He'd been
too busy trying to survive to lose his place.

Funny what one brown-eyed woman with a conscience
and a family could do to you, and how little time it took
her—and her relatives—to do it. What was it Alice had once
said to him about family? *Crash, bang, clatter, then suddenly silence.* And strange as it was, she'd said, she hated the
silence worst of all.

With more of a sense of irony than surprise, Gabriel realized that through his own experiences in law enforce-
ment, and earlier at the missions, he pretty much
understood what Alice meant. The hoopla, however nerve-

racking, made you feel necessary, part of something, as if you belonged. And for a man who'd never particularly felt as though he belonged anywhere, finding out that he could was both intimidating and calming. It meant that he might be good at something besides stinging and arresting life's sleaze, but it also meant risking something more than his life to keep on belonging.

He rubbed a hand across his mouth and folded last night's bed back into a couch. What the hell, huh? he thought. Life wasn't designed so you could hang on to your heart forever; eventually someone or something got to it. If he hadn't known that before, Alice had certainly taught him that last night. Where she was concerned, his heart was well and truly hooked. It was the timing that bothered him, the insidious twist of providence that had led them to find one another when they were both most confused about who they were and what they wanted to happen next.

Well, he amended wryly, that wasn't entirely true. He *did* know some of what he wanted to happen next; it was a matter of whether or not he'd stay alive long enough to see that it did. And that was probably the simplest way he'd ever thought about his job.

"Becky?" a voice at the half-open front door queried.

Gabriel felt his muscles flinch and tense with surprise, even as he kept his features blank. He turned on the balls of his feet and bounced slightly, ready from reflex to deal with an unscheduled intruder.

"Becky," the voice said again. "Please, honey, talk to me."

The screen door groaned open, eased shut. Gabriel got a profile look at a surfer-blond youth of about nineteen wearing blue hospital scrubs. He estimated the kid was at least a head taller and forty pounds heavier than he was, and was the kind of good-looking athletic type Gabriel had found most teenage girls would drop their eyeteeth to date. This must be the husband, he thought.

"I don't know what I did, Becky." Michael's voice was young and soft with approaching maturity. "Whatever it was, I'm sorry. Can't we work it out?"

"She can't hear you, Mike," Gabriel said. "She's not here. She and her mother went—"

He stopped when Michael jumped and turned, hands open and positioned in front of him, feet balanced wide apart in a martial-arts stance. Eyes steady on Gabriel, he knocked the inside door all the way open, out of his way. Gabriel recognized instinctively that the stance was not a bluff, and that if he himself didn't talk fast and move quickly, he was likely to find himself in a world of hurt.

He extended his hands wide from his sides, palms up, open and unthreatening. "Mike," he said cautiously, hoping—not for the first time—that using a man's familiar name would prove as disarming as police school said it would. "Take it easy, Mike, you don't want to do this."

"Where's my wife and her mother, man?" The lost immature quality was gone from Michael's voice, replaced by the hard edge of a man who meant business. "What have you done with them?"

"Nothin', Mike, really. They're fine. Look, I'm Gabriel, I'm a friend of Alice's. Becky came home about five-thirty this morning crying. She and Alice talked, but there were so many extra relatives parked here last night that Becky was having a hard time explaining to your mother-in-law what was wrong. They went up to Big Boy to see if they could get to the bottom line over a cup of coffee. That's all. They've been gone a couple of hours. I imagine they'll be back soon." At least I hope so, anyway, he finished silently.

"Yeah?" Michael wasn't convinced. "Well, *Gabriel,* if you really knew so much about it, you'd know Becky's mom doesn't trust any men friends to be in her house."

Gabriel felt a tiny rush of pleasure sing through him at the announcement. He liked the idea of being the first man allowed in Alice's home. However he'd gotten there. He touched his chest over his heart, raised his right hand like a man under oath. "God's truth, Mike. I'm part of the wedding party and everything. I know all of Becky's aunts, and I've met Skip and Phil. I spent the night here with Aunt Kate and Uncle Delbert, and George, Mamie and the boys. And this may be kind of low, Mike, but I also know how bad Alice felt when you and Becky ran off and got married, and then couldn't face her in person with the news that Becky was pregnant."

Michael's hands wavered. "Man, that wasn't my idea. She raised the woman I love single-handed and did a helluva job. I got a lot of respect for her. I wanted her blessing. But Becky...she's still halfway a kid. She's a little immature sometimes. I guess after what she figures her dad must have done to her mother, she wanted us to have a little time to get used to the idea of what we'd done ourselves before we invited what she calls 'open commentary' from the families." He shrugged, at a loss for excuses. "What can I tell you? I love the girl. I agreed."

He dropped his hands, suddenly surrendering to Gabriel's presence, and rubbed a hand across his eyes. The face he presented to Gabriel was once again young, bewildered and vulnerable. "Everything seemed fine yesterday," he said. "We're trying to save up some money, so I worked a double shift last night. She kissed me goodbye, happy as could be. I got home this morning and she was gone, and there's this note: 'Mike, it won't work, I'm sorry, I'm going home. I hope you have a good life. Love, Becky.'" Michael sat down on the couch and dropped his hands between his knees in defeat. "What the hell kind of Dear John is that?" he asked. "'I hope you have a good life. *Love,* Becky'? I don't even know what it means—how can I fight it?"

"Do you want to?" Gabriel asked.

"Hell, yeah!" Michael was on his feet, jabbing the air with his hands for emphasis. "I was going to ask her to

marry me after graduation no matter what happened. I
didn't want her to get pregnant yet—I mean, don't get me
wrong, I'm real happy about the baby and everything, but
it'd probably be easier for her if we'd waited. I mean I meant
to, but—'' he ducked his head apologetically ''—things
kinda got away from me. You know?''

''Yeah, I do.'' Gabriel nodded. ''I feel kind of the same
way about her mother—like things are getting away from me
before I want 'em to.'' He jerked a thumb toward the
kitchen. ''You want a cup of coffee?''

''No, you got any juice?''

''Dunno. Take a look.'' Gabriel headed for the kitchen.

Mike followed him. ''Say, Gabriel—man, that's a
mouthful of a name your parents stuck on you, isn't it?''

''Biblical. Named me for an angel. Should've saved
themselves the trouble.''

''Yeah, man, parents do things for weird reasons, don't
they?'' Mike agreed from the refrigerator. ''I'm not doin'
that to my kid. He's going to have a regular name—John,
Pete, Tom—something nobody's going to tease him about
on the ball field.''

Gabriel poured himself the last of the coffee. ''Yeah, if I
ever have a kid, I think that's what I'd do, too.''

''You think you might?''

''What?''

''Have a kid?''

''I don't know.'' Gabriel viewed him with surprise. ''I
never thought about it.''

''Well, you know you should,'' Michael-the-expert said.
''I mean if you're gonna have one, you oughtta do it soon,
right? Before you get too old to do it any good. I mean, you
gotta play with it, teach it things, keep up with it. I'll tell
ya—'' he took a long pull straight from the apple juice bottle ''—it's not just women got clocks ticking. Men got 'em,
too, only they're in their knees—which reminds me. You

really feel the way you say 'bout Becky's mom, maybe you and I could do each other some good. . . ."

Thirty minutes later, Alice pulled the station wagon halfway into the driveway, pausing to take a good look at the red Fiero parked in front of the house. Beside her, Becky shrank in her seat.

"Mike's here," she whispered, half-pleased, half-anxious.

"What are you going to do?" her mother asked.

"I don't know. Talk to him, I guess?"

"Sounds like a plan," Alice said with a nod. She finished pulling the car up the drive and opened the door.

"Mom?"

Alice paused. "Hmm?"

"You—you'll stay around while I talk to him, won't you? In case I need you . . ."

Alice glanced at the porch where Michael stood poised in the doorway. Then she leaned across the car and gave her daughter a hug. "Of course I will," she murmured. "Whoever else you become, you'll always be my daughter, and I'll always be here for you. Now go on, there's Mike. He's waiting for you."

The early-afternoon breeze blew hot across the backyard.

Alice was sitting on the lower platform on the play structure. She linked her arms around a corner post and lifted her face into the wind and the heat, closed her eyes to the cool mist the wind tossed across the fence from a neighbor's sprinkler. Beside her, ice cubes tinkled against glass like wind chimes when Gabriel swirled his tea.

"Do you think they'll be all right?" she asked.

Gabriel shifted his weight off his legs, dangled them over the edge of the platform. "If Mike has anything to say about it they will."

"They're so young to think they know what will last forever."

Gabriel nodded. "I envy them."

Alice's arms slipped from the post. "So do I."

They were silent a minute.

"She's not pregnant," Alice said.

Gabriel's hands tightened around the edge of the platform. "Are you glad?"

"I guess maybe. I dunno." She fitted her hands down beside her thighs and stiffened her arms, making her shoulders rise. "If I'd had a minute to think about it, I might actually have gotten used to the idea of someone calling me Grandma by now. But lately I keep feeling like I'm running from one crisis to the next all the time. Seems like I never have time to stop and collect my thoughts. There's a part of me that keeps wondering what would have happened if I'd thought about it before I let Michael drive us—"

"Matt," Gabriel corrected.

"What?"

"Didn't you mean 'before Matt' drove you?"

"That's what I said."

"Uh-uh." Gabriel shook his head. "You said Michael." He watched Alice swallow. "He's not Matt, Alice."

"I know."

"I think he's afraid that's why Becky ran home, because she suddenly got scared that he'd leave her the way Matt left you."

Alice pressed herself up on the heels of her hands again, staring at the back of the yard and this year's garden. "He came back," she said softly.

"Mike?"

Alice shook her head. "No. Matt. Twice. Once the day the girls were born, once when he graduated from college. He asked me to marry him again both times. I didn't love him anymore and I didn't think I'd ever trust him, so I said no. When he started earning money, he tried to get me to take child support from him, but I wouldn't, so he set up a trust fund for them that I couldn't do anything about. They'll get it when they're twenty-one.'' She paused. ''He's married now, but he still calls about once a year to find out how they're doing. I never call him. He's never tried to contact them, but I think he used to pull by the grade school sometimes on his lunch hour, watch them playing at recess. He couldn't miss them, I suppose. Except for the hair they both look like him. I was always glad about that.'' She laughed wryly. ''Funny. The one thing we ever did well together was make pretty babies.''

She looked at Gabriel. ''I never told anyone that before. Not even the girls.''

''Maybe it's time you did.''

Alice looked at her hands. ''Maybe.''

Gabriel leaned toward her and drew a line down her jaw. ''Alice . . .''

Alice turned to him and her mouth curved to meet his. His kiss was chaste and lingering. Seductive. Alice closed her eyes, savoring it.

''Why,'' she sighed when he drew away, ''does everything always seem like it's going to be all right when I'm with you?''

''I don't know.'' Gabriel took her hand and drew her off the play structure to stand between his thighs. His gaze held hers captive, conscious, while his thumbs sketched her cheekbones, smoothed her lips. ''Why do I,'' he asked quietly, ''feel like I belong to you?''

Chapter Eleven

Alice pulled her bottom lip in over her teeth and bit it, trying to steady herself. Every square inch and nerve of her quaked like shaken jelly. She didn't ask him to repeat what he'd said. She'd heard him perfectly well. She didn't ask him what he meant. She understood exactly. She didn't ask herself what she wanted to do about it because she didn't know. Or rather, she did know, but the very idea terrified her.

She rocked back on her heels thinking about trying to run away from him, but he was everywhere. His hands held hers; his legs surrounded hers; his mouth tipped upward at the corners, inviting hers to play; and his eyes . . .

His eyes saw clear to the bottom of her soul and weren't afraid of what they found there. She'd never felt so naked. Or been so impressed. It took an unusual man to ask a question that made such a statement, despite the fact that he'd been cast full tilt into the jaws of her family during a family wedding. Despite the impediments time and occupation put between him and Alice.

I wish— Alice thought.

"I wish—" Gabriel whispered, thinking aloud.

But I need time to figure out who I am—

"It's going to take time to really clear up this case—"

—to get used to being on my own—

"—and there'll be countless court dates and publicity and traveling back and forth—I'm not even from around here. I'm just an undercover on loan. I've got an apartment—" with nothing in it, he thought mutely "—and a job and most of a life—" well, part of a life, he amended silently, but no dog, no girlfriend and no family "—in New Jersey—"

—I've got to find another job and get back on my feet, see where I'm going—

"—and I can't ask you to pack up and travel with me because this being an internal-affairs case, there'll be threatening phone calls and maybe other kinds of threats—"

—and I have to do this on my own. I can't just let you take up the slack for me, because letting you come in like the cavalry to rescue me from loneliness and financial insecurity is too tempting—

"—I can't expose you to that and I want to walk away from this job, but I can't walk away until I can do it with a clean slate—"

—and after only a week I can't ask you to just hang around waiting for me to feel comfortable with my pride and . . . and everything else. I mean, if I met you two years from now, maybe it'd be different, but I guess I've never done anything in my life at the right time before—

"—and, based on three days, I can't ask you to wait around for what might take me two years or more to do—"

—but now I've got to. And this is just not the right time for you in my life.

"—so, you understand, it's the wrong time for me to ask you into my life."

"What?" Alice shook herself, all at once aware that he'd been speaking to her.

"Nothing," Gabriel said, unaware that he'd said anything out loud at all.

They studied one another uncomfortably for an instant. Then Gabriel squeezed her hands and rubbed her wrists once with his thumbs and let her go. Alice touched his mouth with two fingers in an equally wordless goodbye and stepped away. Becky and Michael came around the side of the house hand in hand, glowing.

"Mom!" Becky dropped Michael's hand and darted across the grass to throw her arms around her mother. "It's all right. Mike doesn't care that I'm not pregnant. He wants *me*, not just a baby."

Alice glanced at her son-in-law with amused approbation. "That's wonderful, darling, I'm so glad."

"But, Mom." Becky danced excitedly out of Alice's arms to catch her husband's hand again. "That's not all. Mike thought that maybe, if you think it'd be all right, since Grace and Phil might just not show up at the church Saturday, that maybe we…" She took a deep breath and looked up at Michael, starry-eyed. He squeezed her hand.

"What she's trying to say, Ms. Meyers," Michael said, "is that I'd like permission to marry your daughter again in front of the whole family on Saturday. That way she'll never have to be sorry we ran away, and it'd save the show for the guests, too."

"What about your family, Mike?" Alice asked. "Won't they be hurt if they're not included?"

"Most of my family lives in the area, anyway. It might be short notice, but they could get here if they want. No, Ms. Meyers, I just want to be with Becky and have her be happy. If my family can't understand that, well, that's everybody's loss, but it won't change what I do or how I feel. No, you give the word and I'll call my folks, let them take it from there."

"Well…" Alice glanced at Gabriel, then from Michael to Becky, not sure how she felt about the whole thing, but already making a mental checklist. "We'll have to talk to Grace, call Grandma, notify the church, plead with the caterer to add a few more places—" she looked at Becky "—get a dress, figure out how we're going to work the attendants." She turned to Michael. "You'll have to get your marriage license, and—" she offered a hand to Michael, palm up "—I guess you'd better start calling me Mom."

Feeling alone once more, Gabriel slipped off the play structure and followed them into the house.

The house was still, silent. The mother of the new bride had made her phone calls and put the wheels in motion for Saturday. She and Becky had made a date to go shopping for a dress Friday, after Thursday night's rehearsal-dinner madness. Then Michael and Becky had left to find some clothes for Michael and a motel where he could get some sleep before they put in an appearance at the family "do" tonight.

Aunt Kate and company had returned from Detroit sunburned and loaded down with shopping bags and souvenirs and, after George had made a single phone call, gathered their belongings meekly together at his direction and departed for the hotel that had allegedly messed up their reservations. On their way out the door, Mamie chucked Alice's chin and gave her a conspiratorial wink, and Aunt Kate fixed Gabriel with a baleful stare. Then they were gone, as noisily as they'd come.

And now the house was quiet; blissfully, blessedly, awkwardly without sound. The time, space and privacy Alice and Gabriel had wanted last night hung between them now. They shared an instant's elation at the possibilities, then an immediate denial. They hadn't touched, they hadn't spoken, but they'd said goodbye. Gabriel looked at Alice with regret. Alice picked up the last forty-five seed pearls and the veil that Grace might never wear and looked at Gabriel with a sigh. Her family's timing had never been more off.

The afternoon wore slowly on. Alice sewed seed pearls; Gabriel found his case file and tried to read. Alice finished the veil and got up to wash this morning's dishes; Gabriel followed her to the kitchen and silently dried them. When Alice decided to vacuum, Gabriel moved the furniture for her. In wistful silence they stripped the beds and changed the sheets together, eyeing one another with longing. Each shared look was like a guilty touch, an arousing self-conscious frustrating stroke along the emotions and the skin they'd bared to one another last night.

Working blindly, trying not to get in one another's way, they collided in the narrow space between Allyn and Rebecca's beds. Gabriel caught Alice to keep her from falling. Alice caught Gabriel to prevent the same. As though they had a mind of their own, his hands slid up her arms. Her body seemed to reach unconsciously for his without even consulting her brain. He bent toward her; her wrists locked around his neck.

"We shouldn't," she whispered.

"I know," he muttered in despair. "I can't protect you."

"Oh, Gabriel, what are we going to do?"

He set her away from him. "Nothing," he said tightly. "Not one damn thing." He strode out of the room.

Alice collected the stuffed animals she'd put on the floor and finished making the girls' beds alone.

Gabriel went outside and struck the tent the boys had used, then cleaned the grill. Alice finished with the beds and consulted her list of things she had left to do before Saturday only to find that there was no more she *could* do until Friday except get dressed for tonight's gathering—but it was even still too early to do that.

She stepped to the window of the girls' room to watch Gabriel scrubbing the grill rack with steel wool, then turned blindly to straighten up the twins' dresser. It wouldn't be long before they'd box up their clutter and move it to their own places. Alice looked around the room, at the bookshelves loaded with everything from Nietzsche to Trixie Belden, at the shelves they'd used to store every stuffed animal they'd ever been given, at the cosmetics and brushes and hot rollers and curling irons. What she'd have after they left was a clean house and time on her hands.

Involuntarily she glanced out the window to see Gabriel again. He was still working on the grill, scrubbing it like a man who had a bone to pick with the world. Alice watched him with concern, wondering what his life would return to after Saturday, what he would go back to and where he would be assigned. Vaguely wondering exactly what Mamie's boys had gotten all over the grill as she tried to stop thinking about Gabriel. If she were seventeen, she acknowledged dully, she'd have said she loved Gabriel—and known, even after such a short time, that it was true. In high school it had been possible to form a bond to last a lifetime, to fall in love forever during one long night spent laughing and talking and touching the stars. It had been so easy to trust the moment when she'd been seventeen. Too easy, maybe. Yet she missed the adolescent idealism that had allowed her to fling herself into the world with confidence and enthusiasm despite the fact she'd had no idea what she was doing.

Now experience demanded that she cautiously analyze everything, then weigh it against tomorrow before she did it. For the first time in her life she wished, not to be seventeen again, but to have back just a little of the trust-yourself know-it-all arrogance and innocence of youth. To believe, just for the moment, that the world was her oyster and that the future held no obstacles that optimism couldn't climb.

Then she wouldn't feel the least bit insane for wanting to spend the rest of her life with Gabriel after only three days.

With a muttered "Quit being such a fool, Allie," she picked a stuffed puppet off Allyn's dresser, prepared to set it back on the corner shelves where it belonged. The same stiff, cellophane crinkle that had made her pause and look through the wash last week stayed her now.

Whoa! she thought with shock, then gently squeezed and released the puppet once more. Again she heard the crinkly-crackly sound of cellophane or plastic. With a gulp, she set the toy back on the dresser, stuck her hands in the pockets of her skirt and looked at it, not wanting to appear too anxious. At the same time she thought she heard both her heart and her libido let loose ragged whoops of anticipation. Thought she really ought to think about chastising her daughters for hiding things from her instead of hoping she'd found what she thought she'd found.

Like a bomb-squad rookie, she poked the bunny puppet tentatively as though afraid it would go off. Then she gathered her courage about her and anchored the puppet with one hand while she eased the other inside. And withdrew six square innocent-looking cellophane-wrapped packages.

For a fraction of a second Alice rocked back on her heels wishing she'd possessed Allyn's nerve and sense of reality, as well as her curiosity about the physical wonders of the body, when she herself had been seventeen. Right or wrong, good or bad, protecting herself from the consequences of her irresponsible prom-night act of insanity would have saved everyone a lot of grief.

Then one side of her mouth drew a line of bittersweet irony into her cheek. If she'd been more responsible all those years ago, she wouldn't be standing here in Allyn and Rebecca's room wondering how she might have been a better parent at the same time as she wondered if she dared present these packages to Gabriel. Especially since their relationship was only temporary. Maybe if she found some wrapping paper and ribbon...

She whistled sharply through her teeth and flicked the condoms to the far side of the dresser, not particularly happy with the irreverent drift of her thoughts. Wow, looking at these things sure did make you think about what you were doing, didn't it? she asked herself. Took the wind right out of your emotion and brought you right down to the basics: she could go get Gabriel and be downright "bad" and get away with it. Physically, that is. Mind and emotions, she had a feeling, would be another story.

She swallowed and eyed the bright pink packages again. It wasn't a crime to want to love Gabriel no matter how short a time they'd known one another; to think about it, to want to set the scene and be ready for him. And the bottom line was, she was getting pretty damn tired of always being so tightfisted with her emotions. She and Gabriel were going to be living together for at least the next three days and it was getting harder and harder to be near him without wanting to touch him and hold him—and love him. All he had to do was look at her to make her feel complete; yet with his eyes he also seemed to touch places inside her, make her experience feelings she couldn't express to him in words. And she wanted to express those feelings, needed to share what he gave her by offering them to him in the most expressive way she knew. He'd already said more than once that he had no way to protect her. But now, truth be told, she could protect them both. And since her emotions, as well as her body, seemed to be in league against her common sense...

Alice took a deep breath and stuck the condoms in her skirt pocket. Just in case.

The contents of Alice's closet lay on her bed.

It was a gloomy collection of neutral shades and conservative styles purchased for its inexpensive and washable durability rather than for show. Alice stared at it in dismay. She'd sort of hoped to wear something pretty tonight for a change. Dress, maybe, for Gabriel. Pretend that the family picnic was a kind of date with the potential for more dates. The clothing on the bed was all "nice" stuff, but there wasn't a bright or truly attractive item in the whole lot. Just

A-line skirts and cotton blouses. She didn't even own a sundress or a pair of blue jeans. Jeezo pizza! she muttered under her breath, when had she become such a drudge?'

"Moving?" Gabriel queried from the door.

Alice glared at him. "Just getting dressed."

"Ah." He nodded, grinning. "The layered look."

"Did you want something?"

Gabriel cocked his head and ran a lazy eye up the length of her legs, made a thoughtful appraisal of her hips and belly, shook his head with an appreciative "mm-mm-mm" over her breasts and met her eyes.

Alice blushed. "Cheap," she said. "Very cheap."

He grinned wickedly. "You asked."

"That's not what I meant and you know it."

"Yeah, well . . ." Gabriel cleared his throat. "What time do we have to leave for your mother's?"

"Five-thirty."

"Good. Gives me time to grab a shower." He started to turn away, paused, eyeing her.

"What?" Alice asked hopefully.

"Oh—" Gabriel gave himself a reluctant shake "—nothing. I'll just go shower now."

"Good," Alice snapped. "I'll just get dressed."

She ransacked the twins' closet, wondering why she was mad at Gabriel. Because you don't really want to go to your mother's, she answered herself, but you also don't want to make the first move and invite him to do something else. Alone. Just the two of you.

Aw, come on, she argued with herself, go to your mother's. Doing something alone, just the two of you, will only invite trouble.

But I *want* trouble.

No, you don't.

Yes, dammit, I do!

She gave up talking to herself and returned her attention to the girls' closet. It was too hard to argue with a fool.

Between them, Allyn and Rebecca had covered the fashion bases. Alice shoved aside a leather miniskirt she distinctly remembered telling someone not to buy, shuddered over the sixty-dollar price tag that had been left on a pair of jeans with artfully frayed holes all over them, and stopped at a vivid tangerine-colored sundress with a lot of tiny buttons down the front. The dress was made of some wrinkly gauzy fabric that looked as if it would be cool and clingy, modest and provocative at once. The weatherman had promised a hot night.

Alice chewed her lip for an instant. The dress straps were too slim to hide her sturdy white bra straps, but the bodice was lined. Maybe she could do without a bra. Dare to jiggle, she told herself, then shut her eyes and shook her head. She was out of her mind.

She confiscated the dress, anyway, searched the bottom of the closet for the sandals Becky usually wore with it, then sifted through the twins' communal jewelry box for a pair of earrings. She wound up with a pair of rose-shaped posts that matched the dress, a flat gold-chain necklace with a rose pendant that hit the hollow of her throat, and a slim gold bracelet. It was, she realized, probably more jewelry than she'd worn at one time since before the twins were born. After appropriating some of the twins' discarded makeup, she went into her own bedroom and shut the door to get dressed.

When she emerged a short time later, Gabriel was waiting for her in the living room dressed in slacks and a sport shirt. He turned and saw her, and all the *wow!* looks she'd ever read about, imagined or seen men give women in movies or TV paled in comparison. He inhaled awe, then exhaled a "yeah" of absolute awareness. Then his mouth curved, his eyes glowed and he took on the pleased somewhat puffed-up expression of a man who knew this woman had dressed for *him*.

Alice's heart fluttered. She dragged her top teeth over her bottom lip and turned one foot on its side behind the other, a gawky teenager on her first date. Gabriel smiled at her, a man smiling at a woman, not a boy smiling at a girl, and all at once the inept adolescent inside Alice was gone. She lifted her chin and drew herself up, reveling in the buzz of awareness that ran through her. Gabriel reached out and touched the dark comb she'd used to pull her hair up and back over one ear, let his fingers drift to her chin.

"Beautiful," he murmured, wanting her more than he ever had before, needing more than anything to spend some time with her alone so he'd have something of her to take away with him.

"You, too," she said.

"Do you have to put in an appearance for your family tonight?" Gabriel asked. He might never get another chance to have her to himself.

Alice hesitated. "I probably should, to save Becky and Michael from—" She stopped abruptly, suddenly realizing she was about to throw away an opportunity to spend time with him that she didn't want to miss. She tilted her face up to him. "No."

"Sure?"

"Absolutely."

Gabriel's smile widened at the positiveness of her tone. "Good," he said. "In that case, Alice Meyers, will you have dinner with me? Someplace with deep dark intimate booths, good service and a lot of privacy?"

"I know just the place," Alice said, and handed him the keys to her car. After all, if he was going to take her out on the first real date she'd been on in twenty years, she was darn well going to let herself succumb to the sexist proprieties of the event and let *him* drive.

Grinning, Gabriel took the hint and held the front door open for her.

They drove across Pontiac to picturesque between-the-lakes Keego Harbor, dining at Gino's Pizzeria restaurant—a cozy spot with dim lights, plenty of atmosphere and good basic Italian food. Dinner was an intimate, sometimes intense, no-holds-barred laughter-filled affair. Conversation was frank, funny and revealing—a nonstop yak-fest between two people who felt as if they'd known one another forever, but who'd never had the time to really sit down and simply get to *know* one another. Alice told Gabriel what it was like to grow up in a big family, and then to raise two children on her own. Gabriel reciprocated by telling Alice what it had been like to grow up in Quaker missions.

The minute he began to talk, it was as though Alice had somehow opened a dam inside him that had been backing up for too long. All at once he needed her to know him the way no one else ever had, wanted her to understand what made him tick. Wanted to tell her all the things about himself he'd never told anybody.

He told her about the nun who'd given him the St. Jude medal and then died. He told her about the growing-up dreams he'd had of carrying on his parents' work in the orphanages of Southeast Asia. He told her about Aunt Sarah, about going back to Vietnam and winding up a prisoner of the North Vietnamese for three days. He told her about becoming a conscientious objector who felt he had a peaceful contribution to make in a war zone, about becoming a medic at the evac hospital, about watching the guys come in and go out, about how difficult it was to remain a nonviolent nonparticipant in the face of so much violence. Of the first time he'd ever held a gun in his hands and been tempted to use it. Of the thing that had snapped inside him when someone else had died because he hadn't.

Dispassionately he told her of how he'd decided to become a participant, a gun-toting cop, when his self-made hell over that incident and the many others that had seemed to resemble it too closely became unlivable. He told her about the demon that had started to grow inside him not long after he'd started to handle undercover cases and that had eventually destroyed his relationship with his parents. He told her how the job had managed to shake his belief in everything except man's ability to heap treachery on top of treachery on top of betrayal. He told her about wanting to quit the cynicism of his profession, and he told her about Markum.

Alice listened. She couldn't have stopped the flow of his story if she'd wanted to, but she didn't want to; she'd begun to realize how much she'd told him about herself the past few days without learning much of anything about him. Now she understood why; it had simply taken him longer to depend on his instinct to trust her with his life than it had taken her to be open with him. But that was the way it generally was with Brannigans. To be open with total strangers about emotions and details, but to keep them at arm's length when it came to any deeper involvement until they'd been around "long enough"—which meant anywhere from two minutes to ten years.

After dinner they drove around nearby Sylvan Lake, peeking at the lake between the houses built along its shore, stopping to trespass in the moonlight bathing the subdivision's private beach. Carrying their shoes, they walked along the water's edge in comfortable silence, close without touching. In the silky water that washed up, then receded, around their ankles, they stopped to watch the stars come out. When Alice shivered involuntarily during a sudden off-the-lake breeze, Gabriel automatically moved in behind her and wrapped his arms around her like a shawl, tucking her tight to the warmth of his chest. Wind lifted her hair to tickle his nose, filled his nostrils with her scent.

Sensation flooded him. He buried his face in her hair, letting her fill his senses as she filled his heart. He didn't think he'd ever be able to get enough of her. He couldn't remember ever feeling the way she made him feel—whole, free, replete, a part of something larger than he'd ever been a part of before. Family. She'd made him a part of hers. And without meaning to, she'd made him a part of her. That was the way it went. When you weren't looking for a thing to happen, when you couldn't afford it to, boom, that's when it caught you. He was used to snap judgments; they were a hazard of his profession, and he made them and lived by them every day. But this was different, this was deeper, a knowledge he'd somehow carried with him all his life, a sense of recognition. He loved Alice Meyers.

He'd expected to shock himself with the admission, but he wasn't shocked. Unnerved, maybe, uncertain about how to work love and Alice into his future—and himself into hers. But not stunned.

He felt her take a deep breath of lake air and sigh it happily away. "It's beautiful, isn't it?"

He rubbed his face in her hair. "Very." God, he wanted her. Wanted to brand her as his.

Alice turned in his arms, slipped her own arms about his waist and tipped her face up to him. He made her feel sexy and secure at the same time, but she didn't want to be "safe" with him tonight. Tonight she wanted to flirt with the dangerous side of him, to know if she could tame it.

I want to touch him, she thought. I want to hold him. I want him to touch me, be with me. Just once before he leaves. Before I let him go.

She drew herself up with a mental start. He couldn't leave her if she let him go. It was that simple. Why couldn't she have understood that eighteen years ago with Matt, and last week with the girls? Love didn't mean binding up—it meant freeing. It meant choosing to release. It meant choice.

"I never said thank-you, did I?" she asked aloud.

Gabriel touched the moon shadow on her cheek. "For what?"

For coming into my life, she thought. For listening to my complaints. For waking up my body. For touching my heart. "For dinner," she said aloud. "For whatever you said to Mike this morning."

The set of her lips in the moonlight fascinated him. He couldn't take his eyes off her mouth. "Dinner was my pleasure. I didn't say anything to Mike. He doesn't need anyone to say anything to him where Becky's concerned. He loves your daughter, Alice. He's not blind to her faults, and an adolescent sex drive hasn't blinded him to himself. He came after the whole woman Becky is—" he grinned "—banana-cake relatives and all."

"My relatives have nothing in common with banana cake," Alice said in mock indignation. "Well," she amended, "except maybe Aunt Bethany. And Aunt Kate. Maybe Helen. Grandma Josephine..."

A gust of wind tossed her hair into her face. Gabriel smoothed it back with trembling fingers. "Alice," he muttered hoarsely, "you're running on."

"Am I?" she whispered. The look on his face made her giddy with anticipation. It made her want to do something she'd never regret. *Touch him,* she thought. *Trust your instincts. Trust yourself.* "Am I really?" she repeated, half smiling.

"Yes." Gabriel nodded raggedly. "On and on and—"

Alice locked her arms about his neck, lifted herself against him and kissed him. He ran his hands down her back and crushed her tight, groaning when she nipped at the soft underside of his lips and dipped her tongue between them.

Just for a minute, he assured himself. *I can do this for a minute, then I'll stop.*

Heat curled and tightened in his belly, clouded his awareness. He struggled for control, but she invaded his mind and his senses, and he lost himself in her. He pressed her to him like some missing piece of himself and let instinct lead him where it would, deepening the kiss. He could feel her against him, her body formed to fit his, soft and hollowed where his was hard and ridged. He wanted her.

Beside his want there was nothing else; it was primitive, uncontrolled, complete. He couldn't remember the last time he'd wanted a woman like this, couldn't remember that he ever had. The ache of his desire for her cut deep. His hands kneaded the soft fabric covering her hips, her name in his throat was an impatient plea. "Alice..." He felt the vibration of her response against his tongue.

"Yes..."

The wind scudded across the lake, sent waves slapping up over his knees to rouse him. Disoriented, he lifted his head to collect his bearings, then felt the waves plaster his pants to his legs again. He looked at the beach, at the lights across the water, at Alice staring up at him as though transfixed, felt the pulse of blood through the arousal behind his zipper. He dropped his head back in angry disbelief and shoved his hands through his hair. Oh, God, he'd promised himself he wouldn't use her and leave her like Matt.

"God, Allie, why did you let me do that?"

"You didn't *do* anything."

"In another minute... Why didn't you stop me?"

"I didn't want to." Alice tried to touch him, but he yanked himself away from her and started back up the beach. "Gabriel, please. Wait."

"Do you know what you're doing, Allie?" He jerked to a stop in the sand and swung about on her. "I could hurt you. I don't want to hurt you, Alice."

"No," Alice said vehemently, fumbling with her purse. "You can't hurt me if I don't let you."

"What turnip truck did you fall off, Alice? I don't know what the future holds past this minute. How can you deal with that when I'm not sure I can? God, I'm not a kid, I should know better. Damn, I'm sorry."

"I'm not." Alice impatiently emptied the contents of her purse in the sand. "I didn't fall off any turnip truck. I'm well aware of what I'm doing. I'm not going to let you hurt me and I promise— Ha!" Triumphantly she snatched up the crinkly packages she'd been looking for and got to her feet. "And I promise to try not to hurt you. Here." She grabbed his hand and put the packages in his palm. "Use 'em in good health."

"What?" He was hysterical, he thought, looking at his hand. He'd lost his mind. But she'd lost hers ahead of him.

"I found them," Alice said with supreme dignity, "inside a bunny puppet when I was straightening the dresser in the girls' room. I wasn't sure what to do with them, but I thought you might be."

Gabriel stared from her to his hand incredulously. "You weren't sure, but you thought I might—"

"That's right." Alice nodded vigorously. "Absolutely. So, what do you think?" Hands on hips, she tapped her foot in the sand. "Should I pitch a hissy-fit and yell at the girls? Should I ignore the whole thing and put them back where I found them? Should I throw them away—" She glanced at Gabriel from the corner of her eye, saw his shoulders begin to shake. "What are you laughing at?"

"Nothing," Gabriel said, laughing harder. "Me, you, the world in general—the way you always seem to hit me in the funny bone to make me laugh."

"I'm not hitting you anywhere. I'm trying to ask you for advice. But if this is the way you're going to act..." She stuck her nose in the air and turned to walk past him.

Too breathless to pursue her properly, Gabriel dropped to his knees in the sand, caught her about the hips and hugged her. "Don't go," he wheezed. "I promise not to laugh anymore. I promise I'll just listen. However difficult you make it."

Ignoring the last, Alice brushed her fingers through his hair. "Will you give me advice if I need it?" she asked softly.

Gabriel rubbed his face in the fabric across her stomach. "Absolutely," he whispered.

"In that case..." Alice framed his face between her palms, lifted it toward her and looked down at him, loving the play of moon shadow across his features, the revealing shift and play of it in the breeze. Her heart swelled and contracted with emotion and excitement, but no doubt. "I want you, Gabriel," she whispered. "I need you. I've thought about it, and I know the promises I can't make, and I understand what you—I know these things—" she stroked a hand down his arm to find his hand "—don't give me any license beyond that, except..." She touched two fingers to his mouth and smiled shyly. "Please, Gabriel, I want to make a memory with you. I want something of you to keep—a secret I won't ever have to share with anybody but you. Please. Let me love you while you're here and I can."

All laughter gone, Gabriel pressed his face into her stomach and hugged her tight. If she wanted him he was hers body and soul. He would make her his for as long as possible. He reached for her hands to pull himself out of the shifting sand, bent and kissed her. "Let's go home," he said.

Chapter Twelve

Inside the darkness of her bedroom, they fumbled together, laughing, until their clothing lay in puddles around their feet.

"Nervous?" Gabriel asked, running the tips of his fingers up and down her arms.

"A little." Alice smiled tremulously. "I've never had an adult lover, Gabriel. I had a high-school sweetheart, a *boy*friend. I don't know if I'll—"

Gabriel stilled her self-doubt with a finger to her lips. "You'll be fine," he whispered. "Incredible. I'm the one who should worry about disappointing you."

"But you won't," she protested.

"No," he promised softly, "I won't."

A moment of awkwardness passed between them. Then Gabriel smiled and bent toward her, and Alice stretched to meet him, fit him.

Bared to one another for the first time, they moved slowly, hands tracing every line and curve. No shrinking violet when she'd made up her mind to something, Alice found the appendectomy scar on Gabriel's abdomen and examined it thoroughly, making Gabriel smile when she bent to kiss it, making him inhale sharply when she drew a line from the scar to his navel with her tongue and paused there for a few tantalizing moments before continuing on. In his turn, Gabriel lowered her to the bed and took his time, exploring every inch of her, finding the sensitive nerves in the arch of her foot, the ticklish spots at the inside of each knee, the places that made her giggle and try, not very hard, to get away from him. The spots that made her gasp and sigh and twist her hands in his hair with longing.

When his mouth finally found one of her nipples, Alice moaned with relief. It felt—it felt— It just *felt!* There were only so many breasts and so many ways to describe the sensation of a lover's mouth suckling them. Alice had read them all, from the chaste to the blatantly erotic, from series romance to bodice-ripping historicals to literary erotica to the trashy earthy passions of glitz. She'd read them to sell them, to escape reality, to fuel fantasy. None of them came near to describing how exquisite it felt to have Gabriel's mouth, his tongue, on her—she gasped, half rose when his head dipped below her waist—*in* her.

His name grew urgent on her lips. "Gabriel, come to me. Gabriel, please, now!"

And Gabriel complied.

Heat curtained them from the world, fused two into one, created a perfect nucleus with swift bold strokes. Hot mouths, hot hands, hot skin; his on hers, hers on him; his in hers, hers around him. No longer separate, he was part of her, and they were one. One movement, one heart, one pulse, one complete universe, newly formed, freshly landscaped, virginally beautiful. Touch, hold, kiss, caress; senses cottoned, senses exploding—

"Gabriel, please—"

"Allie!"

"Don't stop, don't stop, don't—"

"Allie . . . Allie . . ."

Ripples washed outward, reversed suddenly to whirlpool in, suck them down, drown them, then toss them out toward the shore, together, full and empty, replete and complete. Gabriel heard Alice's pleasure in her breathless laughter, felt the echoing spaces inside him fill up with her. Suddenly shaking, he wrapped himself around her, holding on to her and their moment for dear life. It would be over too soon. He would go back to where he'd come from six months ago and she would go on without him, her life too full to remain interrupted by thoughts of him. And he—

All at once he thought he heard Markum's voice in the back of his head. It slunk in through the chinks loving Alice had left in his armor, poking at him where it would do the most damage.

You come in alone, you go out alone, it insisted, as Markum always said to newcomers to the academy. *Trust no one. Always expect the worst.*

"No," Gabriel whispered grimly, trying to bring Alice closer by sinking deeper into her embraces. "Not this time." Markum's voice was relentless.

You can't stay with her, it reminded him. *You're an undercover. You've got no life, no family, no friends. You aren't even the echoes in an empty room.*

"No." His denial was louder this time, startling Alice.

"Gabriel?" Her voice was anxious beneath him. "What's wrong?"

"Nothing, Allie, I'm sorry. It's nothing."

Like hell, Markum's voice retorted inside his head. *You wanna walk away, but you can't walk until you clean it up— until you deal with me.*

Not yet, Gabriel thought, not tonight. Tomorrow I'm coming to get you, Si, but not now. He lifted himself on his hands, wanting to see Alice, to fill his eyes with her. She lifted her chin, smiling, and tightened her legs around his hips. Gabriel looked down at her through eyes filled with wonder, terror and awe, acknowledging commitment and responsibility, his possessor, his possessed. He had branded her. She was his.

And God help them both, he was hers.

In desperation he rolled away from her, reaching for the packages they'd tossed somewhere on the bed. Alice came up after him, running her hands up his back. "Gabriel—"

Ready for her, Gabriel caught her around the waist and lifted her into his lap, pulling her legs around him. He would lose himself inside her just for tonight, keep her with him, keep the world at bay. She didn't judge him the way he judged himself, merely took him into her and drove the night away hard and fast, out of control. He needed most to lose control sometimes, fiercely, savagely, thoughtlessly. The medicine of her body healed him; her spirit cloaked his, sheltered and renewed. He needed that right now, needed her, couldn't wait.

"Gabriel," she murmured again, caressing his face, then clutched his shoulders hard, gasping and arching into him when he rocked upward, filling her.

"Hold me, Allie." His breath was harsh against her breast. "Hold me, Alice. Love me..."

Toward dawn they slept.

The scent of Alice roused Gabriel. Evocative, welcoming, it drew him from his dreams, causing him to reach for her before he fully awoke, to bury his face in the hair furled on his pillow. His body knew her; she was woman, she was life. Buried inside her was strength and peace, quixotic, healing. In her arms, desperation faded.

Smiling sleepily, Gabriel arched and stretched against Alice. Even in her sleep she responded at once, snugging her hips to his, rotating them. Her breast swelled to fill his hand.

Late-morning daylight eased around the edges of the window shades, brightening the room and hiding night's terrors.

Fully awake, fully aroused now, Gabriel jacked himself up on an elbow and turned Alice's face toward his. She murmured warm unintelligible greetings against his mouth before opening it to the delicate pressure of his tongue. Smiling and drowsy, she twisted in his arms and slid a hand down his belly as she opened for him. Gabriel shuddered beneath the lightness of her touch, arching into it. So sweet, he thought, tasting her mouth again, like honey. Alice's hand closed on him, stroking. Gabriel groaned at the tension coiling too fast inside him. He wanted to wake her slowly. Take his time. Make it last. We've got time, he thought, plenty of time.

Obviously being a cop had not equipped him with the instincts of a parent. The phone jangled with importance just as he dipped his head to find Alice's breast. The mother-whose-children-are-not-at-home instantly came awake inside Alice. She rolled away from Gabriel before she even realized what she was doing, snaking out a hand to grab the phone off the nightstand next to her side of the bed.

"Let it ring—" Gabriel began, but it was already too late. With a groan that was half-frustration, half-chuckle at the ever present and inevitable interruptions of Alice's life, Gabriel flopped onto his back to listen.

"Hello." The word came out scratchy, so Alice cleared her throat. "Hello?"

"Mom?"

Alice sat up, recognizing Allyn's quavery, you-were-right-Mom little-girl-lost-in-the-middle-of-the-night voice at once. She reached instinctively across the bed for Gabriel. "Lynnie? What's wrong?'' She listened a moment. ''Are you all right?'' she asked sharply, and Gabriel slid across the bed to support her back.

''What's wrong?'' he asked. ''Where is she?''

Alice shook her head, listening. ''Did something happen? Did you lose your money? Where are you?'' She shut her eyes gratefully and covered the receiver with her hand. ''Sounds like she's okay, just scared and mad. She's at the bus station in Colorado Springs,'' she told Gabriel. ''Her friends dumped her and took off before she could grab her money or her clothes. She wants to come home. Says she's got enough traveler's checks for a ticket to Kansas City, but—''

''Find out if she's somewhere safe—transit officials around or whatever—and get her phone number,'' Gabriel said. ''You'll call her back. Let me make a call. I think I know somebody who'll look after her until we can get her home.''

Alice narrowed her eyes. ''Who do you know?'' she asked. ''Some woman?''

Gabriel grinned at her and climbed out of bed to pull on his jeans. ''Nope, an ex-fed who quit civil service and went out west to become a born-again ecologist and mess up the logging industry by pounding railroad spikes in trees.''

''Oh, God.'' Alice covered her eyes. ''And you think the people I know have a lot in common with banana cake? He won't, um, preach his eccentricities to her, will he?''

''He's not big on people. I doubt he'll say anything.'' He leaned on the bed and kissed Alice squarely. ''Now, *Mom*,'' he said, ''get the kid's number and get the hell off the phone so I can do what I'm good at and bring her home.''

Already near noon, the arrangements for Allyn took longer to make than Alice expected. True to Gabriel's prediction, the ex-fed-turned-ecologist who lived near Colorado Springs was willing to keep an eye on Allyn while he kept her company. Allyn said he was kind of quiet and reminded her of Marlon Brando on a bad day, but that he was better than some of the other creeps who hung around public-transportation facilities. Still, it was late afternoon before Alice was able to complete wiring a bus ticket and food money to her daughter, whose bus would not leave until close to midnight and, with layovers, be several days getting home.

With a sigh, Alice realized it was the best she could do. Allyn had gone off in search of adventure, and now she was getting it. Alice only hoped this trip would not discourage her daughter from striking out on her own again. Soon.

"I used to want twenty kids," she told Gabriel with a sigh, when they lay propped on their elbows on the bed later. "But that was before I had two. God, my mother was crazy—or a saint—to have seven of us. And all accidents at that. 'Course—" she glanced at Gabriel wickedly "—I suppose even accidents have their silver linings."

"You're the best accident that's ever happened to me," he assured her gravely, but his eyes twinkled. Then he turned serious. "Do you think you'll ever want another one?"

"Accident?"

Gabriel fixed her with a mock evil-eyed glare. "Baby."

"Why?" she asked, avoiding the answer to his question with one of her own. "You wanna have one with me?" When Gabriel merely stared at her, refusing to rise to the bait, Alice rolled onto her back and faced the wistful envy that rose every time one of her sisters had a baby. "I dunno," she said truthfully. "Sometimes, I guess, but not while everything's so up in the air with me. I don't even know if I'd be able to support a baby. And I wouldn't want to do it alone—I've done that. But maybe if I could pick the time, the place, and the husband. Why?"

Gabriel shook his head. "Just something Mike said made me think about it."

Alice rolled up and ran a hand down his side. "And what did you think?"

"That I shouldn't think about it until my chances for living to help a child grow up are better."

"Do you think about dying a lot?"

His eyes were blank. He shrugged. "Hard to avoid it some days. Especially days when I realize there's got to be a better way for a grown man to earn a living."

Alice inched closer to him and kissed his throat, wanting to ease. "Do you have a lot of those days?"

Gabriel tucked an arm about her waist and pulled her under him. "Lately, yeah. Fact, I'm having one now. I think it's going to last awhile."

"If you find a better way to earn a living—"

"You'll be the first person I call."

For a long moment Alice's dark brown gaze held Gabriel's, sharing hope, regret and maybe. Then Alice drew Gabriel to her, and they didn't speak again for a long time.

The double wedding rehearsal was nearly over by the time they got to it. Helen, who had somehow been coerced into spending the day baby-sitting Mamie's boys, made I'll-get-you-for-this faces at Alice the minute she stepped into the church. Alice, who was feeling fairly invincible with Gabriel's hand at her waist, smiled gently back at her. Grace and Phil huddled with Becky and Michael near a side altar, apparently in the midst of a heated argument. The groom's parents and the groomsmen sat on one side of the church looking bored, except for Skip, who wandered aimlessly about wearing a painful-to-witness I'm-in-love-and-she-doesn't-know-I-exist expression. The rest of Alice's sisters sat with their families whisper-laughing and chatting, taking brief meaningful glances at Alice and Gabriel, Helen and Skip, and Grace and Phil, then turning back to one another and giggling.

Michael's parents sat alone in a back pew, looking as though they weren't sure why they were there. Alice gulped when she all of a sudden realized they were not here as the in-laws for one of her sisters, but for her *daughter*. No matter how often she'd thought about Becky's marriage the past few days, the reality of it hadn't sunk in until now.

Serene, dark-haired Julia Block Brannigan floated gracefully to the back of the church, hand outstretched to Gabriel. In her thoughtful laughing way, she assessed the man who made her eldest daughter glow, gave Alice an intense knowing perusal and went off to speak to the deacon who'd conducted the rehearsal.

The dinner afterward in a side room at Mitch's Tavern seemed to include a lot of everybody's relatives who weren't actually part of the wedding party. The families were noisy and jovial and, jumbled together by circumstance, even the in-laws found they enjoyed one another's company. At least briefly.

Alice felt more comfortable than she had at any family gathering in years. In the past, being with her family had tended to make her examine her conscience and wonder what sins she'd committed lately. Because even after years on her own, when she was with her mother and her sisters, she was still the eldest, the one to "set a good example," after all. But tonight she felt none of that; tonight she had Gabriel at her side and— She felt his arm brush hers and she glanced at him, smiling, then touched him with concern. There was something in his eyes, his expression, that was almost indiscernible, something Alice sensed before she saw it. He seemed restless, distracted, and she thought his concentration on what was going on around him lapsed a beat now and then.

When she tried to ask him about it, he shook his head, unable to tell her that she'd caught him in the worse case of the "wishfuls" he'd ever had. Wishing he could stay with her, wishing he could be as close to his family as Alice was to hers, wishing this whole damn undercover was over so he could go back to New Jersey and figure out a way to get out or go on. Unable to tell her the only three words he really wanted to say to her, because not knowing if he even had a future after the lies Markum had spread about him made them stick in his throat.

Instead of saying anything, and hoping to distract her, he kissed Alice thoroughly in full view of her mother and her daughter, then went off with Michael to talk to Phil about turning up at the wedding. Openmouthed, Alice gazed after him for a long minute, then treated her mildly amused mother and her heartily flabbergasted daughter to an unrepentant stare before going off on her own to browbeat Grace about Saturday. Grace, however, had already been guilt-tripped into submission by Becky. She offered Alice her inimitable do-I-know-you stare and politely asked big sister if her veil would arrive in time for the wedding, since, as far as she knew, everything else would. In thirteen seed pearls, Alice assured her guiltily, the veil would be there, too. Then she fled.

Skip stopped her halfway across the room to repeat his office-building-bookstore proposal without Helen prompting him. He had, he said, checked out Alice's background, talked to her former employers and been able to present a glowing report on her potential to his partners, who had then agreed unequivocally to back her in opening three bookstores over the next three years. Bent on finding Gabriel, whom she could no longer spot anywhere in the room, Alice nodded at what she hoped were the appropriate spots, accepted Skip's card and told him she'd get back to him in a couple of weeks. Then she squirmed purposefully through the rest of the crowd and went in search of Gabriel.

"No," Gabriel said sharply into the phone, "I don't want to wait, Jack. Sonovabitch has got me where it hurts. Besides, we wait and there's no way to keep him from finding out about the warrants. Whatever else the bastard is, he's not a fool. If you got the warrants, we gotta execute 'em."

Listening for Jack Scully's response to his tirade, Gabriel glanced uneasily around both sides of the telephone kiosk in the crowded parking lot outside Mitch's, hating not having a wall at his back. A lot of untidy emotions were running around inside him, and he didn't intend to get caught out in the dark because of them. Being with Alice had made him realize he had a lot of old baggage to deal with, starting with reconciling with his parents and coming to terms with why he'd become a cop in the first place. For the first time in a lot of years, he had something more than the next case to keep him going.

"No, Jack, back off, I'll bring him in," he snapped now. "You gotta pay for the truth, isn't that what you always say? This is my case. I'm paying. You knew what I was going to find—that's why you sent me on it. So when I corroborated what you suspected about Si you'd have his daughter's godfather for an unimpeachable witness."

Again he listened briefly, stabbing the inside wall of the kiosk with a finger. "You and the rest of the suits just be there when I get there, Jack, and bring some decent backup," he said and, after slamming the phone down, went back inside the restaurant. Whether he wanted to or not, he couldn't leave without saying goodbye to Alice.

He found her in the hallway between the tavern's general seating area and its private rooms. There were no words. He looked at her, and she knew at once. He took a step toward her, and she was in his arms. Why, Gabriel wondered savagely, did you always know for sure what you were looking for when it was time to leave?

"Alice—"

"Please, Gabriel—"

People were staring at them. He found a door, pushed it open. The closet was dimly lit and private. Alice clasped her arms around his neck. Her mouth was open on his, desperate. He pushed her away.

"I've got to go."

"It's too soon. Don't go yet." She didn't mean to say it, couldn't stop herself. She hid her face in his neck. "I'm sorry. Strike that. My mouth got away from me."

Gabriel took her chin between his thumb and forefinger and lifted her face where he could see it. "One of the best things about you is your mouth," he said. "Don't apologize for it. I like always knowing where I stand with you. In my business, too many people deal one way to your face and another to your back. I needed a good dose of your honesty to help me put my priorities in perspective."

Alice tried to laugh. Failed. "Gee, you make running off at the mouth sound like a virtue." Her eyes teared suddenly and she hugged Gabriel hard to keep him from seeing. "Thank you for giving me a new perspective, too."

Gabriel's arms tightened around her. "It's entirely my pleasure," he whispered.

They clung to one another for a long moment. Then Alice raised her head and Gabriel's hold on her loosened.

"I'll—" He stopped. *I'll be back.* The phrase hung in the air unused. He didn't want to make her a promise he might not keep.

"Come—" *Come back to me.* She didn't say it because she didn't want to load him down. She eased herself out of his arms. "The wedding's two o'clock Saturday," she said softly.

Gabriel rested his forehead against hers, brushed her cheek with his fingers. "I'll remember that," he returned. Then he was gone.

Alone in the hallway once more, Alice wondered what she would do if he was still gone tomorrow.

Chapter Thirteen

The rest of the dinner dragged on forever.

Phil's brothers kidded Grace's sisters until both sides were locked in an increasingly obnoxious battle of retorts. Skip plied Helen with words of love, a set of emerald earrings and the whispered promise that the matching necklace would be hers on their wedding day. He then moped when Helen firmly informed him that she wasn't going to marry him, would never want to marry him, and if he truly loved her, he would know the way to her heart was hardly precious gems—especially *green* ones even if he only gave them to her because they poetically matched her eyes. She was in the army, for God's sake, and saw more green than she wanted to. She was also, she said, not particularly interested in managing his life as she had quite enough to do managing her own and her sisters, and that any man who might eventually capture her heart and the rest of her, as well, would know, understand and encourage that. He would also, she

stated definitely, be able to knock her off her feet by looking at her, be capable of standing toe-to-toe with her in verbal combat—and occasionally win—and be understanding
enough to volunteer—*on his own*—to hire the caterer and
the maids even if there was only the two of them to enter-
tain for dinner. And he would never, ever, under any circumstances, on any occasion whatsoever, wear a three-piece
suit.

The night grew long.

Since the wedding had expanded to include her daughter
as the second already married bride, Alice felt obligated to
stay and maintain appearances—which was not something
she did well. She made only cursory small talk with the in-
laws, only half listened to what was going on around her and
had no idea what she was eating, because her palate had
gone flat. She couldn't get Gabriel out of her thoughts.
Every time she turned around she thought she saw him out
of the corner of her eye, thought she felt him behind her. In
four days he'd invaded her life completely; they'd become
"a couple," and more. She was unfinished without him.

When you find him, you'll know, her mother had said. *It
won't take long. You'll know.*

Well, she *did* know finally, dammit, and now she wanted
to tell him, show him, but he was gone.

When her family started to whisper about his absence,
then to ask her about him, she had nothing to say. Wasn't
sure what she could say that would neither compromise nor
jeopardize him. What could she say? Sorry, guys, he had to
go to work? He's an FBI agent masquerading as a bad cop
to catch some dirty cops who sold information about up-
coming operations to the bad guys—and who, as a sideline,
execute other cops who get in their way? Only really what
he's doing—but he didn't know this at first—is being used
by a man he's worked under for ten years to trip up a man
he's loved and trusted for fifteen years who's been using him

for the past five or six years to cover up a trail of drug theft, corruption, murder and embezzlement? And the sting is going down tonight?

She shook her head. Somehow...

It occurred to her out of the morbid blue that if she were married to him she'd probably have to learn how to lie all the time about who he was, where he was and what he did. *He's an insurance investigator,* she imagined herself saying. *He works for Lloyd's. They keep him traveling a lot.* And the fact of the matter was that she, his wife, wouldn't know who he was, where he was, or what he did. Not specifically. She wouldn't be allowed to ask him any of those questions, wouldn't be able to share that part of his life. Even if he wanted to, he wouldn't be allowed to tell her. She'd have to learn to live with a man who could never be entirely forthright with her, one who might sometimes bring his hidden life to bed with him, who flirted with death on a daily basis and survived because he was good at it. A man who might have to be gone for days, weeks or months at a stretch without even being able to call first and tell her he was going. A man who could die in some anonymous place without even his supervisors knowing for sure he was gone.

She closed her eyes and clenched her laced fingers around one another. She'd never asked him what it was like for him "out there"—hadn't thought of it really. Hadn't wanted to know maybe. The way she'd found him had seemed explanation enough. But now she remembered the news stories, the recent slew of books on the dangers of undercover work, the television "movie of the week" docudramas about the customs agent who'd been tortured and killed in Mexico. She'd been fascinated by the intrigue, but of course movies, nonfiction books and even the news never seemed real. Nothing seemed real unless you lived it. And if she couldn't even ride anything more rigorous than the little Ferris wheel on Bob-lo Island, how the hell would she survive a life with Gabriel? No matter how she felt about him.

Sick as it made her feel, it was good to think about these things now, she decided, while she still had a chance of kicking him out of her system. Before she had time to get too attached to thinking about him. Remembering him. Wanting him.

Needing him.

When she finally got home from the rehearsal dinner, she didn't sleep at all that night.

Gabriel stared unseeingly through the pane of glass that separated him from the squad room. All he could see was the look on Lillian Markum's face when he'd arrested her husband, the hatred in his thirteen-year-old goddaughter's eyes when he'd been forced to handcuff her father in front of her last night. Silas Markum had betrayed him, but Gabriel felt as if he'd been the one to take the bite of the Judas apple. The fruit left a bitter taste in his mouth, and he wished he could spit it out.

He scrubbed a hand across his aching eyes and found the cut, now a scab, over his temple. Body, mind and soul, everything hurt. He'd been up for thirty hours. He needed a shower, a shave and some food. He felt like hell. If that damn Scully didn't get in here to finish debriefing him soon, Gabriel was pretty sure he wouldn't think twice about pitching Jack's desk chair through his window just to see if that wouldn't get Jack's attention.

He turned his back on the window when his supervisor finally headed for the office, beaming.

"Hey, Book, we got him! Four counts first-degree murder, three counts conspiracy to commit murder, six counts conspiracy to deliver narcotics, two counts actual delivery, embezzlement—"

"I'm out, Jack," Gabriel said flatly.

Jack Scully stared in disbelief at the most dedicated and successful undercover agent he'd ever worked with, and moved behind his desk. "Come on, Book," he soothed. "We all know Si was your friend, but don't go off the deep end over this."

"This is not the deep end, Jack," Gabriel snapped. "This is the damn shallow part of the pool you keep throwin' me into headfirst."

Scully spread his hands generously in front of him, automatically doing what he was paid to do well—placate his agents. "C'mon, Book, you had a hard night, but we've all been screwed by people we think are friends. Don't mean nothin', right? Don't let it get you. Go someplace, get some rest. You did a good job—it was worth it. Few weeks this'll be a bad dream. Give it time."

Gabriel flattened his hands on Scully's desk and leaned over them. "In a few weeks," he said, "I'll be sitting in the witness box talking to the prosecution and looking at Catherine Markum listening to Uncle Book tell the world what a piece of scum her father is." He laughed shortly. "No, Jack, trust me, it's not worth it anymore. I'm sick of being lied to and cheated and stabbed in the back by people who're paid to tell me what to do and who I gotta trust before I even get into the street. No." He straightened. "You do whatever paperwork you have to do to get me out. I'll clean up my files, stick around long enough to close out whatever's pending, but that's it. No more game."

"You're serious."

"Dead right."

Scully sucked air through his teeth, letting it squeak against the roof of his mouth. "Awful sudden," he said. "You think about this?"

Gabriel stuck his hands in his pockets and turned his back on Scully to look through the inside office window again.

"Long enough." In the window's reflection he watched Scully rub his chin, thinking. It looked like hard work.

"How long since you've had a vacation?" Scully asked suddenly. "Two years? Three? You've been logging a lot of hours. Why don't you take some time off, think about it— No, no—" he pointed a couple of fingers at Gabriel's snort of disgust "—hear me out. You take some vacation—back vacation, as much time as you need—and let things cool down. Clear it with the prosecutor, apprise him of where you'll be, but that's all the contact you keep with us. Kick back and clear your head. Think about it. I think you'll find this stuff's in your blood, and you can't live without it. You'll be back."

Gabriel faced him grimly. "You pay me for it, I'll take the vacation. But I've got better things to do with my life. I won't be back, Jack. Guaranteed."

Saturday dawned, bright and picturesque, with robins and sparrows chirping outside Alice's window, and turtle-doves cooing above it on the telephone lines. June swept its dew-fresh morning breeze through her open window to tickle the shades, making them flap gently at her. Alice opened one eye and glared at the world, then turned over and pulled the pillow firmly over her head. Of all the things she didn't need right now, a bright, sunshiny all-the-world's-in-a-good-mood-except-you day was right up there among the least of them. What she did need was about twelve hours' sleep, fewer dreams about Gabriel and a less heartless conscience.

Friday, if she recalled correctly, had been an absolute bitch. No sleep and no Gabriel Thursday night had left her moody and broody—and somewhat of a pain for Becky to shop with. Fortunately her daughter had been far too engrossed in her search for the perfect fashion statement to make at the wedding to pay much attention to her mother.

Alice had unwisely used the six hours they spent shopping to remember how readily Gabriel had responded to every crisis *she'd* faced in the preceding four days. How patient he'd been with Mamie's boys. How he'd done whatever he'd done with Michael. How quickly he'd gotten someone to accompany Allyn around Colorado Springs until she was safely on her way home. His generosity when they'd made love.

And she'd considered holding something as inconsequential as his life-threatening profession against him. What a humbug she was! Why, it had been that very life-threatening profession that had brought him into her life in the first place. It wasn't the possibility but the actuality that counted.

Right?

With a snort of disgust at herself and her fickleness, Alice switched ends of the bed, hoping to escape the birds' singing without having to close the window. But the birds were having none of it. Neither was her head. It poked and prodded her unmercifully. If he's gone for good, it asked her, will you be happy? Isn't some of the best worth a little of the worst? What do you want, Alice? An excuse to stay the same staid old reasonably unfulfilled person you are?

No, she thought, that isn't what I want at all.

Then dare to be great, that niggling little demon inside her urged. Come on, Allie, dare. Who knows, maybe it's all academic anyway. Maybe he's not coming back. Maybe you'll never see him again. Maybe—

"Shut up!" Alice snapped aloud and sat up, spilling her pillow onto the floor. The glaringly familiar room seemed to stare at her, beckon her examination. Blue carpet, matching bedclothes, homogenized white walls . . .

She looked at the walls, and the years melded around her. Sundays spent in the kitchen fixing pot roasts, chickens, turkeys and potatoes, carrying out a tradition of Sunday dinners only her daughters had seen. Evenings spent alone in front of the television set, sighing over the tube's bad-boy heroes. Sticking her head through the girls' bedroom door after the evening news to listen to them breathe. Taking only fantasies with her when she headed off to bed.

Daytimes spent at the bookstore answering hesitant, revealing, too poignant questions about the latest how-to bestsellers posed by people who seemed to confuse the local bookstore manager with their bartenders or their shrinks. Afternoons spent unloading and shelving books, building a career on the sale of someone else's adventures, wishing they were her own.

Stirred together as they were, the years became time spent looking forward to, and preparing for, a someday she'd never expected to see; a never-never that was suddenly near. An opportunity that had been here. And gone.

What was it Allyn had so churlishly advised her a few days ago? *Ah, Ma, get a life...*

Not so simple, Alice thought. Easy to find a life, hard to hold on to it. Harder still to hold on to whoever came with it. Hard to know if the tribulations were worth it until you tried. Faith, she thought, I've got to have faith in me and in him.

She chewed her lip fearfully for an instant. All her life she'd wanted something extra; all her life she'd dreamed of something just a little more. Reality was the safety net she'd clung to for years; it had never become what she dreamed. Until Gabriel. She would never, she realized suddenly, have a greater adventure than this past week with Gabriel. Unless she somehow finagled a future with the man.

What did you do, she thought with a sigh, when your reality suddenly exceeded your dreams?

Take a deep breath, she thought wryly, as her father used to say, then punt. Whatever happened after that, at least you'd taken your best shot at the goal.

* * *

She dressed carefully, slowly, full of nerves and anticipation. She dressed neither for Grace, nor to impress the thirty-three-year-old nudge-nudge, wink-wink Skip who once again was slated to accompany her down the aisle. She dressed for herself, as a reminder of Gabriel, to take a stab at a tiny dream she hoped it wasn't too petty to have. Just once she'd like to command attention, have all eyes on her—however briefly. Just once she wanted to be knock-'em-dead beautiful, instead of plain old dress-for-propriety-but-not-for-show Alice.

She dressed for Gabriel and an optimistic *maybe. Maybe* was a word with so many possibilities behind it; such a hopeful, do-anything word. Maybe he thought about her once in a while. Maybe he pictured her; maybe he dreamed about her. Once in a while. Wherever he was. How long had it been? Night before last—a long time ago when you had too many questions to answer on your own and nothing definite to answer them on.

She raised her chin defiantly. Maybe he would come. And maybe he wouldn't.

She dabbed the foundation brush down her nose. After all, why should he come to the wedding? What was four days out of an entire life? Nothing, really, except a vague memory, a bittersweet smile to take out on February evenings when the television shows got too boring, and the post-Christmas blues became too much. Certainly, four days was not enough to base an entire future on.

Certainly not.

And yet at the deep end of her heart, against the odds, for no rhyme or reason, Alice hoped.

"Mom?"

Alice turned and caught her breath. Pale and nervous, Rebecca fidgeted in the doorway, gloved hands locked at the waist of the washed silk cream-on-cream two-piece suit they'd found for her yesterday. The matching cloche with its tiny half veil perched atop her head; her hair was brushed to a fine sheen and French-braided down her back. She looked sophisticated and sure, beautiful, ready to face the world. A woman, a wife, not Momma's little girl. Watery-eyed and wordless, Alice opened her arms, and Rebecca threw herself into them.

"Momma, I'm scared."

"I know, baby. I am, too."

"This isn't like eloping was, this is really thinking about it. This is really getting married, Momma."

"I know." Alice stroked her hair, her cheek, held her daughter away from her. "You don't have to do this, Becky. If you want to wait, if you're not sure, I'll be here for you whatever you decide."

"I know, Ma, but I'm sure." Rebecca used a gloved finger to brush the moisture carefully from the corner of her eye. "I get confused about me, sometimes, but I'm sure about Mike. He fills me up and he makes me whole and he sets me free. Running away with him made me feel funny, like I was doing something wrong that hurt everybody, but this..." She drew a tremulous breath, smiling. "This is right, Ma."

How can she know what I've only begun to learn at twice her age? Alice wondered. Rebecca was so young to know, so positive. But at eighteen, that's what the future was— bright, positive, optimistic. There for the taking. Optimism as a revolutionary concept. Doubt grew with age. Doubt deterred love. Doubt was the thing Alice most wanted to do away with. And soon.

With sudden decision, she headed for the phone to try to find Gabriel.

The church vestibule was crowded with relatives who preferred to talk rather than find their places. Chaos ruled.

"No, Aunt Bethany," Julia Brannigan soothed *her* mother's sister in front of the double doors at the interior entrance to the church. "I think you look beautiful. How could anyone know you'd buy the same dress as Phil's mother? Twink—" she caught her daughter's arm "—tell us honestly, dear, what do you think? With the hat and her corsage, do you think anybody's going to notice—"

"No, no," Grace moaned, blocking the stairway to the church's vestibule. "I knew I shouldn't let anybody talk me into this. I can't walk in these heels and everybody's going to see I have brown bobby pins with a white veil. I'm going to fall flat on my face in the middle of the aisle and Phil's parents will have heart attacks and you guys'll all laugh and—"

"Shh, Grace, shh." Meg patted her arm. "You'll get through it. You won't fall. Alice is bringing the white bobby pins. You'll be beautiful."

At the steps on the other side of the vestibule, Helen supervised the delivery of three mammoth bags of birdseed.

"Yes, I know birdseed isn't traditional, Aunt Kate, but it's better for the ecosystem. We don't want the little birds that come down to clean up the church steps after the wedding to start dropping out of the sky dead because the rice we tossed swelled in their stomachs and— No!" She turned hastily and poked a commanding finger at Mamie's boys who were chasing Edith's children up and down the steps to the choir loft. "Don't run through there, the birdseed bags are—" there was a thud and a hundred pounds of birdseed spilled across the crowded vestibule "—open." Helen rubbed two fingers across her eyes, took a deep breath and hollered, "Broom!"

Julia Brannigan looked at her feet, watching the seed drift in around her shoes. She shook a vehement finger at Alice and Helen. "You two," she said, "promise me. If you ever get married, you'll call me five minutes before the ceremony. I'll come, bring a friend, we'll stand as your witnesses, but you'll elope."

Headed toward the bride's stairs, Alice danced out of the birdseed's path and swallowed a chuckle at the familiar scene and the things her mother didn't know. It was amazing that anyone in her family survived their weddings and willingly attended the next one. Well, she amended, Grace wasn't exactly willing, but who's counting?

While Edith and Meg helped Grace skewer on her veil, Alice pushed open the church's side door a crack to review the stragglers still on their way into the wedding.

"Do you see him?" Sam asked at her shoulder.

"No." Alice swallowed and shook her head, hating herself for allowing herself to be at the mercy of a single absent man she hadn't even known last Sunday. When she'd finally decided that the best person to call about Gabriel would be the local FBI director, it had already been late. When she'd gotten through to the office, they'd told her the director was unavailable on Saturdays. They'd also politely informed her that they'd never heard of Gabriel Lucas Book and were not in the habit, in any case, of giving out information on agents. "No," she said again. "I don't see him."

Sam rubbed Alice's back above the scoop neck of her dress. "Don't worry," she said positively. "He'll be here. He didn't strike me as the kind of guy who'd break a promise. 'Specially not to you."

"I know," Alice said, and she *did* know. "Unless it's something beyond his control—"

"He'll be here," Sam-the-pregnant-volunteer-fireman said firmly.

Torn between fuming at Gabriel for not being able to tell her how she could get in touch with him and worrying that he might be lying somewhere swathed in bandages or worse and unable to contact her, Alice tried to believe Sam.

The chaos in the vestibule sorted itself out slowly, but finally even the brides' and grooms' parents were seated and only the ushers, Becky, Alice and her sisters remained in the entryway, listening while the guitarist and the flutist played wedding preludes, and the singer tested her mike.

"Look," Edith whispered, peeking around the doorway. "There's Phil and Mike, don't they look great?"

"Phil sure looks nervous," Twink observed, poking Becky, "but Mike looks like somebody just gave him a canary. Did you feed him—"

"Shut up." Meg slapped her sister's arm. "Quit making tacky jokes in church. That's what the reception's for."

"Oh, God," Grace wailed suddenly, "my veil's gone and I think my heel's just ripped out the hem of my train."

"No, no, here's your veil," Alice assured her, plucking it off her back. "And here—" she bent over to straighten Grace's train "—lift your foot."

There was a buzz at the back of the church.

"They're ready for us," Helen whispered. "Everybody set?"

"Hold on a sec—" Still silently cursing Gabriel for being absent and pleading with him to be all right, Alice reached to help Edith resecure Grace's veil and froze, eyes locked on the open outside church door.

Looking sleepy-eyed, self-conscious and slightly rumpled, Gabriel dashed up the outside steps and paused, blinking in the sudden dimness. Alice caught her breath and looked him up and down, from his yet unfocused brown eyes to the slightly off-kilter set of his tie, to the spit-and-polish shine on his shoes. Her heart swelled with her lungs. He looked incredibly wonderful.

His eyes found Alice finally. Inhaling, he straightened, telling her what he saw when he looked at her by the quick half-quirk of his mouth, the awed satisfaction in his face, by his inability to look at anyone but her. He took a step toward her.

"Gabriel, there you are!" Helen bustled forward, grabbing the last boutonniere off the table at the side of the foyer. "Here, let me just pin this on and—"

Alice slipped forward and gently traded Grace's veil for Gabriel's flower. "This one's mine," she said firmly. "I'll do that."

"Yours?" Gabriel queried softly, looking down at her with laughing eyes and an expression that said *just checking*.

Alice stabbed the flower pin into his lapel with decision, nodding. "Absolutely mine," she affirmed, shoving his chin out of the way so she could adjust his tie. Then she lifted her eyes to him anxiously. "I mean if that's all right with you?"

Gabriel brushed her lips with a finger and went to get in line with the rest of the groomsmen. "I think," he said thoughtfully, looking back at her and grinning, "that maybe for the next seventy-five years or so I could just about handle that."

Epilogue

Sunlight filtered through the funnel of maple trees, spread in lacy shadows over the ground. A summer breeze drove the scent of charbroiling hamburgers and hot dogs into neighboring yards, lifted the dangling curtain of blue oilcloth that was spread over the long picnic table, sending paper napkins and plates flying. Alice's mother, sisters and daughters reached hastily for them, collided laughing, then weighted the flyaway utensils with pickle jars and mustard pots before turning their attentions back to the babies—Grace's six-month-old daughter and Becky's six-week-old son—tented in mosquito netting, sleeping in the shade. Deeper in the yard, young voices rose and fell, shrieking, laughing, bickering; the swing chains and trapeze rings on the play structure clanked to the rush of children through them.

"Look what I did! Bet you can't do it."

"Bet I can."

"No, you can't. You're too little."

"Can!"

"Dare ya! Dare ya, dare ya, dare ya!"

"Mom!" The word was a singsong aimed at Twink. "Sarah's teasing me. Make her stop."

"Sarah," Edith admonished her eleven-year-old youngest, "quit teasing your cousins. Act your age."

"Oh, that's good, Edie." Meg swatted her sister playfully. "You never could figure out what that meant when Ma said it to us, and now you're saying it to your kids?"

"Just wait." Edith said slyly and patted Meg's burgeoning belly. "You'll learn. Sometimes it just comes out. I get lost trying to think of new things to say all the time."

"Sure." Helen grinned. "That's what they all say." She turned to her own mother beside her. "Right, Great-gram?"

Julia Block Brannigan, mother of seven, grandmother of ten, great-grandmother of one and, at age sixty-one, two weeks away from beginning a twenty-four month stint as a teacher in the Peace Corps, folded her hands in front of her and smiled serenely. "I'm just glad they're yours," she said, and her daughters laughed.

Above them in the bedroom window overlooking the backyard, Alice smiled, eyes pausing briefly on each sister in turn. A lot had happened to all of them in the past two years; a lot more was about to happen. Meg was pregnant for the first time and nervous as hell about it. Helen . . .

Alice grinned, watching her high-handed, gung-ho sister tickle her grand-nephew when she thought no one was watching. Poor Skip had swallowed his sense of propriety, stopped wearing three-piece suits and hung around the family for weeks hoping the major would relent and come back to him. Helen, of course, had been unsympathetic to his plight despite the phone calls from her sisters urging her to have a little heart and at least reconsider the man. She had, however, invited a pretty petite, sassy-mouthed

Southern Army Captain home with her for Thanksgiving, winked at her sisters and introduced the captain to Skip.

Skip had gotten the last laugh on that one, though. By the end of the holiday weekend he had, much to Helen's supreme consternation, requested an immediate transfer to his company's Seattle office and married the captain on Valentine's Day ten weeks later.

As for Helen herself, Alice suspected she was finally about to receive her own comeuppance in spades from the Navy photographer who'd recently thrown the major for a full loop. Sad to say, the rest of the Brannigan girls were having a field day at the newly discombobulated major's expense, but on the other hand, Alice decided, it was about time Helen succumbed to the hearts and flowers she'd once tried to bury her sisters under.

With a final mental thumbs up to the course of justice, Alice's eyes moved on.

Edith had gone back to school and become a visiting nurse-practitioner. Twink still managed the same law office but now had another son. Sam was unendingly *Sam,* authority's tester; she was also now the first, and only paid full-time female firefighter in the area. And Grace...

Again Alice smiled. Quiet, crowd-hating Grace strapped her toddler in the stroller, her infant in the backpack, picked up her walking stick and hollered for the dog, then spent her days walking the wooded back roads of the Upper Peninsula for Michigan's Department of Natural Resources, studying the physical drift of the land.

So much to celebrate, Alice thought gladly. Each of her sisters were still marked individuals whom love had tempered but stolen nothing from.

Her attention shifted proudly to Allyn and Rebecca, sitting close together on one side of the picnic table, still not quite comfortable at being included among the adult women. They'd grown, too; changing, shaping themselves to fit their own futures. Becky and Michael still had differences to outlast, but they seemed to be learning to sort out those differences on their own instead of running home to Alice with them all the time. Their son, Alice's first grandchild, had been baptized today.

Allyn, the formerly frightened and defiant wanderer who couldn't decide who she was, had suddenly discovered an untapped determination in herself, collected her nerve and signed up for a six-month stint as part of the galley crew aboard a marine study vessel in the Pacific. Her doggedness at winning the post for which she'd had almost no concrete qualifications still amazed Alice, who'd never known about her daughter's passion for marine biology. Now Allyn was well on her way to getting her bachelor-of-science degree in aquatic studies with honors, had chosen to pursue her master's degree through the coast guard, and was already putting out feelers that could take her to Woodshole or Pensacola to work on her doctorate.

And Gabriel.

Alice took a deep breath trying to quiet the giddy beat her heart still took on every time she thought about him. He'd gone straight to New Jersey from Jack Scully's office after Markum's arrest to get his great-great grandmother's wedding ring out of storage, and it had taken him exactly three minutes after Grace's and Becky's wedding to find out that he wouldn't have to get it sized for Alice. It already fit. Later, at the reception, no one had been the least surprised when Becky's mother and her escort were mysteriously unavailable for their dance.

Even at the memory, Alice blushed. She and Gabriel had spent a decidedly wanton few days getting to know one another properly in every room of the house. On the fourth day, while Alice guiltily greeted Allyn who had arrived home at last, Gabriel sat on the edge of the bed and gingerly pulled his mother's last letter out of the pocket of the jeans he'd shed in favor of the tux for the wedding. The paper was crumbled, dirty and hard to read, having spent six months wadded into a ball in the basket at his apartment, but it didn't matter. The letter still said what he remembered, that his parents loved him and wanted to see him, no matter where—or who—he was. They were taking a sabbatical from their mission and would spend the summer with family in Iowa. He hadn't much time.

By the time Alice had finished her heart to heart with Allyn and come searching for him, he'd found the suitcase she kept tucked in the back of her closet and had it half-packed. He'd eyed her sheepishly for half a heartbeat, then he'd well and truly swept her off her feet, spiriting her away to meet his parents and marrying her at a simple Quaker ceremony inside of a month. Alice had already decided to live with him no matter what, but true to his word to Jack Scully, he'd tied up his loose ends and left the Bureau to become a crisis counselor at nearby Oakland University, putting both his experience and his educational background to use. His transition from undercover agent to husband, stepfather and a mostly eight-hour-a-day career life had not always been smooth, but every instant of it had been worthwhile, had served to cement the bond between him and Alice.

Alice's own life in particular seemed to have struck a reckless course for new horizons, sailing far beyond the edges of her most unrestrained desires. She no longer hid her competence under a waffling exterior and had made a deal to buy the string of bookstores Skip had once asked her to design and oversee. Under Gabriel's gentle encouragement she'd become a firm believer in risking everything to achieve a dream. She still found it incredible when she thought about how their lives had settled and changed together, weathered disaster, grown and blossomed. There was only one dream that they'd agreed to postpone until everything else settled. And with two years behind them, and Gabriel's undercover life—including any leftover testimony he'd had to make during the last twenty-four months—out of the way, Alice decided firmly that it was time to make one more dream come true.

"You look pretty complacent." Gabriel slid his arms around her waist, rested his palms on the flat of her belly. "What are you doing, counting our blessings?"

Alice rubbed her husband's chin with the back of her head, nodding . "Feels good to know where I belong, who I am."

Gabriel's arms flexed tight around her; he buried his face in her hair. "God, does it ever," he muttered fervently. "You'll never know."

Alice turned in his embrace, reaching to hold him, too. "But I do know," she said. "If I hadn't found you that day, I never would—"

Gabriel kissed her quiet. "You've always been stronger than you think," he returned softly. "Even without me you'd have been all right. You'd have grown and survived and become who you are, anyway. It's me who was lucky that day..." His eyes shut, a prayer of thanks. "I've gotten so much from you, Alice, I can't say. My own family back, a whole new family here—sisters, daughters, a grandchild. A real life."

"But if it wasn't for you," Alice argued gently, "I'd be a lonely brittle frustrated not-quite-forty-year-old. You make me—"

"Whole—" Gabriel kissed her. "Complete—" His tongue made a lazy tour of her mouth. "'And these two shall be as one.'" He quoted the words from their marriage ceremony as tongue and lips traced the familiar but always new trail along her throat, up the sensitive area below her right ear. "'One heart, one mind, one spirit, one body...'"

"Two minds," Alice murmured, arching her neck for him. "One heart, one spirit, *two* minds and one body."

"As long as we come back to that," Gabriel muttered, skimming his hands over the sides of her cotton-covered breasts. "I don't care if we have six of everything else."

"Mmm." Alice's arms locked around his neck, and she pulled herself up to meet his mouth. "I think you've definitely got something there—"

There was a thump in the hallway.

"Alice, aren't you going to bring the— Oh!" Edith gasped, embarrassed. "I'm sorry, I didn't think—pardon me."

"Ah-ah-ah, Alice," Helen teased from the doorway. "This may be the place, but it's not the time. You've got guests in the yard, an open window and you didn't even shut the—"

"Thank you, Helen, I'll take care of it," Gabriel said firmly, then closed the door in her face and locked it.

"How rude," Helen commented.

"Are they actually going to stay in there now?" Edith breathed.

"Looks like it," Helen said.

"Well!" Edith exclaimed, affronted, and then ruined the effect by giggling. "At least one of us has found a man who can handle Brannigans."

"In his sleep," Helen agreed, and the two of them went off, laughing.

"Well, that's taken care of." Gabriel turned back to his wife with an irresistible come-hither smile and a look of unabashed anticipation. "Now, where were we?"

Alice backed away from him. "No, Gabriel, we can't. Not now. They're all going to—"

"They'll talk about us no matter what we do. You've got to face that, Alice."

"But—" Alice scrambled across the bed "—don't you think we should go—"

"Yes." Gabriel knelt on the bed, leaned over and caught her hand, drawing her toward him. "I definitely think we should."

"Now?" Alice felt the buzz of warmth through her muscles, felt them melting. She resisted Gabriel an instant longer, prolonging the anticipation. "Shouldn't we go do it now?"

"Wrong verb, Alice." Gabriel tugged suddenly, and Alice sprawled on the bed. He knelt over her, pulling impatiently at the tiny buttons on her sundress. "I think what you meant was, shouldn't we *stay* and do it now."

"Yes." Alice sighed. She arched to him, reveling in the instant coil of tension inside her, wishing she hadn't put all these damn buttons between them today, wanting him inside her now. She stilled his hands by wrapping her hips around him and pulling him down to her. "I suppose that's exactly what I meant."

She shifted beneath him, touched moist feminine heat to the fly of his light summer pants. Gabriel groaned softly and caught her hips, rubbing himself against her. Alice pulled herself up by his shoulders, hips matching the rhythm of his, pressing them tighter. "Come to me, Gabriel," she whispered against his mouth. "Come into me *now*."

Her eyes were dark, full of passion; her demand left him hard, impatient, trembling, ready. With a hoarse oath Gabriel tried to ease himself away from her, reaching for the decorative can on the shelf beside the bed. "Oh, God, Alice, I will. Just let me get—"

"*Now,* Gabriel, please," Alice breathed, tugging at his pants, unsnapping, unzipping, freeing him. "I'm ready *now*." She reached between their bodies, guided him past the silky barrier between them, and with a twist of her hips sheathed him inside her.

Gabriel's breath grew ragged with his effort to stay still inside her. "Alice—God, you're killing me, Allie. Let me protect—"

Alice rocked her hips, moaned at the feel of him, hot, slick, sliding. She looked up at him through heavy-lidded eyes, arched her throat and moistened her mouth with her tongue. "Don't want to be protected," she gasped, lifting herself toward him again. "We've waited two years, everything's taken care of. It's time, Gabriel, it's time..."

Realization dawned slowly. A low animal growl emanated from deep in Gabriel's throat, and he laced his fingers in her hair, pulling her head back where he could see her. Love and passion filled her face, but there was something else, too. Invitation, fierce and joyful; surety and expectation. Gabriel's lungs constricted.

"Are you sure you want this?" he asked carefully. "You're not just doing this for me? You're sure?"

Instead of replying, Alice rolled her hips around him once more, eliciting another groan from him as her body took him deeper. With the last shred of his self-control, Gabriel wrapped his arms about her waist and held her motionless. "Alice. Please. I need to know."

She brushed his face with the palm of her hand, an act of love. "I'm sure, Gabriel. This is for me, too. I want everything with you, you know, the whole shot. Parenthood, midnight feedings, diapers, sleepless nights, toddlers and teenagers. I want—" she grinned and touched her mouth to his "—to wash baby spit out of your shirts and watch baby fingers pull your hair. And I want to see your face while you watch our baby born, see you hold him, see you..."

Her breath faltered when Gabriel cradled her in his arms and laid her back on the bed, bending over to unbutton her dress with his fingers, lips, teeth. Alice pressed him to her, feeling the coil of heat begin to expand and swell inside her, wanting to hold it in, wanting to explode. Her throat made sharp unintelligible sounds of excitement, her body moved, her hands tightened in his hair. Gabriel held her still.

"What else?" His voice was an erotic stroke against her fevered skin; his tongue provoked, teased, withdrew. "What else do you want, Alice?"

"I want to see your eyes in his face," she whispered thickly. "I want to share everything with you that I did with Allyn and Rebecca alone. And I—" She gasped and her entire body convulsed when he clutched her hips and came into her hard, at the same time dipping his head and finding a nipple, suckling it deep. "Gabriel, please," she pleaded, her train of thought lost as the volcano began to erupt inside her. "I want you there, too. Don't let me go alone. Come with me. Come—"

"I am, love. I will," Gabriel assured her fiercely. "Always, anywhere you want to go. I'm with you."

And then there was no more talk, only breath and movement and hot sweet sensation, the song of their future being born.

* * * * *

SILHOUETTE·INTIMATE·MOMENTS®

NORA ROBERTS
Night Shadow

People all over the city of Urbana were asking, Who was that masked man?

Assistant district attorney Deborah O'Roarke was the first to learn his secret identity . . . and her life would never be the same.

The stories of the lives and loves of the O'Roarke sisters began in January 1991 with NIGHT SHIFT, Silhouette Intimate Moments #365. And if you want to know more about Deborah and the man behind the mask, look for NIGHT SHADOW, Silhouette Intimate Moments #373.

Silhouette Books®

Silhouette Special Edition®

This April,
Silhouette *Special Edition* is pleased to present

ONCE IN A LIFETIME
by Ginna Gray

the long-awaited companion volume to her bestselling duo

Fools Rush In (#416)
Where Angels Fear (#468)

Ever since spitfire Erin Blaine and her angelic twin sister Elise stirred up double trouble and entangled their long-suffering brother David in some sticky hide-and-seek scenarios, readers clamored to hear more about dashing, debonair David himself.

Now that time has come, as straitlaced Abigail Stewart manages to invade the secrecy shrouding sardonic David Blaine's bachelor boat—and creates the kind of salty, saucy, swashbuckling romantic adventure that comes along only once in a lifetime!

**Even if you missed the earlier novels,
you won't want to miss
ONCE IN A LIFETIME #661**

Available this April, only in Silhouette *Special Edition*.   OL-1

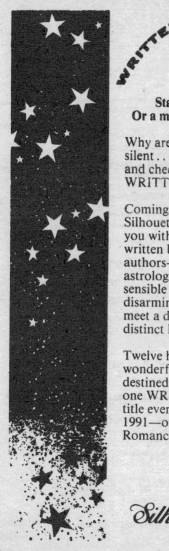

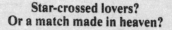
WRITTEN IN THE STARS

**Star-crossed lovers?
Or a match made in heaven?**

Why are some heroes strong and silent...and others charming and cheerful? The answer is WRITTEN IN THE STARS!

Coming each month in 1991, Silhouette Romance presents you with a special love story written by one of your favorite authors—highlighting the hero's astrological sign! From January's sensible Capricorn to December's disarming Sagittarius, you'll meet a dozen dazzling and distinct heroes.

Twelve heavenly heroes...twelve wonderful Silhouette Romances destined to delight you. Look for one WRITTEN IN THE STARS title every month throughout 1991—only from Silhouette Romance.

STAR

Silhouette Books®

SILHOUETTE'S "BIG WIN"
SWEEPSTAKES RULES & REGULATIONS

NO PURCHASE NECESSARY TO ENTER OR RECEIVE A PRIZE

1. To enter the Sweepstakes and join the Reader Service, scratch off the metallic strips on all your BIG WIN tickets #1-#6. This will reveal the potential values for each Sweepstakes entry number, the number of free book(s) you will receive and your free bonus gift as part of our Reader Service. If you do not wish to take advantage of our Reader Service but wish to enter the Sweepstakes only, scratch off the metallic strips on your BIG WIN tickets #1-#4. Return your entire sheet of tickets intact. Incomplete and/or inaccurate entries are ineligible for that section or sections of prizes. Torstar Corp. and its affiliates are not responsible for mutilated or unreadable entries or inadvertent printing errors. Mechanically reproduced entries are null and void.

2. Whether you take advantage of this offer or not, on or about April 30, 1992, at the offices of Marden-Kane Inc., Lake Success, NY, your Sweepstakes numbers will be compared against the list of winning numbers generated at random by the computer. However, prizes will only be awarded to individuals who have entered the Sweepstakes. In the event that all prizes are not claimed, a random drawing will be held from all qualified entries received from March 30, 1990 to March 31, 1992, to award all unclaimed prizes. All cash prizes (Grand to Sixth), will be mailed to the winners and are payable by check in U.S. funds. Seventh prize will be shipped to winners via third-class mail. These prizes are in addition to any free, surprise or mystery gifts that might be offered. Versions of this Sweepstakes with different prizes of approximate equal value may appear at retail outlets or in other mailings by Torstar Corp. and its affiliates.

3. The following prizes are awarded in this sweepstakes: ★ Grand Prize (1) $1,000,000; First Prize (1) $25,000; Second Prize (1) $10,000; Third Prize (5) $5,000; Fourth Prize (10) $1,000; Fifth Prize (100) $250; Sixth Prize (2,500) $10; ★ ★ Seventh Prize (6,000) $12.95 ARV.

   ★ This presentation offers a Grand Prize of a $1,000,000 annuity. Winner will receive $33,333.33 a year for 30 years without interest totalling $1,000,000.

   ★ ★ Seventh Prize: A fully illustrated hardcover book published by Torstar Corp. Approximate Retail Value of the book is $12.95.

   Entrants may cancel the Reader Service at anytime without cost or obligation to buy (see details in center insert card).

4. This Sweepstakes is being conducted under the supervision of an independent judging organization. By entering this Sweepstakes, each entrant accepts and agrees to be bound by these rules and the decisions of the judges, which shall be final and binding. Odds of winning in the random drawing are dependent upon the total number of entries received. Taxes, if any, are the sole responsibility of the winners. Prizes are nontransferable. All entries must be received at the address printed on the reply card and must be postmarked no later than 12:00 MIDNIGHT on March 31, 1992. The drawing for all unclaimed Sweepstakes prizes will take place on May 30, 1992, at 12:00 NOON, at the offices of Marden-Kane, Inc., Lake Success, New York.

5. This offer is open to residents of the U.S., the United Kingdom, France and Canada, 18 years or older, except employees and their immediate family members of Torstar Corp., its affiliates, subsidiaries, and all the other agencies, entities and persons connected with the use, marketing or conduct of this Sweepstakes. All Federal, State, Provincial and local laws apply. Void wherever prohibited or restricted by law. Any litigation within the Province of Quebec respecting the conduct and awarding of a prize in this publicity contest must be submitted to the Régie des Loteries et Courses du Québec.

6. Winners will be notified by mail and may be required to execute an affidavit of eligibility and release, which must be returned within 14 days after notification or an alternate winner will be selected. Canadian winners will be required to correctly answer an arithmetical skill-testing question administered by mail, which must be returned within a limited time. Winners consent to the use of their names, photographs and/or likenesses for advertising and publicity in conjunction with this and similar promotions without additional compensation. For a list of our major prize winners, send a stamped, self-addressed ENVELOPE to: WINNERS LIST, c/o Marden-Kane Inc., P.O. Box 701, SAYREVILLE, NJ 08871. Requests for Winners Lists will be fulfilled after the May 30, 1992 drawing date.

If Sweepstakes entry form is missing, please print your name and address on a 3" ×5" piece of plain paper and send to:

In the U.S.	In Canada
Silhouette's "BIG WIN" Sweepstakes	Silhouette's "BIG WIN" Sweepstakes
3010 Walden Ave.	P.O. Box 609
P.O. Box 1867	Fort Erie, Ontario
Buffalo, NY 14269-1867	L2A 5X3

Offer limited to one per household.

LTY-S391D

HARDEN
Diana Palmer

In her bestselling LONG, TALL TEXANS series, Diana Palmer brought you to Jacobsville and introduced you to the rough and rugged ranchers who call the town home. Now, hot and dusty Jacobsville promises to get even hotter when hard-hearted, woman-hating rancher Harden Tremayne has to reckon with the lovely Miranda Warren.

The LONG, TALL TEXANS series continues! Don't miss HARDEN by Diana Palmer in March... only from Silhouette Romance.

LTT-1